THE
FORGOTTEN
WORLD

the BLUE FLOWER trilogy

THE
FORGOTTEN
WORLD

R. GENE CURTIS

For Anna

Retreat

Shouts and the clang of metal against metal rang out over the rumble of the storm that had been brewing since supper time.

The princess. They had come for her.

Cylus pulled his weary body out of his chair and reached for the cane leaning against the wall. This was no time for slowness, but old age put lead in his feet and made his joints creak as he made his way to the window. With a burst of energy, Cylus threw the window open, and was greeted by the wind, blowing from the west in a terrible gale. Bits of the fall harvest rushed through his hair and pulled at his robe. Raindrops smacked his face.

But, his eyes focused on the lights. Torches. Thousands of men had come from the outside and were standing at the castle gates. From what he could gather from the screams of the city's dying guards riding the wind, the king was not with them.

The small city guard didn't stand a chance without the power of their Azurean king beside them. Where was he? Dead? Incapacitated? It didn't matter which. The resistance would be minimal. Without the king, the invaders had a clear shot to the princess.

It was time for the contingency plan. That last-resort, fool-hardy desperate plan, the king had entrusted him with. The plan he had promised Cylus would never have to be used.

The promise was broken, and Cylus alone carried the key for the princess's escape. The king had been too kind-hearted, too willing to forgive. His weakness had put his entire family in jeopardy, and he had known that. And now the king wasn't here in the midst of a crisis. Hopefully, the princess was safe in the castle with the staff. They knew the plan, they would know Cylus was coming.

Cylus had to get to the castle before that army.

He forced his old body into action, moving away from the window to the door. He stopped on the threshold only a moment to gaze back at the small home where he had raised his family. With too little time for nostalgia, and no time to wonder about his grown children, Cylus grabbed the hourglass from its hiding place and stepped out his door for the last time.

Shouts from the battle at the gate filled the wind. The cries of pain and fear pushed Cylus faster as he trudged through the mud to the tree that held the secret passageway to the castle.

The passageway inside the tree had been Dee's passageway, though tonight would be the first time Cylus would use it. He had discovered it only by accident last year, long after the affair was over. But if the army was any indication, the affair wasn't over, at least not its consequences. Cylus could not let his conscience rest, not even after he had given so much of his life to atone for his mistakes. If he failed tonight, nothing else he had done would matter. All the people he had tried to protect would be dead.

Cylus reached for the tree as his boots slid in the slick mud and his old body tumbled to the ground. His shoulder slammed against a protruding root, forcing his arm out of its socket. He gasped with the force of the pain.

Then a crash sounded and the shouts at the gate stopped.

The army was in the city. And Cylus was on his back, lying injured in the mud.

Swearing under his breath, Cylus hooked his remaining good arm around the tree and pulled himself up, his clothes heavy and wet. His hand hit the knot on the trunk. Upon contact, blue light flashed out from inside the bark, and the trunk split open. Cylus stepped out of the rain into the dimly-lit passageway that led to the castle.

He hurried forward as fast as his old body would move. The passageway wasn't nearly as long as the actual distance that separated his house from the castle. By using Dee's tunnel, Cylus had a chance to beat the army to the princess. Still, the minutes dragged as he pushed his body through the dimly lit corridor.

The crisis had come on so suddenly. Only two days ago, the king had shut the castle gates and announced a terrible sickness in the royal family. Even so, everyone had expected a quick and full recovery. No one expected anything less from an Azurean.

But that was the last anyone had heard from the king. The dread in the pit of Cylus's stomach wasn't going away.

Where was the princess?

If only Cylus could move faster.

Cylus walked until there was nothing in front of him but a stone wall. He slowed and looked around frantically, but could see no other way out. Frustrated, Cylus banged his hand against the wall, but his arm never hit anything solid—it went right through the wall, which wasn't a wall after all. He stepped out of the passageway into a castle stairwell. He squinted down the stairwell, trying to make out where he was in the dim light.

The passageway had brought him to the wrong tower. Cylus swore and stumbled down a couple stairs to the main floor. He pushed himself through an empty ballroom and shoved open heavy wooden doors to go back outside into the rain.

Strong wind greeted him on the causeway separating the two castle towers. The wind pushed him back and moved his limp arm in ways it was not supposed to move. Through the rain, he could see the lights of the army in the distance. They were moving quickly through the maze of city streets. The race was on. He needed to find the staff. He needed to find the princess.

At this rate, he wasn't going to make it.

The rain came down in sheets. Cylus tried to walk faster, his eyes focused on the large doors at the other end of the causeway.

When he got to the doors, he flung his cane aside and pulled. His one good arm was no match for the heavy door. He pulled again. And again. He wondered if he would pull his other arm out and end up standing in the rain with no arms at all. But then the door started to budge. Another pull. The door opened enough for him to slip inside before the wind slammed it shut behind him, nearly knocking him over.

His bad arm hurt so badly he could barely think. He was too old for this.

The main entry hall was silent. Where was everyone? A lantern glowed weakly next to the doorway. Cylus grabbed the light and swung it forward. He stopped cold as the light filled the large hallway.

Bodies. On the ground. A serving maid lay at his feet, her hair wet with vomit, her lips blue. Just beyond her were two guards, slumped over, also covered in vomit.

The room reeked.

Poisoned. All of them. The castle staff was dead.

Cylus swung the lantern around again and again, but the royal family was not among the dead. Was there a poison that could kill an Azurean? Before tonight, Cylus wouldn't have believed it, but he wasn't so sure now that he was looking at all of the staff lying dead on the ground. The king had been missing for so long already.

Cylus started to run, faster than he thought possible. There wasn't time to mourn the dead or worry about slipping on the vomit-covered floor. He stepped over bodies and climbed the stairs, ignoring the corpses that littered the stairwell.

A crash sounded downstairs as Cylus reached the top step. He jumped into the king's bedchamber and slammed the door shut. His breath was rapid and heavy and the pain from his shoulder was taking over his consciousness. The quick ascent up the stairs had pulled muscles he hadn't used in decades. But he had to keep moving. In a few minutes this would all end, whether he found them here or not.

The room was as quiet as a tomb; nothing moved except Cylus as he crept forward, dreading what waited for him at the king's bedside. The light moved with him, each step bringing the edge of the light a few feet closer to the dark forms across the room.

Cylus stood at the bedside. Light illuminated the still forms of the people he loved so much. The queen lay curled around a bundle, and the king's hand rested across her bosom, his body kneeling on the floor, his head slumped on the bed.

Neither body moved. Cylus reached out tentatively. The king's hand was cold, icy in the still room.

He hadn't saved the king. After all he had done. The king was dead. Tears ran down Cylus's worn face. And the baby? Was all lost?

A faint, muffled cry made its way through the thick blanket.

The cry of hope momentarily disbanded his despair and filled Cylus with determination. The lantern dropped, and the flames engulfed the bedsheets. Cylus reached into his robe with his good hand and pulled out the small hourglass. It would save the baby. He would go with her. They would be safe. Everything was not lost. Not yet.

Shouts echoed in the stairwell breaking the silence. Cylus pulled the princess from her mother's cold bosom. The baby wailed as he pulled her close to him, balancing her against his bad arm.

Hand shaking, he hit the hourglass on the side of the bed. It didn't break.

The first soldier banged on the door. Cylus lifted his hand again and struck with everything he had left. The glass shattered, and Cylus winced as splintered glass sunk into the flesh of his palm. Blue sand poured over the princess and his lap.

The door crashed open, and an arrow flew through the air. Cylus heard the crying stop, he felt the arrow hit his chest, and he fell to the floor with a thud. He gasped as the soldiers pulled his dying body off the floor, but his hands were empty. The Azurean princess was gone.

1 Raining

Lydia

Bright lights in my eyes. Rain on my face and running down my arms.

Screams and chants from the crowd fill the damp air. I dig my cleats into the ground and account for the opposing players around me.

My clothes are soaked through from the drizzle, sweat, and mud, and smell even worse than they look. I suppress a shiver and put my hands on my knees, squinting through the lights to watch my teammates on the other side of the field. Maria fakes around a defender and dribbles toward the goal, but she opts out of a shot and passes back to Rachel.

I swallow hard and look at the stands for the hundredth time. Coach Fant is still sitting there, even in the last minutes of this game, watching my every move. I've done well tonight, but she has a reputation of being critical and playing favorites. I'm from the wrong school to be one of the favorites, too many kids at Newport High are from wealthy families, which automatically makes me spoiled and lazy.

"Your lead won't last much longer, Thala." Joana Hart from the other team, Issaquah, jogs up to join me.

I wish she would leave me alone. I wish I would never see her again after tonight, but I don't have that kind of luck. Joana is the only other girl on the field that will be playing for U-dub next fall, and from what I've heard, Joana is one of the coach's favorites.

"My name is Lydia," I say, and I take a step back. Five more minutes in this game, and with Coach Fant's eyes on us, there's no room for error. And, we're only up by 1.

Joana laughs. "That's a human name. You looked more Neanderthal than a human. Neander-Thala. Are you sure the University of Washington is really going to let a Neanderthal play for them next fall?"

I take another step back; the action is moving toward our side of the field.

"Where are your parents, Thala?" Joana has her back to the ball. I can't see around her.

"Not here." My eyes follow Joana's gaze toward the stands. To Mom's empty seat. It's been empty for four years now. She would have loved to see me play in the championship game. The last time Newport soccer won the district championship was when she was in school.

Joana cuts and her body flies past me, pony tail extended. I spin and run after her, but the ball flies over our heads and lands right in front of her. She angles off to the side and shoots, and we've lost our lead. The game is tied at 1.

Joana runs around the field, hugging her teammates and laughing.

I kick at the dirt and try to ignore my teammates. Up in the stands, Coach Fant scribbles in her notebook. Will she cut me before camp? With so little time left in the game, how did I let myself get distracted?

"Don't sweat it," Shelly calls from her midfielder position. "There's still a lot of time."

I try to return her smile. The team is counting on me to keep my head in the game.

Coach calls us over and outlines the next play. Issaquah is just as tired as we are. We can get another goal. We can still win this game.

We put the ball into play, but the play fails and results in a goal kick. Still 1-1. Two and a half more minutes.

The Issaquah goalie kicks the ball to one of her midfielders. She gets the pass and jukes around Shelly. As she moves downfield, I follow Joana, who takes off running laterally toward the sidelines. The midfielder forces the ball downfield to her, but I'm ready. I break in front and send the ball upfield. Maria jukes around her defender and puts us up 2-1. 110 seconds left. We're up 2-1 with less than two minutes left.

I breath a huge sigh of relief. "Great job ladies!" I shout.

"So, Thala. Why is your nose so flat? I've never seen one like it. Is it like your Mom's?"

Will she just shut her mouth and play the last two minutes? Ugh.

"And your hair is so curly. Doesn't your dad have straight hair?"

I'm ignoring her. Just a few more seconds and I won't have to see her again until fall camp.

"Maybe you're an alien, and not a time-traveled Neanderthal after all. What do you think, Thala?"

Watch her hips. She can't fake past me if I'm watching her hips. Don't look at the clock. The seconds will tick off whether I'm watching them or not.

Sweat mixes with rain and stings my eyes, but I keep them open and focused on Joana. My legs ache from exertion, and my pulse pounds in my ears. Despite what Joana says, Mom would be proud if she was here. She never missed a game. Soccer was her life. Our life.

6

Joana's hips move, and I jump into action.

The crowd roars and the ball sails towards us. Only me and the goalie stand between Joana and our goal. I stay stride for stride with Joana as the ball comes in gently. She takes control and sprints, trying to outrun me.

Not this time. My cleats dig into the soft, wet turf as I run stride for stride between her and the goal.

Joana slows as the space between us and the goal disappears. Her ponytail flips back and forth as she jukes, rain drops fly out of her hair and glitter in the light. Time to end this before she gets past me.

I jump into a slide. Water sprays off my cleats and bare legs as my body flies across the turf. My foot hits the ball with a thud, and it rockets off the field. Joana leaps over me and trips on her own feet, falling face first into the mud.

There can't be more than 30 seconds of the game left now.

My teammates scream, and I let myself smile, too. I hope Coach Fant saw that one.

I push my hands into the muddy grass and stand, wiping the mud on my already soiled shorts. These shorts started the game colored yellow, and they even were comfortable, too. I offer Joana a muddy hand.

She glares at me and puts her own hands into the mud. "I don't think so, Thala. What if I touch your hand and end up looking like you?"

"It's Lydia," I say softly as she runs away to get the ball back into play. Seconds later, the whistles blow and the game is over.

District champs.

My teammates race to midfield in a screaming, hugging mass.

I smile and walk slowly until I'm a few yards away from the team. I stand awkwardly on the outside, where I usually am. On the outside, waiting for Mom to come out of the stands and find me.

But this time, Maria leaves the pack and throws her arms around me. My body stiffens, but I try to smile as she jumps and screams.

"We're district champs!" she yells. Her blonde hair is matted against her face and her uniform is as dirty as mine. "I can't believe you stopped Joana!"

I'm not sure if I should hug her back, so I stand stupidly with my hands hanging by my sides.

"This is great," I finally think to say. Maria laughs and runs back to the rest of the team. I play with these girls, but I'm not one of them. Like Joana said, it's like I'm on the team, but not really on the team. Like I'm an outsider.

Like I'm Neanderthal?

The rain slows to a drizzle, and I close my eyes and let myself enjoy the moment. I'm a champion. No one else hugs me or yells at me. That's okay. I'm not sure what

I would do if they did. I belong with them on the field, but when the game ends, we all go home.

Each girl meets her family and leaves. Eventually I stand alone, in the rain.

The stands are empty except for the people cleaning up. It's quiet except for the sound of rain hitting the benches. And there's Joana at the side of the field, talking to Coach Fant. I walk to the stands and climb up to Mom's empty seat. I don't sit in it, but I stand there, stare, and remember. The rain stops, and a gust of wind sends shivers up and down my wet body.

If Mom were still alive, she would have been here. Her face would have been painted red and gold. She would have cheered louder than anyone. She would have come down to celebrate with the team.

"I'm going to do it Mom," I whisper. "I'm going to play soccer, like you did. I'm going to make something of myself. I won't disappoint you."

My cleats clink on the bleachers as I turn away and start back to the bench to get my bag. Mom is not here, and I have no one to blame for that but myself. Instead, Coach Fant was the one to watch me tonight. She probably didn't notice how well I played. She saw how I got beat and nearly lost us the game.

I risk a look, and she's heading away. That last stop was a good one. Hopefully she saw it. At least she's leaving without talking to me, which means she's not revoking my scholarship tonight.

I pick up my bag. It's time to head home.

"Hey Thala."

Why is she still here?

"I'm just curious. Have you ever seen your birth certificate? Will you show it to me before we're teammates next fall? If you end up making the team, that is."

I'm going to make the team.

"I just want to make sure you're really human."

Mom's empty place at the top of the bleachers calls to me, and I look up into the stands where she should be, my fingers touching my flattened nose, my oddly round face, my ears without earlobes.

I am different.

2 Revelations

Lydia

I step out of my car and slam the door. Rain patters lightly on the tin roof covering my parking spot. I shift my bag on my back and squint through the spotlight that turned on when I arrived. I can't see any lights on in the house. Maybe I got lucky and beat Dad home.

I step out of the carport and head out into the rain to walk to the front door. An engine revves behind me, and a white beat-up car barrels down the street. I jump off the driveway and onto the porch in time to see it swerve in front of the house and nearly crash into the garage.

Not so lucky. Dad just got home. My timing couldn't be worse.

He gets out of the car and stumbles toward the door.

I step to the side into the overgrown rhododendron bush—maybe he won't see me. He stumbles out of the car, mumbling and nearly slips in a puddle. Is he angry tonight?

Probably. He's been angry since Mom died.

"What are you doing out so late?" Dad grumbles. He saw me.

"District championship for soccer."

"In the winter?"

We've had this conversation before. More than twice.

"They had to postpone the fall sports tournaments because of the teacher strikes. My college coach was at the game tonight."

"What did you say?" His voice echoes down the quiet street. "Can't you ever speak up?" He's really angry tonight. I consider bolting for my car, but that wouldn't go over well.

He mumbles something and fumbles with his keys some more, but I don't help. I've tried helping before and ended up on my butt.

I feel like Mom spent her life trying to convince me that Dad was an amazing man. I'm not sure I ever saw—he was always stressed and anxious about his work when she was alive, and her death finished him off.

9

"Get yourself to bed." Dad finally gets the door open and stumbles inside. "It's late. I can't believe you insolent little brat—running all over the town at this late hour. You should be more grateful that you have a roof over your head. I wouldn't've ever treated my dad with such disrespect. Coming home late, lying about soccer..."

He stumbles into the house, still cursing, and wanders down to his bedroom, passing the master bedroom on his way. No one has opened that door in over four years.

The light to his bedroom flicks on. I hear a crash and then a thud as he passes out on his bed.

I close the front door and shiver in my wet uniform.

That went better than usual. I've learned to avoid the landmines and keep the peace—and avoid the bruises. I'm quick from years of soccer, but Dad is stronger than me, and the last time I saw him sober, was probably the last time anyone opened the door to the master bedroom.

My flip-flops snap down the hall to my bedroom. I flip on the light and strip off my wet shirt. I maneuver through my cluttered room and drop it in my laundry bucket. I'm just as bad as Dad, in a way. I'm not sure I've cleaned my room since Mom died. Stacks of paper and mementos line the window sill and the furniture, most of them from when she was alive. On the top of the stack next to the laundry basket is the last note she ever wrote to me.

Sleep well my soccer star! I'll kiss you when I get home. Dream of making that winning goal, and someday it will happen.

I sit on my bed and pick up the cell phone from on my bed stand. It's old now and won't turn on unless it's plugged into the wall. I haven't used it in years, though it's become my constant companion off the soccer field. I turn the phone slowly in my hands and let my fingers probe the divots in it while my mind wanders back to the soccer game.

If Mom were here, I would ask her about what Joana said. Why do I look so different? Did I have some kind of surgery? Was I adopted? Some rare genetic condition?

It isn't the first time I've wondered, of course. I've always been different, but I never asked about it before Mom was gone.

I want to think that I have some of Mom in me, and I do from the hours we spent together. But, the thought that we might not have the same blood running through our veins makes me colder than the cool night air against my bare skin. Mom played college ball, and if all goes well, I will, too. But, is that where the similarities end?

I slide off my muddy shorts and throw them into the laundry basket with the rest of my clothes, and then I slip on my bathrobe and turn on my heater. Dad stopped paying for gas months ago, so we only have electric space heaters now. I huddle down next to it, positioned so it spits warm air into the robe.

My shivering stops, but my mind wandering does not. Dad keeps important documents in his bedroom—in the small cabinet next to his bed.

I should look at my birth certificate. It seems like something I should do anyway, though I'm not giving Joana a copy. After all, I will be an adult in a few weeks, and I haven't looked at it in ages.

But I don't go right away. I stay crouched down, enjoying feeling warm, and let the minutes tick by. Long after I've stopped shivering, I snuggle into the warm robe and leave the space heater.

Thankfully, Dad loves TV too much to stop paying for power. I don't know how much money he still has, though. He collected a check from Mom's life insurance and stopped working, but there's no way he's using the money responsibly. And, I know I'm not ever seeing any of it.

My feet pad lightly on the wood floor as I walk down the dark hall. I don't turn on any lights—Dad hates it when I leave lights on unnecessarily.

Dad's light is on. I move slowly, and peak around the corner into his room.

He's fully dressed, passed out on his bed just as I expected. A large string of drool drips down his mouth into a puddle next to his head. So gross.

Quieter than a cat, I slip into the room and open the cabinet. There aren't very many documents in here. Mom's birth death certificates, her marriage certificate, Dad's birth certificate. My lungs start to burn from holding my breath. But, there it is. My birth certificate with Mom and Dad's name on it. But, if I was adopted, would it say anything about it? I don't know. It all looks in order.

Dad swears and I nearly jump out of my bathrobe. I close the door to the cabinet and slowly peak over the edge of the bed. He moved his head out of the drool puddle, but he's still asleep.

I tiptoe out of the room and down the hallway before I let myself start breathing again. My shower is short—cold water showers are never very fun in the winter.

But when I lie back in bed, I can't fall asleep for a long time. My birth certificate looks fine, but does that mean anything?

* * *

My phone buzzes.

Absently, I look over at the now-lighted screen. It's a new email: College Entrance Survey for Registered Adoptees.

What?

I shove my homework to the corner of my desk. I hate chemistry.

I pick up the phone and my finger hovers over the small screen. The light dims, and then the screen goes back to black. If this is spam, then Dad is still my dad, and nothing changes. I'm stuck here with him, he's my blood and flesh, and I have to take care of him. That option is straightforward. And depressing.

But what if I'm not who I think I am? It doesn't make sense, though. Why wouldn't Mom have told me? Who am I, if not Sandra Miller's daughter?

I turn the phone back on and stare at the screen again. I think of Mom teaching me how to be aggressive. We spent hours together on the soccer field at the park near our old house. She would try and get past me, and it was hard to find it in myself to stop her, it was so fun watching her maneuver around me. She would get so mad whenever she beat me! "This ball is yours, Lydia!" she'd say. "Just take it."

The screen goes black again.

It's probably just spam.

I turn the phone on again and open the email.

It looks legitimate. They even know I'm registered to start school at U-dub this fall.

The flood of emotion pushes me off my bed. I drop the phone and grab my old phone and twirl it in my hands. Then I push it close to my heart. I bite my lip as the tears start to flow.

Next thing I know, I'm standing in front of the master bedroom. I don't open the door, but I don't need to open it to smell the room, see the pictures of Mom on the wall, feel the warmth of snuggling next to her in her giant bed. I don't need to open it to remember speculating who was going to win the World Cup or who was going to make the national team.

Momentum carries me down to the family room, which is connected to the kitchen. Dad sits in his recliner, watching a late-night basketball game with a can of beer in his hand. Does he know where I came from?

Warning bells sound in my head. I shouldn't be here. But I can't leave. I stay and stare at the man who isn't my biological dad. Who hasn't been my Dad for years.

The game goes into a commercial break. "Hi Sean," I say.

"What?" Dad mumbles, not looking away from the racy hamburger commercial. I should have waited for a different commercial.

"What!" Dad shouts. He turns away from the TV, which has switched to showing the hamburger instead of the naked lady. His eyes are bloodshot.

"Why are you crying?"

Because I couldn't stop myself. My emotions are too strong, too real. "I just wanted you to know that I know you're not my dad," I finally make out.

Dad jumps out of his chair and grabs my shirt. "What did you say?" The smell of alcohol washes over me.

I should shut up and try to get out while I can, but something inside me keeps me talking. "I just got an email from the university."

"Speak up!"

12

I yell the words at him. "You're not my dad. Why did you ever tell me? Why would you keep something like this from me?"

"You idiot girl." His spittle smacks my cheeks; the bitter taste of beer burning my mouth and nose. He pushes me. I stumble and then fall backward. My arms flail out, but there is nothing to grab on while I sail backward through the room. My head hits the cabinets. Hard. Lights flash in my eyes and I gasp from the sudden pain pulsing through my head.

"Your mom didn't cheat on me, if that's what you're implying."

I shake my head and push myself up, but Dad kicks my shin and then then my abdomen. I fall back onto my hands and knees. "No," I say. "I'm not."

"Your Mom wanted babies so bad," His voice is loud enough to wake up our neighbors. "She couldn't bear the fact that the man she loved came home from the war injured. She couldn't accept me. So she adopted you."

She. Not we. The words hit me harder than his boot. Dad didn't want me.

I'm back on my feet now, but when I turn to leave, he follows me until I'm cornered in the kitchen. When I look back at him, all I see is his fist. The blow hits my left eye, and I stagger backward, tripping over the open dishwasher and hitting my head again, this time on the wall.

My vision goes fuzzy, but I try to concentrate on getting out of here. Dad yells fill the small corner of the kitchen, though his access to me is now blocked by the dishwasher. I try not to listen as he rants about being replaced, soccer matches that Mom insisted on seeing, a girl who is ungrateful and lazy.

Still, each word hits me harder and harder.

He hates me.

Tears burn my eyes.

Dizzy from the pain, I push off the wall and jump through his legs. His beefy hand catches me, but my leg jerks free when he kicks me on my upper thigh. I scream and shove myself onto my feet. I limp-sprint out of the room.

Dad's drunken shouts follow me as I run away from him. But not fast enough.

"Because of you," he yells, "I lost Mom before she died."

I burst out the back door onto the porch. The evening rain falls lightly as I stumble around the house.

"I never wanted you! You've made me lose everything!" Dad slips in a puddle.

I make it to my car, glad I still have my keys in my pocket. I yank the door open and hit the gas—hard. Dad regains his balance and runs after me, screaming at the top of his lungs as he disappears in the rear-view mirror. I drive fast, windshield wipers going full throttle. Blood and tears run down my face, but I don't care. I drive through neighborhoods, over hills, and around shopping centers until I finally pull into a small office park and stop the car.

My shirt is ripped and soaked in blood. I grab a handful of it and hold my nose. My head hurts. I'm alone in the dark, in a car in the middle of a silent city. Rain splatters on the roof of the car. I check my nose, but the blood still hasn't stopped.

Mom would tell me that things are going to work out. She'd tell me that comeback story from college when her team was down two goals with only ten minutes left. "You can never give up," she'd say.

But she isn't here anymore. I reach into my pocket and pull out my old flip phone. The last time I heard her voice was on this phone.

3 Respite

Lydia

I'm not sure when I fall asleep, but when I wake up, it's light outside and the parking lot is mostly full. Rain hits the top of the car and runs down the windshield.

I'm not going home.

I don't have anywhere to go.

The girls on the team are the only people I really know. We moved here shortly before the accident, and I still don't really know anyone well enough to ask for help. I'm skipping work today, and school. I can't go walking around like this, and I can't go home when Dad is waiting for me.

I search my brain for an option, any option that doesn't involve me running out of gas on my way. Finally, I settle on Maria's house. We had a team party there last week, and I think I could find my way back. We're not close, but she would probably let me come in and get cleaned up.

She's my best option.

Now to wait for school to end. I start the car and leave the office park and drive until I find a nearly deserted parking lot next to a library. I lower my seat and wait as the sun comes out and the clouds blow away. My stomach rumbles, and my head aches, but I don't dare step out of the car with how much blood is caked on my shirt. Moms come with toddlers and go in and out of the library, but I shrink deeper into my seat and they don't see me.

Why didn't Mom tell me I was adopted? Lots of people are adopted. If I'm a registered adoptee, why didn't I ever know? Maybe Mom told me, but I didn't realize it? Maybe she would have told me if only I had listened.

When study groups from my school start showing up, I pull my seat up and start toward Maria's house, glad to finally have something else to think about.

I can't see Maria's house curbside because there are hundreds of trees and more than 30 steep steps going up to her door. There's no way I'm going to drive my car up her driveway, though. One, I don't think it can make it up that steep of a hill, and two, it would leak oil all over. 30 steps it is. I just hope no one else I know will see me on my way up there. And, that I won't have to turn around and come back down before getting cleaned up.

I take a deep breath and step out of the car, intending to sprint up the steps. Instead, after spending all day hiding in my car, my vision goes black and I lose my balance. My arm flies out and I manage to grab the side of the car, gasping as my body falls against it. Slowly this time, I push myself back into a standing position. My right leg barely moves where Dad kicked it, and my head aches from the exertion of standing up. I start up the stairs. My sprint is more like a crawl, and I'm sure the entire neighborhood has seen me by the time I limp up each stair and get to the door.

I ring the doorbell.

Will Maria be home? Does she have siblings? What if a brother answers the door?

What if no one is home?

The door opens and it's Maria.

Something finally went right, though she's wearing a neon pink bikini.

"What are you wearing?" I blurt out at the same time she asks me about my appearance, which I'm sure is no less shocking, though the rearview mirror only tells part of the story.

She waves me in, and I limp inside. I wipe stupid tears out of my eyes as she closes the door behind me.

"I'm really sorry. Are you just leaving to go swimming or something? I don't mean to interrupt."

"You're fine!" Maria puts her arm around my shoulder and gives it a squeeze. "I've been on the back porch, sun bathing."

"Sun bathing? In the winter?"

Maria laughs. "I take advantage of every opportunity we get sun. And I mean *every* opportunity. Don't worry—I have a space heater out there with me—it's a pretty awesome setup. But Lydia, you look awful. What happened?"

She's moved away from me, and her eyes are averted. I'm avoiding her eyes, too.

"I, uh..." I shrug when nothing else comes out.

My face burns and I wipe at my eyes, frustrated by the emotion. I want to crawl under her table and curl up in a ball. I choke down a sob and try again.

"I was hoping you wouldn't mind if I got cleaned up? I don't want to be a bother or anything, but...I just need some help. Just for a minute."

I feel about as big as an ant.

"Of course." Maria does meet my eyes now, and she gives me another hug, getting blood on her swim suit and her shoulder. "You can use my shower. Clean up, and then will you come outside with me? It's such a beautiful day! I've been out there wondering who I could share it with."

16

Fun isn't the word I'd use to describe the awkwardness of the situation, but I agree. I'm putting Maria out, but if it's fun for her I should stay for a bit. I've never worn a bikini and I can't imagine that it will be comfortable. But nothing is comfortable about today.

Maria takes me upstairs to her huge bedroom. Half of my Dad's house would fit inside this one room, and that house isn't small. Not only is the room huge, but it's immaculately clean, with its own bathroom and shower. Maria pulls out a neon green bikini for me and tells me to take my time. I hope she doesn't see me gawking at her room.

I take the world's fastest shower, careful not to look at myself in the mirror any more than I have to. My face is swollen, and my eyes are puffy. If I didn't look like a Neanderthal yesterday, I do today.

Maria's smile keeps me from running back to my car as I step onto the deck, the remnants of my fight with Dad displayed all over my nearly naked body. This was such a dumb idea. I should have just hopped in my car and left, but then I would have had to say no, and I would have had to figure out what to wear.

"I'm so glad you're here," Maria says.

I don't believe her, but I sit down anyway. I brought my old phone with me, and I grip it until my knuckles turn white.

Maria and I have been on the soccer team together for three years, but I barely know her. We're complete opposites, and really have nothing to talk about. Ever. Her blonde hair is always styled, her nails are always done, and the tanning salon must be her home away from home given how tan her skin is through the dreary Seattle winters.

As for me, I don't have money for make-up, and I'm lucky that my clothes fit me. I look different than anyone else in the school, and I'm definitely not pretty or stylish. I don't have half as many friends as Maria. I don't have any. And if even one boy looked at me for every date that Maria has, I'd call myself lucky.

I settle into the lounge chair, grateful for the space heater, but awed by the view. The deck looks straight west. Lake Washington stretches out in front of us, turning into the Seattle skyline, and finally the sun as it beats on our skin.

I stretch out my legs and try to soak in the entire view. It is a beautiful afternoon. My body aches, and I realize that by stretching out my legs, I've put them on display. My right thigh sports a huge bruise, and my shin on my left leg is badly scraped. I bring up my knees and hug them to my chest.

"You know," Maria says, and I brace myself for the questions. "You have the coolest tattoo I have ever seen. I don't know why you always keep it hidden."

I've been so subconscious about my bruises that I forgot about the blue flower.

"You think it's a tattoo?" It's just above my right breast, reaching up to my collarbone.

"Where did you get it?"

"It's been there as long as I can remember." The mark is more detailed and real looking than any tattoo.

"It looks like you have a flower permanently glued onto your skin. No, not onto your skin, living in your skin."

Talking about this is only slightly more comfortable than talking about my bruises.

Maria blows a bubble with her gum until it pops. She licks the gum off her face and starts chewing again. "Well, I can't think of what else to call it besides a tattoo."

She sits up and leans over me, so she can see it better. I blush and pretend to see something interesting on the Seattle skyline that wasn't there seconds ago. If I pull my legs any tighter, I'll hit her in the head with my knees.

"It's so cool."

"Yeah." The flower is a reminder that my parentage shouldn't have been a shock. I should have figured this out a long time ago. Mom would have never gone to such great lengths to put a mark like that on me.

"Speaking of cool tattoos in sexy places." Maria blows another bubble with her gum and then keeps talking as she licks it off her face. "I heard that Trent Smith is going to ask you to Prom. You should totally get a low-cut dress and show that baby off."

My face turns red. I'm not showing the tattoo off. Ever.

Then, what she said fully registers. "Trent? Ask me?" Trent Smith is the most popular guy in school.

"That's the rumor. I guess there was a tiff with Hanna, and he's looking for someone who will make her really jealous. He decided to find a soccer girl, and given your performance last night, he's got his eyes on you."

I don't want anyone's eyes on me right now. "There's no way I'd say yes." Despite what Joana might think, I'm definitely not that desperate.

"Seriously, Lydia, he's gorgeous. It doesn't matter what his reasons are."

Yes, it does. "Do you think that Trent has ever had one intelligent thought in his entire life?"

"He's really good at football."

"That's not intelligence. Besides, so was my dad. I think he even played in college." I don't know why I brought up Dad. I shut my mouth and bite my lip to stop the tears.

"I'm so excited for college," Maria says. "It's so awesome you made the team."

"For now." I can barely keep my voice steady. I bite the side of my cheek to distract myself.

"Yeah, I hear it's pretty cut-throat. But getting a scholarship is awesome. You worked so hard for that!"

"My mom played college ball. It was her dream that I would, too." With the situation with my dad like it is, I wonder if I can afford to go to college, even with the scholarship.

"That's so totally cool. You're so great, Lydia!"

I swallow hard and change the subject. "What are you excited for? About college I mean."

Maria giggles. "Do you think it's as fun as they say? Just think—all the beer, boys, and parties that you could ever want. Without parents!"

I look away at the mention of beer. I'm not going to any parties with alcohol. And, I'd give just about anything for parents right now.

"You'll have to go to some parties with me."

I shake my head. College will be soccer, studying, and feeling sorry for myself. No parties, no boys. I'll be just as much a loner there as I am here. Besides, I can't fix my appearance, even if I didn't mind the alcohol.

"Come on, Lydia. Please?"

"I don't want to be by beer," I say. "Ever." The word comes out with more feeling than I intended.

And then I start to cry. Pull yourself together girl.

I can't burden Maria with this. I stand, but Maria jumps up too and grabs my arm.

"Did someone drunk beat you?"

My sobs get harder. Words aren't going to come back for a while.

"Your dad?"

She saw right through me.

"Have you called the police?"

I shake my head.

"I'm calling right now. Do you have a place to stay?"

I shake my head again, and finally manage to find words. "Don't call them. I don't mean to be a bother. I'll go now."

"Sorry, but you need to stay here." Maria doesn't let go of me when I try to pull away. "All summer."

"I have somewhere to go," I say.

"Where?"

I'm pathetic. Another sob escapes, and Maria takes me into her arms. Tears fall on her bare shoulder. At least it isn't blood this time. Cold wind blows the heat from the space heater away and we both shiver.

"You're staying here," Maria says again. "The first thing we'll do is call the police."

Dad will kill me if I call the police, but do I really ever see myself going back?

19

"It's the right thing to do. Stay here where you're safe. You'll be welcome all summer."

I nod dumbly. I don't have much of a choice, but it feels awkward to accept the offer. "How could I ever repay you?" I ask.

Maria gets a glint in her eye. Then it breaks into a full smile. "Actually, this is perfect! You should stay here the summer of course, but the way to make it up to me is if you'll room with me in college next year."

"Room with you?" Why would Maria want to room with me?

"Yes," she says. "Last night my dad threw down the gauntlet. He said I have to live at home this year. But, this is perfect. If you need someone to room with, and if you're not going to parties, Dad will have to change his mind. This is so perfect, Lydia. You work harder than anyone on the team, and you're really nice."

I can't think of one positive thing about the situation. "I'm not always like this. I grew up in a stable house, with a good mom. Then I got this strange email saying I was a registered adoptee. That's what started all of this. If I hadn't been curious..." I'm blabbering.

"Lydia, listen to me. This isn't your fault. You're safe now. You'll stay with us and living on campus will be so awesome! You have to do it."

"I can't afford the dorms..."

"My dad has contacts, and we can help you get a great job for the summer. Not a problem. You've worked too hard to get on that team." Maria grabs her phone and calls 911.

When she puts the phone down, I'm still sniffling. "Do you have clothes I can change into before they get here?"

All she has are jeans. Apparently, Maria thinks stretchy pants are out of style. Still, jeans are better than a bikini I put them on and wait for the police.

The last time I talked to police was the night Mom died. I clutch my phone. The screams, the silence. The endless ticking of the clock as I sat by the window watching the rain fall. Then the police arrived.

I don't sit by the window this time.

Maria squeezes my hand. "It will be okay. We'll get your Dad thrown in jail, and we'll find out where you came from. And we'll make sure you play soccer for U-dub."

I force a smile and nod, but my eyes go down to my feet. I don't want Dad in jail, and I don't want other parents. I just want Mom back. I want her to see me play college ball and know that all the time she spent with me on the soccer field was worth it.

4 Research

Karl

I wipe my sweaty palms on my pants. I take a deep breath, but my nerves don't relax. I mean, would a fly caught in a spider's web relax while it waited for the spider to show up? No. When things are about to get messy, things get uptight.

And things are about to get messy.

Through the doorway, Sam towers over Rahul. Sam's voice gets louder with each word as he goes on and on about what Rahul should do next. I've been sitting here long enough to know he wants Rahul to throw away the last eighteen months of work and start over.

Figures. Advisors always want their students to start over. They don't care if any of them ever get out of school. When an advisor looks at a graduate student, prestigious publications and continued funding flash before their eyes. Especially if it's a good student. Funding sources, big publications, ideas coming to fruition. And graduation is the enemy.

I rub my temples. Waiting outside Sam's office to get yelled at, is almost as bad as being in the hot seat. I stare blankly at the brand-new Gates Center floor. I'm almost a mile away from my office at the old Mellon Institute, so it's not like I can rush back to my office and grab my computer and work until he's ready. And I don't foresee a day when I lug that huge machine all the way up to keep me busy when Sam doesn't keep my appointment.

And I'm the one who is waiting to get yelled at for not making progress.

Sam will finish eventually, and I'll lumber out of my seat and take my growing body into the torture chamber. What kind of facial expression should I assume today? Scared? Determined? Maybe I should make a joke about how much weight I've gained this month and see if that lightens the mood.

The floor doesn't offer any advice. It starts to click, though, as tanned legs, high heels, and a short skirt meander until they stop in front of me.

"Mr. Stapp, aren't you looking lovely today?" the owner of the legs says in an English accent.

I didn't know we had anyone in the program from England. I thought everyone was from China or California.

I take my eyes off the floor. The girl is pretty. Really pretty. Eventually I recognize her as a first year from my program.

A first year. The recognition sends my eyes back to the floor. Even though I wouldn't mind looking at her face for a while, on principle I don't fraternize with first year students. During graduate school, you make and learn from mistakes. I made the particular mistake of befriending a first year during last year's retreat, and I ended up losing a lot of the fall semester helping him with assignments. Not this year.

I keep my eyes locked on her toes and wait for her to leave. Someday she'll understand.

She giggles and sits next to me, crossing her legs. "You waiting for Sam?" she asks.

Obviously. People say the dumbest things to start conversations. I nod, and this time I struggle to get my eyes back on the floor. The girl has a slender frame, short red hair, and a shorter black skirt. I like the way her hair brings out her green eyes, which light up when she smiles.

The first year who befriended me last year was tall and lanky and waved his arms around when he talked. Not nearly as nice to look at. Maybe I should reconsider my principles.

"Do you have an advisor yet?" If she has a good advisor, I can justify spending a little time getting to know her.

"Yes." She blushes and extends her hand. "I'm Tara."

Totally not helpful. "I'm..."

"Karl Stapp, of course." The girl, Tara apparently, laughs. "Everyone in the program knows who you are. Everyone with half a brain, anyway."

Gossip travels fast! I knew Sam was upset with me, but I didn't realize that the rumor mill was already churning.

Tara's smiles fades. "You look concerned. I only mean it in the best way. Everyone knows how brilliant you are, and how you've flown through all the classes."

Only a first year would care about coursework. I've worked as hard as I could for the last three and a half years, and still I'm sitting here waiting for Sam to give me an ultimatum. I need to pick a strong thesis project, or he's done with me. Success in the classroom doesn't matter. Neither do conference publications.

Funding sources and journal publications are what count, and I don't have either.

Rahul comes out of the office looking like a wounded animal. I don't think he even sees us as he scurries by. He must be really riled up—I would have noticed Tara on my worst days. I take one last look at her. One doesn't see many women this beautiful in graduate school. Or anywhere, actually, except maybe TV. And graduate students never have time for TV.

I'll have to try and sit by her at a program retreat sometime.

Tara stands as I do. "I'll talk to you later."

I watch her walk toward the restrooms like she's a movie star or something. She does have a great figure.

Just before she rounds the corner, she turns and winks at me.

My face gets hot.

"Karl?" Sam's voice brings me back to reality.

Most people would probably say the most terrifying place on earth is their father's den. Those people have never had a graduate school advisor.

Sam waits for me behind his desk, scribbling furiously in his notebook. As usual. Poor Rahul. He really is a good student. His latest machine learning model did have some holes in it, that was obvious last group meeting. But, at least his ideas were decent. The group had some good suggestions for him, too.

I sit down and wait for Sam to finish his notes.

Sam isn't scribbling as fast anymore. His hands move over the paper like the ink suddenly turned magnetic and is pulling the pen onto the paper. Sam is a fast-paced guy. He does everything at double-speed. Slow writing isn't in his playbook.

I shift uncomfortably in my seat and clear my throat. Sam glances up at me, and his head moves in slow motion.

I clear my throat again. "Are you feeling okay?" I ask.

Sam shakes his head, slowly, but keeps writing. When he finishes, he blinks a few times before glaring at me.

"Did you pick your thesis topic?"

No reason to beat around the bush. "Not yet." I didn't like any of his ideas. I didn't come to graduate school to spend the rest of my life here. I would spend the rest of my life here before I could finish even the simplest idea he had. There has to be a way to apply some of the models he's proposing to real world problems instead of always trying to figure out the next theoretical extension.

Sam takes a deep breath. Too deep. Is he trying to show me how frustrated he is? I shift in my seat. Something is not right with Sam. Not that it's going to make the beating any less severe.

Sam's mouth opens, and I know what he's going to say. That I've been in the program for nearly four years now. That I need to pick a thesis topic now, or he won't keep funding me. That it doesn't matter if I've published four papers at different conferences, I need real results on impactful problems. That even though I could probably graduate with the work I've done so far, he will fight me every step of the way until I have something real I can show him.

I brace myself as he leans forward. His face darkens, contorts into a scowl, and then he falls out of his chair. I watch in disbelief as his head slams against the desk with a loud crack. It bounces off the desk and then his body slumps and collapses onto the floor.

"Sam!?"

I jump off my chair and crouch down behind the desk. I lift his head. Bad idea. Warm blood oozes through my fingers. His eyes open weakly, and he tries to say something. The weak moan echoes through the small office.

My lecture is over.

I place his head on the ground and stand, unsure of what to do. My hands are covered in blood. I can see how this is all going to go down. Authorities discover a struggling graduate student standing stupidly in his advisor's office, covered in blood, after being chewed out over his mediocre performance.

Great.

My pants have a large ketchup stain on them from a hamburger I ate yesterday. I wipe the blood by the stain. It blends in okay, though I still have blood under my finger nails.

Sam moans, but he doesn't move.

What is wrong with him? I look around the room stupidly, but I can't think of what to do. Mostly, I would rather be anywhere else but here. Can I run away?

I walk to the door. Tara is back, sitting outside the office door with her laptop perched on her bare legs. Her face is scrunched into a scowl as she pounds away on the keyboard.

She looks up, catching me watching her. Again.

"You're finished already? That has to be some kind of record."

Her words seem to bring back some of my brain's function. "Something is really wrong with Sam," I manage to get out.

She gently sets her laptop on a chair and walks over to stand by me. I step away so she can see what happened. Her shriek fills the office and leaves my ears ringing.

For a minute, I think she might faint and bang her head as well. That's just what kind of day it seems to be right now. She stumbles over to the door and grabs the frame with both hands. I hear her take a few deep breaths, and then she stands up and turns around.

"We have to get him to a hospital," she says.

"No. I think we should call 911." I don't want to get sued for helping my advisor get to the hospital.

"That will take too long. We need to go now, and I have a car close by. The ER at the UPMC hospital is just down the street."

If she has a car close by, that is the better option. At least for Sam. I nod.

"Any idea what's wrong with him?"

24

I shake my head.

"He's bleeding badly." Tara crouches down next to him. She isn't dressed for a rescue operation, but she looks good doing it. "Karl, stop gawking at me and take his other arm."

The drive to the hospital is short, but it feels like an eternity. The sound of Sam's raspy voice fills the car as Tara zips down the road. I try not to look at him or think about him. And I hold my breath so I don't smell the blood. The thought of sitting this close to death paralyzes me. How could Sam, a healthy, middle-aged man, collapse like that?

He'll be fine, I tell myself. There's nothing to worry about.

I close my eyes and try to ignore the rasps and the sound of death. I clench my hands and hold them against my ears. Sam's rasping breathing still resonates loudly in my ears. I shudder and close my eyes. What if he dies?

Tara slams on the breaks and jumps out of the car—high heels and all—and runs into the ER.

I get out of the car, but I don't follow her. I don't want to see anyone in the ER.

Seconds later, a few EMTs run out with Tara and take Sam away on a stretcher. I stand dumbly by the car. The wind picks up and blows bits of snow against my face. I shiver, realizing I left my coat back in Sam's office.

Tara's arm slides across my back, sending shivers through me. Instinctively, I lean into her warm skin.

"Do you want to stay?"

"No." I don't even want to be here now. I open the door and slide back into my seat.

Tara walks around the car to the driver's side door. I need to get away from this place. I need to get back to my office. I have a lot of work I need to do this afternoon. Like that conference paper I need to submit tonight. But Sam won't have time to go over it now. He hates it when I submit things without his approval. As sick as he seems, though, it might not matter.

I'm sure they'll figure out what's wrong with him. He'll be fine.

Tara stays quiet as she drives the few blocks back to campus and parks the car on the street next to the Mellon Institute. The stately building sits above us, its proud columns black on the side towards Pittsburgh and white on the east side.

If Sam dies, I'll have to start all over with another advisor. Sam really hasn't been that bad, even if I haven't made much progress in his eyes. I stare out the window, wondering why they never tried to clean the columns after they shut all the steel factories down. The building probably looked nice a hundred years ago.

Tara clears her throat, and I look over to find her smiling at me. "Did you want to stay in the car? I can get a power adapter for you. Is there anything else you need? I will do anything for you, Karl. Whatever you want."

The words are oddly flirtatious. A rush of something goes through me, but I push it aside and open the car door. Tara was out of my league before I put on 150 pounds after starting graduate school.

We take the stairs to the entrance and I swipe my student card to open the door and hurry out of the cold.

"Thank you for your help. I'm sure Sam appreciates it, too."

Tara smiles. "I'm glad I was there. I think you might have died with him otherwise. Perfect timing, I suppose. I had decided to head back down here when I got the call from Candice that I'm now your new office chum. So, I came back."

Office chum? No way. I haven't shared an office with anyone all four years of graduate school. The huge stack of papers on Steve's unused desk, the clutter around the office. It's worked for years.

"I'm sorry," I say. "What do you mean, office chum?"

"I'm moving into your office. Our office."

"You're moving into my office?" I repeat dumbly.

A playful grin tugs at the corners of Tara's full lips. Why does it seem like she's always laughing at me? "Steve doesn't use the office. Did you know that? All the stuff on his desk actually belongs to you. I talked to Candice about it, and she told me to move in right away."

Share an office with a first year?

By now we've walked through the building to the offices for the program. Carefully, I insert my key and open the door. This office is not the same office I left two hours ago on my way to meet with Sam. Steve's desk shines as if it's been recently polished, and a dozen pictures of orchids hang on the walls. All of my fast food wrappers from the last four years sit in the corner in a huge trash bag. The room smells like some kind of perfume. And Clorox. A pile of my dirty clothes has been collected into a laundry basket in the corner.

A laundry basket? This has got to be some kind of joke.

Tara laughs and gives me a small push. "Welcome to your new home, Mr. Stapp."

I take one step inside, but the smell is too much. "I need to get something to eat."

"I'll come with you."

No way. I haven't eaten a meal with a girl since Andrea.

"No. That's okay."

"Please?"

Tara's laugh follows me as I run down the hallway. "Where are you going?"

Away. From here, from the smell, from the reminder that Sam is in the hospital. I'm not sure where I'm going, but I'm going. Maybe I'll talk to Candice and see if I can get Tara out of my office. Maybe I'll take a walk and finally figure out what I'm doing for my thesis work.

5 Review

Karl

Two days.

That's how long Sam lasted in the hospital. Two days.

Tara and I might as well have left him in his office.

I'm finally going to delete the email from Khanh, our program director. It's been sitting in my inbox for more than two weeks. Khanh said nice things about Sam, all well deserved. He gave his life to his research. His wife left him years ago, but Sam never noticed. He mentored over 250 students during his career and published more than two dozen high-impact papers. His research was a big part of the latest breakthroughs in machine learning, and he was a renowned leader worldwide. He gave his life to his work, and he expected his students to give even more.

It's over. He's gone.

Something is happening behind my eyes. Tears? Not today. I delete the email. I have work to do. I need to find another advisor, and I need to figure out what research to work on now.

But one more email from Khanh needs to be deleted from my inbox.

I read the subject line again: *Funeral Arrangements.*

A funeral. More than a week ago. My muscles tense and my throat constricts.

Funeral.

I should've gone.

I couldn't go.

My hands won't move. I realize I'm holding my breath and my head feels fuzzy. I start breathing again and stare at the email, but I don't open it. I haven't opened it once.

It's been four years since the funeral, yet the email has kept me back there like it hasn't been any time at all. I'm in a church building. The music is haunting, the room still. Andrea sits next to me. She holds her arm around my back, even though she knew then. She hid her secret, pretended to care. On my other side, Dad sits still as a statue, stone-faced and pale. Pearl sobs to his side. Her face is red and blotchy.

27

Crowds of people tell me how sorry they feel. They crowd around me, drowning me. There is no escape.

Mom's body lies at the front of the church. Inside that casket. She knows. She knows it's been four years now. The promises I made before she passed are promises I haven't kept.

I delete the email and force myself to stand. My legs are wobbly. I slam the computer shut. Thoughts try to force their way into my mind. Who went to Sam's funeral? Did his wife come back? Did his children come? Any of the students or other academics that he worked with go?

Or, did people cower in their offices like I did?

The door swings open and Tara walks into the office.

"Hey Karl," she says, her presence as strong as her perfume.

"Hi." I sit down and put my eyes on my computer. It's time to get busy. It's already late, and I'm need to start another project before I go home tonight.

Tara grabs my shoulder, and I jump. Her hair tickles my neck as she leans forward and whispers in my ear.

"This research thing is really getting to you," Her warm breath sends chills down my spine. "You just work, work, work."

Her lips tickling my ear causes a strange change in my mood. I fight back a smile, but I end up losing that battle. "I worked hard before graduate school. And I'll keep working after. It's what I do."

"And eat!" She reaches out and pats my tummy in a way that should be weird, but somehow comes across as cute. She leans across me to grab the arm of my chair. She rotates the chair, moving my view away from my computer and completely onto her. She wears a determined expression, along with a white sleeveless turtleneck that highlights her tightly toned midriff.

"What are you working on?" I ask.

"You wouldn't believe it." Tara walks over to what should be Steve's desk and pulls out her laptop. "Dr. Lee wants us to code up our own Monte Carlo simulator. By tomorrow!"

"That isn't too bad." I remember the assignment. Graduate level homework seems hard at the time, but at least answers exist. It's a whole new ball game diving into research and realizing the problems I'm working on have never been solved.

"Isn't too bad!?" She puts her hands on her hips and pouts. "What do you mean?"

"I mean that it's actually not that hard of an algorithm to code up."

"That's because you're unusually brilliant."

"I don't think so."

She smiles. "You don't think you're brilliant?"

"I'm not narcissistic."

"You don't think I should call myself beautiful?"

"I didn't say that."

"Yes, you did."

"If I did, I take it back." I feel my face get warm.

Tara smiles. She's probably noticed that my eyes haven't left her since she turned me around. I don't even remember what I was working on anymore.

"I have two questions for you," she says. "First, doesn't it bother you that Sam was poisoned?"

My hands become clammy. I swallow hard and look away.

"Karl, it's okay to be distraught. Your advisor died. Was murdered, actually! But, didn't the police talk to you about it when they questioned you? Don't you wonder who did it?"

I shake my head. I didn't ask the police anything when I talked to them. I just answered their questions and left. They didn't tell me anything about how Sam died.

Tara hands me a white board marker. "OK. Suit yourself. We don't have to talk about it anymore. But, as far as the Markov experiment goes, would you explain it to me? My Computational Biophysics class is tomorrow. I think I mostly have it, but I really need help with a few details."

On principle, I don't help first years with their homework. Unless I'm a TA, and then I only help during office hours.

But, most first years aren't Tara. And I need a distraction right now. I stand up and walk over to the white board. "Where do you want me to start?"

Tara smiles and puts her arm around my back. The chills come back. She puts another arm around my stomach and her body presses into mine.

"Why don't you start at the beginning?" She's whispering again. "I'll stop you when I have questions."

"Sure."

* * *

It's well past 1:00 AM when I finally shut off my computer for the day and leave the office. I have a sleeping bag under my desk for occasions like this, but I haven't been to my apartment for a few days, and my supply of clean clothes at the office ran out last week. You can only wear a shirt three or four days before you start to notice the smell.

Tonight, I'm going home, sleeping in a bed, and doing some laundry. It's a pain, but sometimes one must do life, even if it means that some of the mathematical modelling simulations end up failing. Besides, Tara hinted a few times tonight that she thought I would benefit from taking a shower.

Not that I care what she thinks. Even if I did spend three and a half hours helping her with that homework assignment.

29

I walk out of the building into the chilly night and hurry down the steps. Salt crunches under my feet, but that's the only sound at this time of night. I look down the street and see a bus coming slowly up Fifth avenue. It's the bus I was hoping to see. I'll catch it on the corner of Fifth and Craig, and it will take me right to my apartment. It's still several blocks away—going against the one-way traffic in the odd bus lane on Fifth—but it hasn't passed me yet. The last one of the day. Perfect timing.

The cool air of the early spring night makes me wish that I had a bigger coat. I shiver and rub my arms. Even after all these years in Pittsburgh, I still don't bother to think about the weather before I go outside. Once a Phoenix boy, always a Phoenix boy.

I make it to the bus stop and look anxiously back at the bus. It may take another five minutes of shivering before it finally gets to me.

I hear a crunch behind me, and a man steps out from the shadows. His hair is pulled back in a long, blond ponytail. In the dim light his eyes are strangely gray. I shiver and look back at the bus. Still another two or three minutes before it gets here. I hope I don't find out what it means to get mugged during that time.

"Hey," the man says. "I'm Bob." His gray eyes haven't left me. I look longingly down the empty street at the approaching bus.

"Chilly night, isn't it? Want to go out on the balcony for a stroll?"

What balcony? I shiver and take a step closer to the road. Bob can't be a beggar or homeless. He's dressed in jeans that don't have holes in them, and his long coat looks newer than my beat-up T-shirts. Still, one can never be too careful, especially this late at night.

"Heading home for the evening, eh?"

Is this guy from Canada?

I do have my wallet, although I doubt it has any cash in it. If he takes my student card, then I won't be allowed back into the building or onto the bus.

Finally, the bus pulls up to the light down the street. As soon as it's green, I can lose this guy.

"Not very talkative, are you?" His voice is deep, intimidating.

The light turns green.

"That's alright, I'll join you on your ride home. We'll talk more on the bus."

So much for losing him.

The bus pulls up with a screech and the door slides open. I show my student ID card and walk down the aisle. Bob follows me into the empty bus.

I pass three African American women sitting in the front of the bus, chatting about work. At the center of the bus a man watches porn on his phone. I make my way past him to the back of the bus.

Bob follows me all the way to the back and chooses the seat right next to me.

30

I scoot over a seat to give us some space. Common courtesy says never to sit right next to someone unless there are no other options. With the bus as empty as it is, options are plentiful.

"Well, Karl. Now is the time you start talking."

"Excuse me? How do you know my name?"

The man laughs, the deep sound barely audible over the roar of the bus engine as it pulls away from the curb. "I know a lot about you, Karl Stapp. Tell me everything you know about the forgotten world."

I study the man. I'm sure that I have never seen him before. He's tall, taller than me, and muscular. I probably weigh more than him, but for every fat cell I have, he has five muscle cells.

"The forgotten world?"

"Yes," he says, and his eyes light up. "You're a direct descendant of Kinni. What do you know?"

"Kinni what?" I have no idea what he's talking about. How does he know my name? I pull out my phone and pretend to browse my email. Dad tried to call me four times today. One time more than usual.

The man snatches the phone out of my hand.

"Hey!"

He puts it down in the seat between us without looking at it. "I consider it rude to look at your phone when you're talking to someone."

I slip the phone back into my pocket and look out the window. We're still a mile away from my apartment.

"Have you ever been to the world?"

"I don't know what you're talking about."

"Are there others with eyes like you there?"

Is this really about my eyes? My eyes are a bright blue, brighter than anyone I've ever met outside my family. It's a genetic trait. Mom had bright eyes, too, and her grandfather before her. It's a trait that's been passed down for generations, although it skipped my sister.

"I don't know what you're talking about."

"Why not?"

"This is my stop." I pull the yellow cord and push by Bob. He reaches out his foot, and I trip over it, landing hard on my knees in the aisle. The bus stops, and I limp out the door.

Bob follows me outside. There is no way that this is his stop, too. He stares at me, his gray eyes expressionless. I'm not sure what to do except go home. Maybe he'll leave once I'm in my apartment. If not, I can call the police.

I start running, huffing as I hurry up the street toward my apartment complex. Bob jogs beside me. I've never been mugged before. What do I do? Scream? There isn't a soul in sight. We are alone.

Me and this psychopath.

"Hey man," I say, and I stop and put my hands on my knees to catch my breath. "You can't just follow me like this. I'm going to call the police." I take my phone out of my pocket and start to dial 911.

My finger freezes over the call button when I hear the click of a gun. Bob shoves it into my face and pushes the phone down. I stare into the barrel of a pistol, its black opening pointed between my eyes.

"Drop the phone."

I put my hands out, bend over slowly, and drop the phone carefully on the sidewalk. It doesn't break. Good. I can't afford another phone on a grad student's stipend.

"That's better. Now, let's get one thing straight, okay? You don't call the police unless you want to end up dead."

I nod.

"Second thing." I guess he's one of those people who doesn't know how to count. "If you ever make it back to the forgotten world, call me. Immediately. I'll leave you my contact information. I belong to a group, the Sapphiri, and our purpose is to find our way back there."

He hands me a card, and then he stares at me with menacing gray eyes. He lowers the pistol and walks away. I grab my phone and run to my apartment, slam the door, throw the card away, and call the police. Unfortunately, they don't do anything but take down some information and then hang up. I guess they get a lot of crazy calls late at night.

I fall into bed, but I can't sleep. I get up and shower, but I can't sleep after that, either. Between Tara and Bob, I'm not sure what just happened with my day, or what I'm even doing with my life. Who was that Bob guy? Was Tara right and Sam really was poisoned? Why does nothing in my life make sense anymore?

Maybe things will go back to normal tomorrow, and I can get some more research done. Hopefully my jobs will finish tonight. If my latest tweak to my model works, I may actually be onto something.

6 Recognize

Lydia

I barely recognize myself in the pictures Maria took of me standing in her entryway six months ago. I can't believe I completely missed her taking them, but then again, I'm not sure I was myself that day. I also can't decide if I'm mad or glad that Maria took the pictures. With her dad being a lawyer, she assumed that we'd need pictures of my bruising. Maybe she's learned some stealth from being around law enforcement so much, too.

I shove the photos into my bag and summon every ounce of courage left in me to open the car door. The courthouse looms large in front of me. I need to get myself inside that building and into the courtroom where the domestic violence hearing will happen. I'll walk in there. I'll see Dad. He'll see me. The police will show their copies of these pictures to the judge. I can do this. I want to do this.

I close the car door and start the car. Then I bite my lip and shut the car off. This is the fourth time I've nearly turned around since leaving Maria's.

Step 1. Get out of the car. I clench and relax my fists, focus on deep breaths. My surroundings. It's beautiful today. Like most summer days in Seattle, the weather couldn't be any more perfect. A slight breeze offsets the heat from the sun. The sky is clear.

At one time in my life, I spent days like this kicking a soccer ball around at the beach with Mom.

Not today. Those days are over. This summer I've spent every day working my tail off so I can afford college. Until today, and I had to practically beg to get today off, all so I could suffer through a long day in court.

The breeze disappears and the sun beats on me as I walk to the courthouse entrance. My rehearsed testimony rolls around in my mind, and then I repeat it again. I've given this testimony in about ten dreams over the past week, and more times than that with Maria and her dad. They drilled me on it for hours last night. It doesn't feel authentic, having the words memorized. But Maria's dad insisted. He says otherwise you never know what you're going to say when the lights shine on you.

33

Maria's dad wanted to be here with me, but I insisted on coming by myself. He can't take a day off to help me. Not when I'm already sleeping under his roof and eating his food. He won't let me pay for anything, and he helped me get the job that is going to put me in the dorms with his daughter this fall.

Despite all that, now that I'm here walking alone, I wish he were here with me.

"Lydia Miller, I didn't expect to see you here. Though maybe I should have."

I take my eyes off the sidewalk to see Coach Fant, dressed in her usual sweats and U-dub sweatshirt, walking down the stairs toward me.

Seeing her out of context quickly removes all words from my brain, and I stare dumbly at her for a minute before I manage to stand up straight and force a smile onto my face. "Hi Coach, how are you?"

"Awful. I spent most of this week on jury duty. I had to cancel my trip back east, all for some petty rape case. It's been insane. I just hope it doesn't put us too far behind with practice starting in less than three weeks. It's not like my job can just be pushed aside." She lets out a big sigh and rolls her eyes.

"How about you?" she asks. "You here for jury duty?"

I blush and shake my head.

"A run in with the law?" Coach Fant smirks. "So many of you rich kids have problems once you're free from the high school safety net. I guess it's a risk I took when I said you could compete for a scholarship. It's too bad you can't be like Joana, who has had to fight for what she has. A girl like that doesn't get into trouble."

I open my mouth, but Coach raises her hands. "Just leave it there, Lydia. It's better if I don't know any details. That way I can defend my decisions to the department if I ever need to."

"But I didn't..."

"I know, that's what they all say. Make sure you get this all straightened out before camp, okay? I don't have to tell you that I was disappointed with your performance in that championship game. Joana made you look like you hadn't played soccer a day in your life. College is full of girls like Joana. You already have two big strikes against you. Give me just one more reason, and I'll boot you off the team before camp starts. Do you understand?"

My eyes burn with tears. I look away, hoping she won't notice.

"That's a good girl. Now, you trot in there and do what they tell you to do. You're an adult now, so it's time you act like one. I'll see you at camp. 8:00 AM sharp. Don't be late because I won't be scared to kick you off this team faster than you can say Joana. I don't care how much money your papa makes."

With a curt nod of her head she walks briskly by me.

My papa. Just because I live in Bellevue doesn't mean my Dad makes a dime. I may be at the courthouse, but I didn't commit any crimes. Joana may have beaten me once, but that doesn't mean I can't play college ball. If I start at the bottom of the roster, I'll work my way up.

I have to. I've had to fight for everything I have, too.

I wipe the tears from my eyes and start walking again. There will be lots more tears before this day is over.

* * *

Thump, crack. Thump, crack.

My foot hits each ball, sending it flying until it cracks on the back of the net. Five shots, and then I jog in, gather the balls, and start over.

I'm in no rush to get back to Maria's house.

Thump, crack.

My phone buzzes again. It's the fifteenth time Maria has texted me since I left the courthouse. I've told her a hundred times that I don't like phones. But, her dad bought me one and she's used it to contact me all summer.

Thump, crack.

I better respond this time. I shoot another shot and then jog over to sideline where the phone lies on top of my old cell in the grass.

At the park, I respond. That should be vague enough.

Five minutes later her fancy rich-girl car pulls up next to the curb.

Thump, crack.

She wears shorts and an athletic tank top. Even when she exercises, she looks more in style than me. She jogs out to the field and sends the ball closest to the road flying towards the net.

Crack.

"Pass the ball around with me?" she yells.

I kick the ball closest to me to her and then start running. We jog around the field, sending the ball bouncing back and forth between us.

After a few laps around the field, Maria breaks the silence. "You're so lucky you get to keep playing. I'm really going to miss this."

"You could play in an intramural league or something." After my encounter with Coach this morning, that almost sounds nicer than competing to play for the university.

Maria pops a bubble with her gum, which distracts her enough that I have to slow down to receive her pass. "If it's co-ed, that would work for me."

I smile, and it feels good. I kick the ball ahead of her just far enough that she has to sprint to get to it. "Hey!" she giggles.

I laugh, too, and pick up the ball on the return pass. "It's getting dark. We'd better go."

The sun lowers behind the tall green of the cedars the surround the park. The trees hide the houses around us, giving the illusion that we are alone. This has been

35

one of my favorite places to practice for years. Dad found this park shortly after we moved, and then Mom and I spent our summers here.

Maria helps gather the balls, and we start towards the cars. "Was it awful?"

"You bet."

Awful is just as good a word as any. The skeptical look from the judge, Dad's pained expression, the embarrassment of seeing the photos shown again. The shock of the sentence.

"Want to talk about it?"

No. "I don't think so."

Maria tosses the last ball to me, and I kick it hard. It flies across the field and cracks in the back of the net on the other side.

"Nice shot. I thought you were a defender."

"By the time Coach Fant gets through with me, I might not be anything."

"I wouldn't worry about that. My friends tell me that Fant is all talk. You're a good player and a hard worker. You'll be fine."

If I get a chance.

"I don't know if you want to hear this today, but Dad finally got access to your adoption file."

"He did?" My heart stops and all the solace I found on the soccer field is gone.

"I have it in the car."

I look at the car and shudder. "You're right, I don't want to hear about it today."

Maria shrugs. "Okay."

I take a deep breath. "But I want to see it anyway." There's no going back now. We might as well ruin my entire life today.

Once we get to the cars, Maria hands me a big manila envelope. The corners of the envelope are crisp; its contents are thin. I spin it in my hands, wondering if I can handle this. Finally I shrug and tear it open. After all, could things get any worse?

The first page is a record of my vitals. About three months old, birthdate unknown. My eyes linger on that line for a while. I've always loved my birthdate—March 6. It's not my real birthday? It was the anniversary of the day that Mom met Dad. It was the day that we moved into our new house in Bellevue. Mom made a huge deal out of it every year.

I can't believe that she made the whole thing up. I look at the date on the form. July. I probably wasn't born in March.

What else did Mom make up about me?

The next page is handwritten. It's titled *Testimony of where the baby was found.* A single paragraph rests below the headline.

I was out running in the Cougar Mountain Wilderness Reserve when I saw a bright flash of blue light. It was like some kind of explosion or something. I nearly ran away, but nothing happened after the splash of light. Ahead of me I found a screaming naked baby with a mark of a blue flower on her chest. I don't know anything else about where she came from.

The next page is Mom and Dad's application for adoption. Dad's signature is at the bottom next to Mom's.

I put the papers back into the envelope.

"Well?" Maria asks.

I stare out across the soccer field. "This doesn't tell me anything." I'm just as alone today as I apparently was when that man found me.

7 Red

Karl

I'm ready to go home for what is left of the weekend. Maybe I'll even watch TV or something. Or go to bed early.

Or something.

Checking printer, please wait. The machine grunts and makes noises while I stand next to it and wait.

What does checking printer even mean? I know it means, "you can't go home yet." But really. No one has been here all evening. Why would the printer decide to check itself now?

I can't leave without my notes. I'm spending all day tomorrow preparing for my talk at the student seminar. And this talk isn't just any old student seminar talk. Several members of the program committee are going to be there. Based on the talk, the committee is going determine my fate in the program.

The printer groans and churns again. The message changes.

Calibrating.

My phone buzzes.

Tara—she's the only one who ever texts me. Pearl and Dad only call.

It's a selfie; she's lying in the sand at the beach. Rhode Island, I think, is where she tried to convince me to go this weekend. Every week this summer she's invited me to accompany her to some a beach somewhere new, and every time I've declined and instead received a treasure trove of selfies.

Keep working on that talk! You'll knock 'em dead.

I wonder what would happen if people really did die from excitement about a talk. Could the speaker be charged with murder?

"You still here?" Candice, the office secretary, enters the small printer room. She's almost as big as I am, which means one of us needs to leave or else we'll run out of oxygen really fast. This is a small room. Fortunately, my pages are finally printing.

"As always." I grab my notes and squeeze past Candice and out of the room before I suffocate. Candice and I are often at the office after hours. She has too much to do, and I don't have a life outside of work. It makes for a quality friendship.

"I'd thought that since you and Tara hooked up, I'd be seein' less of ya."

"Hooked up?"

"Yeah, hooked up. As in together."

I roll the papers in my hands. "We're officemates. Well, office chums, I guess. But we're not together."

"And why not? You got something against the girl?"

I shrug. Tara is hot, but I don't see us hooking up. It isn't that I weigh a hundred and fifty pounds more than she does, although that is a part of it.

"In case you were wondrin', her grades have sure improved since she moved into that office. The committee decided to let her stay." Candice shakes her head as she rummages through one of the drawers. "That office sure made her smarter."

"What?"

"I ain't allowed to tell you nothin', ya know." She pulls something out of the drawer and closes it. "You didn't hear it from me. But you've done lots for that girl. You ain't gonna find a prettier girl and you've been sittin' in this office night after night for years now."

My phone starts buzzing again. It's Pearl.

Not tonight. I send the call to voice mail.

I look up to respond, but Candice is already halfway down the hall, leaving me staring at the picture of Tara sunbathing as Candice disappears into her office.

* * *

"You know, your talk wasn't that bad," Tara says.

I wipe sweat from my eyes and push myself a few steps to fall into stride with her as she pushes up another hill. "How can you say that? The program director was scowling so hard by the end of it, that I thought his brow would fall off."

"The concepts were good; all it needed was some direction."

"Ha. That's not what the committee said. They put me in Khanh's lab to get me straightened out."

"They should have put you in my advisor's lab. Then I could see more of you."

"Ha! That's the last thing you want, to see more of me."

"Okay, then. Maybe you could see more of me."

I cough, probably from exertion, and ignore the comment. "Besides, I'm not sure your lab would be a good fit, either," I say. "Your advisor doesn't even work on the same planet as I do. Protein folding is more of a computational problem than the machine learning approaches I'm working on. Though I guess I do have a good idea of what your projects are."

Tara laughs. We've spent a lot of time working together lately. The result of our time together has been that her research is moving forward while mine is stagnant. I have good ideas, I just haven't figured out the right application for them. At least not yet, but I will. And then I'll graduate and get out of here for good.

We crest the hill, and Tara walks briskly down the trail. It takes some coaxing before my body starts to move in the same direction. We haven't even been on this hike that long, and I'm completely soaked with sweat and my legs are about to melt into a pile of fatty goo.

I took Andrea on hikes all the time back in college, in the mountains near Prescott. Those hikes were all-day adventures, and I could go all day. Not anymore. I hope Tara isn't planning on going too much farther.

"Keep up, Karl." Tara calls as she sprints up the next hill. I huff and puff and curse myself for agreeing to come. She told me she wanted to get all the details about my academic review with the committee. So far I've done a lot more catching up than she has. Next time, we get caught up in the office.

"When's the last time you exercised?" She calls down from the top of the hill as I trudge slowly up it.

One hundred and twenty-three pounds ago. "Four years, probably."

"Ouch! We should do this more often."

I would have to do this all the time to have a body like Tara's. Her hiking outfit, just a sports bra and shorts, shows a body that suggests she spends a lot less time at her desk than I do at mine.

Graduate school is too hard to spend time exercising. I've given up so much to come here; I have to make my newest model work. I have to find a dataset to apply it on and get some publications. I have to graduate.

The trail descends down yet another hill into a covered area out of the sun. A stream runs through the miniature valley. Climbing out of this place is going to redefine torture. Still, I follow Tara down the winding trail onto a wooden bridge over the stream and look up at a waterfall.

"I've talked to a dozen professors," I say. "I just don't see a good fit in any of their labs. I had a good place with Sam. He believed my work would find a home eventually."

Tara laughs. "We're still talking about that? Well, if you want time to figure things out, Khanh definitely isn't the right person for you."

Exactly. I rest my elbows on the bridge rail. The water races underneath us, hurrying off to somewhere important. I might enjoy this if it weren't so hot and I weren't so tired. And, if I didn't have a huge hike to get myself out of here. Beads of sweat drip off my nose and fall into the stream.

"Do you have any other options?"

"I haven't found them yet."

40

"I guess you're stuck then."

So comforting.

Pittsburgh has so many more bugs than Arizona. Within 30 seconds of stopping, I'm breathing them in. And I hate having bugs stuck in my nose.

"You ready to go?"

I don't move.

"Aside from the workload, how is your lab?" I ask.

She shrugs and leans on the bridge next to me. Her shaped shoulder brushes up against my chubby arm. I nearly step away, but I like the dopamine and oxytocin rush I get from her touch, so I decide to leave it there.

"It's good," she says. "There are some snotty members, but probably not more than most labs. That reminds me, I need your help figuring out how to get started on my next assignment. After we finish the hike here, do you have a few hours?"

"Sure."

"Great. I bought you a new shirt to try out after you shower."

"Sure." I probably will shower today.

"I'm thinking I'll start buying you a new shirt every day. My only requirement is that you shower before you put them on."

I laugh. "It's not worth it."

Our hands are touching on the bridge railing. Were they touching like that before? Did I put my hand on hers, or did she put hers under mine? My fingers itch to wrap around her hand.

"We should come back here in a couple weeks, after the leaves have changed." Tara slips her hand out from under mine and puts it around me. I shudder as her hand glides over the rolls of fat. "Maybe after you help me come up with an idea for my semester project for Computational Genomics. I've heard that class is a bear."

"I have some ideas for your project."

She smiles at me, sunlight sneaking through the trees and caressing her face. She leans close to me and whispers, "I like you Karl Stapp."

"I like you, too." I'm not sure if it's true or not.

She leans into me a little more. I don't say anything, and neither does she. My heart pounds in my chest so hard I'm sure she can feel every beat. A gorgeous girl is cuddled up next to me, and I'm her fat teddy bear with a heart pounding her shoulder hard enough to give her a massage.

I put my chubby arm around her back, swallowing her whole.

It can't be comfortable, and Tara pulls back. Her green eyes are playful, seductive. "Maybe we should skip work this afternoon."

She looks like she's glad to be here. Glad to be with me. I can't imagine why. Tara glances down, and I see her lips. They look soft.

41

Tara closes her eyes and leans her face to the side. I turn my head a little the opposite direction.

My heart rate is faster than it was when we were running up that hill.

She is really pretty.

Our lips are almost touching.

I haven't kissed anyone since Andrea. We were hiking that day, too.

I pull away. I don't want this. Not again.

"Shall we go on?" I pull my hand away. I hadn't realized I was holding Tara's hand again.

"Of course." Tara doesn't seem fazed, though she reaches out and takes my hand again. She pulls me toward the trail. "It will be too hot to bear out here pretty soon."

We walk out of the stream area and back toward the trail.

Holding hands.

It's been years since I walked anywhere holding hands with a girl. I'd forgotten what it feels like—the softness of the touch, the feeling of togetherness. Hard for me to reconcile those feelings with Tara as the girl next to me. Especially when I'm drenched with sweat.

And I almost kissed her.

My phone vibrates in my left pocket. I ignore it and focus on my next step as we start up the hill.

Tara stops and reaches in my pocket and pulls out my phone.

"It's not important." I reach for the phone, but Tara holds it away from me, just out of my grip. I reach across her, trying to take it before she does something crazy—like answering it. Then, I realize where my arm is on her body, and I pull my hand back. I cough and ignore the heat rising in my face.

She swipes her finger across the phone to answer it and puts it to her ear.

"Hello?"

"Is this Karl?" I hear a familiar voice say. It ties my stomach up in knots to hear it. I can't even remember the last time I talked to Pearl. Her voice sounds so much like Mom's.

"This is Karl's girlfriend," Tara says in her normal voice, winking at me. "My name's Tara."

I try to grab the phone from her, but Tara shakes her head and waves me back.

"Karl? A girlfriend? No way. How did you pull that off?" Pearl laughs. Her laugh is so much like Mom's.

"Nothing a little lipstick and eyeshadow couldn't cure."

"Boy, am I grateful for you," Pearl says. "I haven't talked to Karl for more than three years."

"And, dear lady, what is your relation to Karl? Not an ex-girlfriend, I assume?"

I groan and reach for the phone again. Strike three.

42

"I'm his sister. Hasn't he told you about me?" I look at Tara in horror, but she shrugs and gives me a little smile.

"Of course, he has, darling. I was just teasing. He's been telling me how he's just dying to come and visit you sometime. It's been too long, it seems. He talks about how much he misses Arizona all the time. It just isn't as hot here in Pittsburgh, you know."

"Really? He said that?" Pearl is gullible; hearing her voice makes me feel guilty. If I wasn't always in the middle of something when she called, I'm sure I would have answered eventually.

"One thing you need to know about me is that I never lie."

I roll my eyes.

"Well, that's a relief. I was actually calling in hopes that he could come and visit. Is he around?"

"No, he just stepped out to use the restroom before you called. When are you thinking?" Tara looks at me and grins.

"I can't go and visit her," I whisper frantically. Tara waves me away like a gnat and takes a few long strides up the hill until she's far enough away that I can't hear Pearl anymore.

"September 23rd? ... A break in the middle of the year ... For what? ... An international event. Really? ... Yeah, I'm positive that will work."

I stop chasing Tara and sit down on the trail and put my arms over my face.

I can't go see Pearl.

It will take time away from my research.

It will bring back too many memories. I'm not ready to go home.

"Here, let me give you my email, and I'll make sure he gets it. T dot Howell at cmu dot edu. Yeah, that's how you spell it, two l's."

Tara's going to make me do this. I don't have the heart to cancel on Pearl. I would have to talk to her to do that.

Tara finally hangs up and gives me my phone.

"What was that all about?"

Her green eyes are dancing. She's enjoying this way too much. "When were you going to tell me you had a sister?"

"When were you going to tell me that you were my girlfriend?"

Tara laughs. "Does that mean you'll come home with me after the hike? I have some great adult films, if you're interested in those. Or we can watch an action movie, or do *whatever* you want."

I cough and ignore the heat. "I thought you wanted me to do homework with you."

"That can wait."

"I have a lot of work I need to do for Khanh by Friday."

"I'll take a rain check then."

"Yeah. Some other time."

It's a quiet walk the rest of the way back to the cars.

How could she do this to me? What if I see Andrea while I'm in Arizona?

I haven't seen Andrea since the day before I left to come here.

I can still see it—sitting atop the mountain ridge. The trees raced through the canyon, the stunning view augmented by a soft breeze that cooled our sweat soaked skin. Because in the Arizona mountains, the breeze cools you down.

It had been a perfect day.

"Andrea, I want to marry you," I said, leaning over and kissing her. I still remember how comfortable it was kissing her. A promise, a friendship. There wasn't any of this flirty guess-what-I'm-thinking stuff that exists with Tara.

Though, that time the kiss didn't feel right.

Andrea pulled back, and I remember the surprise in her eyes. "I thought after dating me for all these years, you would have had enough."

I laughed and pulled her close. Her hair blew onto my face, but she pulled back before our lips met again.

I wish time could have stopped there. Andrea stood there in my arms, framed with a large pine tree behind her, her hair blowing against my face, her lips slightly parted. I don't know if I'd ever seen Andrea so beautiful or loved her so much.

But the words that came out of her mouth that day weren't the words I expected. She didn't tell me that she would come to Pittsburgh with me.

She told me that she was pregnant with someone else's baby.

And now Tara is going to send me back to Arizona.

8 Reality

Cadah

My body infuses with energy. The sun is up; it's a new day and time to get back on the trail. I roll out of my fuma skin, shivering as the soft, white fur falls away from my naked body. The cold morning air bites my bare skin as I grab my tunic off the fuma fur and pull it over my head. I reach for my tights and pull them on, anxious to be dressed.

"I'm not coming," Ore says, still rolled up inside her fuma skin. "You can pick me up here on the way back."

I laugh. Ore hates mornings—the fuma skin doesn't wake her up as much as most people. "We'll reach the turnoff today," I say. "We're almost done. And then we'll go back home."

Ore groans in reply. "I'm not walking another mile through this forest."

"If we don't get down to the trail soon, you know your father will walk into our little women's camp and pull you out of your fuma."

Ore grumbles, but the thought of her father is enough to push her out of the skin. "I'm glad we'll finally reach the turnoff today. I'm sick of walking."

Walking isn't the only thing she's sick of.

"Maybe Ler will notice you today," I say helpfully.

"Yeah, since he's paid so much attention to me every other day," Ore mumbles. I've lived with Ore and her father for a long time, since my parents died, and so I'm quite adept at understanding mumble. Especially when it's about her crush on the son of the village chief, Ler. He's tall, he's strong, he laughs easier than anyone I know, and he has a strong sense of duty. But, despite the extremely small number of single women in our village Watch, and despite Ore's constant plotting to get his attention, Ler hasn't fallen for her yet.

I shrug and finish rolling my fuma skin into my pack. For all her complaining, Ore was the one who volunteered to accompany Ler over to Keeper for the annual check-in with our sister village. As her best friend, I signed up, and Ziru, our village leader, sent Ore's dad as a chaperone. It's the largest check-in group we've ever sent

45

to Keeper. That's okay, of course. I'm glad to be here, and I'm excited to see Keeper. This is the farthest I've ever been away from Watch.

I just wish Ler would pay more attention to Ore. It would mean everything to her if he would.

Once Ore has finished putting together her pack and supplies, we climb down the trail and find the men.

"Ho! Ladies," Ler calls as we approach. "Did you sleep well?"

Ler is up and ready to go, but Ore's father is still gathering his pack. Apparently, he's a little sluggish this morning, too. Like daughter like father. Ore leads the way over the snow drifts. Our feet crunch in the snow. This is the dead time of the season, when the snow is melted enough to come out of hibernation, but still covers the ground too much for there to be any work done for finding food. We all hope for warm days during this time. Each day that passes with snow on the ground is another day we cannot gather food, and another day we consume last year's supply.

But, the melting snow also gives us time to do things. Thus, the timing of our trip to Keeper.

I shrug my pack off and sit down on a snow drift. While Ore tells Ler about our night's sleep, I break off a piece of snow. The cold makes my fingers swell, but I don't mind too much. We'll be walking soon, and I'll warm up.

"Are you going to throw that at someone?" Ler asks.

I look up, startled. I hadn't heard him come over. Ore is over with her father now, helping him roll up his pack. I can't think of a thing to say to Ler, and so I just smile and shake my head.

"My father said you had a good arm when you were a child. I'd hate to be on the receiving end now." He laughs good naturedly. Ler's voice is as beautiful as he is, if that is possible. Deep, resonating, it makes me happy every time I hear it.

I stand and hold the ball menacingly. "Back off," I say, "or suffer the wrath of Cadah."

Ler laughs, but it cuts off abruptly when we hear footsteps coming from the direction of the valley. Ler gives me an odd look, and I shrug. No one comes from the valley. No one *can* come from the valley, well, besides Sapphiri.

Our ancestors moved here from the valley two hundred years ago, but the barrier blocked anyone from following them. The only ones who can still cross into the mountains are the Sapphiri, the people with bright blue glowing eyes. Wynn, the valley's Azurean king, sends one up here every decade or so to try and kill us. Wynn has ruled the valley for nearly 200 years, and unless the legendary blue princess shows up, he will rule for another 200 years. And, if history is any indication, he'll try and kill us and our descendants for every one of those years. From what I understand about the magic of the barrier, if everyone on the mountain dies, the barrier will break and anyone, including Wynn, will be able to pass into the mountains. Not that we would care at that point, but we've been entrusted with the secrets of the mountains, things that will make it possible for the Blue Princess to one day defeat Wynn.

If she ever shows up. She was supposed to show up 20-30 years after we got here. Instead, centuries have passed, winter seasons have been cold, and we spend our summers gathering food. And waiting. Always waiting. Eating, gathering food, marrying, having children. And waiting. We have a way of life in the mountains. Us, Keeper, and even the people in the Northern Alliance. The environment is harsh, the work is hard, and the wait is long. But we keep living.

And killing every bright-eyed traitor Wynn sends our way.

The footsteps continue to get closer, and Ler pulls a knife out of his shirt. There isn't a better marksman in the village than Ler. If this person is a traitor, he'll die the moment his eyes come into view.

It's a man. He stops when he reaches the trail. He's dressed as we are, and his eyes are dark. Ler hesitates, but then puts the knife back into his tunic.

"Who are you?" Ore's father demands. His pack is finished now, and he stands in front of Ore, his arm holding her behind him.

The man sneers. "I'm Arujan," he says.

"What are you doing out here? So far from any village? This is the year for the Watch emissaries to visit Keeper. Not the other way around."

"I was sent as a spy," Arujan says. "Down to the world of Wynn."

Ore laughs. "That's smart," she says.

"Quiet, daughter!" Ore's father waves his hand at her. Everyone who has ever been sent down to Wynn's world has never returned. Apparently until this fellow, if he's telling the truth.

"Wynn's power has weakened," Arujan says. "It's time for us to leave these mountains."

"Impossible!" Ore's father says. "We cannot leave until the Blue Princess arrives. She, and only she, is the one to lead us."

"A traditionalist, then." Arujan laughs. "Things are changing on the mountains now. You will see. We no longer need to wait for a princess who is not coming. It's been too long. She's forgotten about us. It's time to help ourselves."

"You're a traitor."

"Look at my eyes—are they shining? No. I'm a dreamer. A man not afraid to think of what is possible instead of what holds me captive."

Ore's father pulls a knife from his coat, but Ore puts her arm around him. "Father, don't hurt him. Where are you going now, Arujan?"

"The Northern Alliance."

"Can't he come with us as far as the turnoff to Keeper, father?"

Ore's father looks at his daughter and his expression softens. Finally, he shrugs and puts his knife away. "As long as there is no more traitorous talk."

Arujan smiles and Ore winks at him. I send a questioning glance over her way, but she just shrugs.

We head off. Ore walks in the lead with her father. Arujan stays in the middle. Ler hangs in the back, with me, his hand inside his tunic. Around his knife, I'm sure.

I glance at him curiously; did he choose to walk in the back so that he could watch Ore? Her slender hips sway gently as she carries her pack up a hill in front of us. But, no. His eyes are not on Ore. His eyes are on the stranger, Arujan. And they're on me. I feel my face warm and I look down at the snow. Ler clears his throat awkwardly, but then doesn't say anything and turns his eyes back to Arujan.

Ler always has something to say.

I look back at him, confused. We came on this trip so that Ler would notice Ore. How could everything have gone so wrong? He's not noticing Ore. He's noticing me.

His gaze turns, and his eyes meet mine again. Guilt and pleasure wash over me. I'm Ore's friend, and so I shouldn't love that look. But, I do. I swallow and decide to break the silence and escape my thoughts.

"Do you think the Blue Princess will come?"

Ler smiles pleasantly. "Yes."

"Will she really set us free? Is there really a better life for us somewhere?"

Ler nods. "The Blue Princess will come, Cadah. I believe it. Our ancestors knew King Togan, and they knew his plan. The Blue Princess will come and defeat Wynn. She's the only one with the power to do so. She will."

"But where is she now?" I ask.

Ler shrugs. "All I know is that she will come."

Up ahead Arujan is talking to Ore's father. "I have something I need to show you," he says. "A way for you to see for yourself that the valley is indeed uninhabited."

"I said none of this talk," Ore's father says sternly.

"Just hear me out, you foolish man," Arujan says.

Ore's father bristles at the insult but doesn't comment on it. "Where?" he finally says.

"Just up here. Let the others stay behind and I will show you." Arujan indicates a clump of trees just up ahead. Ore's father sighs and agrees to follow him. The men leave Ore and I with Ler.

Wanting to conceal Ler's attention from Ore, I sit next to her, and engage her in conversation about the organization of the harvest, which will hopefully start within a week or two. The sun rises in the sky as we sit and wait. Eventually, I run out of things to talk about, and we sit in silence. Ler has fallen asleep.

Ore looks at him, then at me, and her eyes grow thoughtful. I panic, not wanting her to bring up the subject of how I spent my morning.

"I'm going to go after them," I say, meaning the men.

"I'm not," Ore says, looking surprised.

I feel bad that Ler is asleep. If he were awake, it would give Ore a chance to talk to him. But, after this morning, another side of me is happy that Ler is asleep. The giddy, happy part of me. The part of me that woke up this morning when he smiled at me.

I haven't traveled too far up the trail when I see them. They stand on a ledge, several hundred feet above me. Arujan is pointing toward the valley, and Ore's father stands next to him. I can hear them speaking, but I can't make out any of the words from so far away.

Ore's father shakes his head and turns to leave, but before he makes it off the ledge, Arujan takes the stick he was using for balance and swings it at Ore's father. The stick hits the older man's legs, and Ore's father stumbles. Arujan pushes the stick hard at the path, and it starts to crumble. Ore's father stumbles as the mountain beneath him falls away. Arujan swings the stick again, higher this time, hitting Ore's father across the temple.

I watch in horror as the father of my best friend falls, his body tumbling down hundreds of feet of rock. Arujan screams and starts running down the trail. I don't turn back to find Ore and Ler. I run to the cliff. I run to find my friend's father, even though I know already he's dead.

It doesn't take long before Ler and Ore catch up to me.

We find him just as Arujan finds him.

"He slipped," Arujan says, nearly out of breath. Ore runs to her father and falls over his dead body.

"You pushed him," I say.

"No," Arujan pants. "I showed him what he wanted to see, and he was so excited he moved too quickly. Then, the mountain just fell from beneath him, and he slipped down. I couldn't stop him in time." He points up to where the path crumbled, the missing trail evident from even this far down.

I open my mouth to protest again, but I remember him swinging his stick and realize he could do the same to me.

"We must call off our mission," Ler says. "And take the body back to Watch."

I nod and bite my lip. Ore, sobbing over her father, turns and looks at me with large, puffy eyes. "Where is the Blue Princess?" she asks. "Why isn't she here now? Why didn't she stop this?"

I look back at her, but I have no answer.

"I'm so sorry I couldn't save him." Arujan puts his hand on Ore's shoulder. She looks at me for another moment, and then she stands and lets Arujan put his arms around her as she cries.

9 Running

Lydia

Sweat runs down my face and the hot sun beats on my skin. Every muscle in my body aches. The whistle blows, and my legs burn as I push myself into a sprint.

"Let's move!" Coach Fant yells. "How come you're slowing down?" The girls around me pick up speed, and I follow suit, staying right in the middle of the pack.

It's the first day of university soccer camp, and we are up near Mount Rainier at a ski resort. When I stepped off the bus into the shadow Mt. Rainier, I thought this would be the perfect week—an escape from all the turmoil in my life. Now, sprinting in the thin air and the heat of the evening sun, it's hard to recall those feelings.

I push myself as we approach the finish line and pass a few girls, letting the thrill momentarily overtake my exhaustion. I bend over and put my hands on my knees and breathe air in huge gulps. Is practice over? I'd like to shower and eat and maybe feel human again.

Joana and another girl stop in front of me. "Hey Thala. I don't know why you thought you could play college ball."

The girl next to her laughs. "We always lose at least one the first day. They get so tired, they just disappear."

Joana laughs and walks away, her pony flipping back and forth. "Guess we know who that girl is this year. Though this time she's going back 30 thousand years to fossilize. Did you hear that her dad was locked up?"

Joana has talked to me several times today, and each time her words are darts, aimed right at my insecurities. Joana's tanned skin says she spent the summer vacationing and getting ready for camp. I spent the summer at work and in courtrooms. I don't even know how she heard about Dad.

I rub my pounding temples and wish that it wasn't so important to me to make this team. A smashed dandelion lies in front of my toe, its head bent over. I poke at it with my foot, but the stem is broken. It will never stand again. Is there any point in continuing to try?

I reach down and pull the flower out of the ground. When I was little, I would pick dandelions like this one for Mom. She put them on the kitchen table. She always believed in me.

Mom. That's why I can't give up. How much of her life did she give so that I could be right here, right now? If I had hung up the phone that night, how much more life would she have had? And wouldn't she have spent all of it on me?

I'll catch up. I'll get back in shape. It's what Mom would want, it's what she gave her life for.

"OK, ladies, bring it in!" Coach Fant is yelling again. All. Day. Long.

Girls crowd in close to hear her.

"You have almost finished your first day of college soccer camp."

Almost? My heart sinks, and I drop the dandelion.

"Just a three-mile run, and we'll be done for the day."

I can't remember a time that a run sounded less attractive. I take a deep breath and think of Mom. She may not be my biological mom, but she raised me to be her daughter. She survived camp; I will too. Three miles. I can do it.

Coach Fant jogs toward a hill at the other end of the field. I hear groans as we follow her—even from the juniors and seniors.

We cross the field and head up a steep incline onto a crooked, rough mountain trail. My quads burn; I focus on the rocks and dirt in front of me and push through the pain. I breathe in as much air as I can with each step. I'm strong. I'm a college athlete.

After a half-mile, we crest the hill, greeted by a gentle slope covered by pines and cedars, out of direct sunlight. The burn in my legs decreases; the pine needles on the trail are soft beneath my feet. A slight breeze rustles through the trees, cooling my sweat and soothing my aching body. The last two and a half miles are almost pleasant. My body moves, in sync with the trail and the trees. "I will do this," I repeat to myself softly with each step. It isn't long before the lodge comes back into view. I almost feel human again, despite what Joana thinks.

"Dinner in 45 minutes at the main building." Coach calls as we get back to the lodge. My first day of practice is over.

I walk slowly to my room. There are an odd number of people on the team this year, and I was the one left without a roommate. Naturally, it was me who was left alone. After all, Coach thinks I had a run-in with the law this summer.

It's fine, though. I'm used to being alone. Still, after living with Maria for the last few months, I realize now that I've grown used to the company. I find myself missing someone to chat with, Maria would commiserate this long day with me.

Back in my room, I take a long, cold shower. The water pounds my back in a solid, hard stream. My body aches, but I'm going to work it just as hard, if not

52

harder, tomorrow. I'm a college soccer player—like my mom. I wonder if she felt as alone.

Probably not. Mom was too cool to ever be alone. She was never the mom who excluded me—when she had a party there were always couples invited with other kids, she made sure of that. And, she loved putting together big parties. Of course, we never had much money, so they were simple things like playing card games with other couples or picnics at the park. Mom would always get Dad to come when she could.

My guess is that Mom was the same way all through college.

And she was on the team. I still have to make the team. And I have my work cut out for me because I'm learning a whole new position. Coach Fant has her own defensive scheme, which relies on a stopper, the "second-to-last" resort position that spends most of its time navigating the field near the goalkeeper and yelling at the defenders. The way Coach has set up the system is unique, which means there is a lot for me to learn. This year three girls are competing for two stopper spots. Haley, who is a junior, me, and another freshman named Brit.

By the time I get out of the shower, I only have two minutes until dinner. I throw something on and jog over to the main building. I'm late and all the tables are full. I sneak in the back and sit down at an empty table. There is an amazing panorama of Mount Rainier out the window. I try to feel happy. I should feel happy right now. I'm one day closer to fulfilling Mom's dream for me.

Someone clears her throat next to me. A short girl with straight black hair. Brit. My competition. She puts a hand on one of the many empty chairs and looks down shyly.

"Can I sit with you?"

"Of course."

"I know this is awkward," Brit says, and she blushes. Her black hair is accented by her skin, which is so white that it looks almost pale. She has soft features, and she's smaller than I am. I especially envy her straight hair; my curly hair is poking out in all directions from my hurried rush to dinner.

"Where are you from?" I ask when she doesn't say anything more.

"Wisconsin," she keeps her eyes averted from mine.

"Really? I didn't know we had anyone on the team from Wisconsin. What part?"

"Near Madison, in a small town in the middle of nowhere."

"Sounds exotic," I say, evoking a little bit of a smile out of her. "I'm surprised that you chose to come out west to U dub." Maybe she'll decide to go home and let me take the other open spot behind Haley.

Not that I'll be that lucky. Besides, Brit seems like a nice girl. She might need the spot just as much as I do.

She shrugs. "It was my best option. I didn't get a scholarship anywhere else that wasn't a really small school."

"Coach Fant always knows talent when she sees it."

Brit blushes again, but she shakes her head. "I'm actually not that good. I'm just hoping to get a scholarship so I can go to a few semesters of school." She looks down again. Her skin is so pale. She must have gone through a gallon of sunscreen to be so white after a full day outside. When I looked in the mirror after getting out of the shower, my entire body was beet red from sunburn. I should ask to borrow sunscreen for tomorrow.

I wish the food would get here, but I realize that I really do want to talk to someone. At this point, Brit is my only option, seeing as how we are alone in the back of the room. "How did you meet Coach?" I ask.

"I went to a soccer camp last summer when I came out here to help my sister with her new baby." Brit answers politely enough, but I'm still not sure if she wants to talk to me.

"You have a sister in Seattle?"

"Not anymore, she and her husband divorced in the spring and she moved to Texas."

Brit is as alone as I am. And she looks really young. I wonder if she graduated a year early or something. If I lose my spot to Brit, maybe that would be okay. At least I could take solace in the fact that someone who really needs the position got it.

Coach interrupts our conversation to make some announcements. Brit gives me a small smile, and we turn our attention to the front of the room.

"By next week, you are going to be fit to be PAC12 champs!" Coach says. Girls around the room yell, but not me—I'll celebrate once I've made it through the next seven days.

They bring the food after Coach finishes speaking.

"I'm so hungry!" I say when my food is finally put in front of me.

Brit laughs, her mouth already stuffed full. "Me too! It was a long day."

"Why did you come sit by me?"

Brit blushes, swallows, and then whispers so that I can barely hear, "There wasn't enough room at the table, so Joana kicked me off."

"Quite the girl, Joana."

"Quite the soccer player, anyway," Brit agrees, smiling back at me. "I'm guessing you know her?" She blushes. "I guess you do because she told all the forwards to stay away from you because of your dad. That he would abuse any girl who gets too close to you. She also told everyone to call you Thala."

I straighten my back and look away. My chances to have any friends on this team just dropped all the way to zero. "I played soccer against her in high school."

"Anyway, that's why I came to sit by you."

54

She came to sit by me because of what Joana said? This girl isn't my competition, she's my friend.

"Did you play stopper in high school?" I ask after regaining my composure.

"No, I was always forward. My high school coach needed someone who could control the ball and try to score goals. I scored a ton, but it didn't work—we still lost every game."

I try to imagine what that would be like. I've been on some losing teams, but every team I've been on has been competitive.

* * *

After dinner, and a very long team meeting, Brit and I walk outside to the practice field. It's silly to play more soccer, and it's almost dark. But we go anyway.

Brit has great ball handling skills and plenty of soccer savvy. What she doesn't have is confidence.

That's probably understandable, given that she lost every game she played in high school.

It's going to be hard to beat her for the spot on the team. Her fundamentals are solid, and even though she doesn't have a lot of practice on defense, she will be great. Defense requires aggression but also raw determination.

Brit has determination.

I'm not a soccer coach, but I've been around the game my whole life. Brit is a great player. My spot on the team is in serious jeopardy. Do I care? Even if Brit is nice?

"You're going to make a great stopper," I say.

Brit laughs. "I was thinking the same thing about you. I don't want to be heading home after this week, but after watching you play, I'm not so sure."

"Well, if you're up for it, why don't we do this again tomorrow?"

"I'd like that."

I sit down on the bench next to the field and she joins me. My competition. Can she be my friend? The sun is behind the mountain now and the sky lights up with splashes of stars. We watch the mountain darken, the pine forest turning into a deep, dark green. I stretch my legs out; the cool evening air feels great on my bare skin.

For a moment, this place hardly seems like the torture chamber it was most of the day. The pine covered mountains stand firm against the darkening sky, the grass blades sway like lissome dancers in the dim light. Parts of this day were rough, but this place is amazing.

We talk about Brit's life in Wisconsin, her single mom trying to make ends meet, her boyfriend who dumped her when she left for Washington, how much she misses her brother, and her insecurities about being so far away from home.

I have a friend! I'm glad she's here. She was assigned to room with Joana, of all people! It isn't hard to persuade her to join me. No more long showers, but I don't mind.

Joana can try being alone.

And this week I have a friend. If only I could shake the nagging reality that one of us are going to be cut off the team at the end of the week.

10 Resolve

Lydia

I'm on the balls of my feet, waiting, ready. Joana jogs toward me, smiling. She looks like she's approaching a longtime friend.

We are teammates; it would be nice if we were friends.

"Hey Thala."

We're not friends.

A forward kicks the ball out to the left side, away from us. I step back. We're practicing defensive schemes when we're outnumbered 2:1. A breeze comes off the mountain and cools the sweat on my skin.

Joana doesn't stop until she's right up next to me, and I tense as her hand rests on my shoulder. Is this what Coach wants her to do? I step away, but she comes right back like a hungry puppy.

I can't see the ball with her there. I move again, and so does she. She wants me to get upset.

"Coach told me she's going to cut you *and* your little friend." I shrug her hand off my shoulder again. "She doesn't want you in the team pictures; your ugliness would make the university look bad. Too bad daddy didn't kill you and save you the embarrassment."

She pushes off and runs to the ball. I grit my teeth and follow her, stride for stride. Joana gets a pass, I move in for the steal, but she kicks it behind her to the field we just vacated.

My heart drops. I wasn't supposed to follow her—I've made this mistake already today. Another forward filled the spot in my absence, and now she has a clear path to the goal.

The whistle blows. Coach jogs onto the field. Right to me. Joana laughs.

"Miller!" Coach yells. "What were you thinking? You were totally out of position. Is your head in the game? Is it even on this mountain?"

I look down at the turf. "Sorry Coach. I won't let it happen again."

"No. *I* won't let this happen again. You're not cut out to play university level soccer. You're dismissed. Come talk to me after practice so we can work out getting you home. It's clear you didn't practice enough this summer, and you're not going to come up here and try and get your lazy butt back in shape on my watch. You're done." Coach Fant turns around. "Sorenson! Get out here."

Brit jogs out onto the field.

I don't move.

Cut?

Coach storms off the field, yelling at the forwards to run the play again.

They start the play and Coach yells at me to move out of the way. Brit doesn't meet my eyes as she runs past me to her position.

I failed. I've just been cut from the team. It's over. I walk numbly off the field. I'm halfway to the lodge before the tears come. It isn't fair. I've worked hard this week, and I've done well. Just as well as Brit or Haley. I got distracted by Joana, but I know how to play the game. It's not my fault I didn't get enough practice time in this summer.

But, fair or not, I was cut anyway.

I shiver at the blast of cold air that hits my sweat-soaked skin and clothes when I step into the air-conditioned room. I face plant onto the bed, letting my sore body collapse onto the soft blankets.

Maria. Mom. I've let them down. They gave so much so I could get here, and I let them down. I've worked and sweated.

And in the heat of the moment I messed up.

After crying a while, I sit up and wipe tears away. I look at the mirror. My face is all blotchy now.

I tried to ignore Joana, but her words were mean. I forgot what I was doing.

She was so smug when Coach sent me running off the field. She finally got what she wanted.

My disappointment turns to anger, and I decide that I won't let her win. Not yet. Not while I'm still here at the lodge. If Coach intends for me to go home, I won't be able to stay. But as long as I'm still here, I might as well fight for a position on the team. Joana may get to me, but she can't make me quit. I won't quit.

This is my scholarship. I'm going to go get it.

Besides, what's the worst that can happen? I've already been cut.

I grab my playbook, wash my face, and jog back to the practice field.

"What are you doing here?" Haley asks when I sit down next to her. "I thought Coach kicked you off the team."

"Maybe she did." I sit next to her. "But I'm not quitting until I'm on that bus driving away."

Haley shrugs and rolls her eyes, pulling up her shirt and shorts to sunbathe while she watches the girls on the field. Brit is doing well; she has a good mastery of the position, moving in sync with the rest of the team. Joana's mouth is moving the entire time she's close to Brit. Brit stays in position.

Ears of steel. That's what I need. Or earplugs.

I flip through the playbook, watching as the players go through each one, moving, flexing, adjusting. It's a thing of beauty to watch. When I'm out there on the field I'm thinking about the plays and position. But the real beauty of soccer is only evident when a person steps back and sees the entire field.

"I thought I sent you away." Coach Fant's voice brings me back to reality. I jump to my feet and face her.

"Yes, Coach. I came up here to play, not sit in my room."

"You're still dressed in uniform."

"Yes, Coach."

"What makes you think that I'll ever put you back out on that field, Miller?"

I shrug. "I don't know that you will, Coach."

"Well, then. Why are you here?"

I keep my voice steady as I speak. "My mother gave up so much time for me to learn soccer, Coach. I can't walk away from that. I'm going to keep fighting for a position on this team until I'm tied up and on a bus back to the city." I look at her eyes, trying to convey confidence despite wanting to disappear under her gaze.

And that gaze doesn't go away. For minutes Coach stares at me, her expression unreadable. My lip almost quivers.

"So, the rich spoiled girl has some spunk in her after all," she finally says. She waits for a reaction. I bite my lip.

"Tell me. Are you better than the other two girls?"

Trick question. If I answer yes, she'll be justified thinking I'm cocky and spoiled. If I say no, then she'll cut me. A coach will never play a player that doesn't believe in herself.

"I think we're all talented. And if I play as sloppily as I did earlier, then you should cut me. But, I already told you it won't happen again."

Coach raises an eyebrow and meets my eyes. She almost smiles. "Maybe I don't have you pegged yet, Miller. You're welcome to stick around for the rest of practice."

I breathe out a sigh of relief and sit down. As soon as Coach's back is turned, my lip quivers and I pull my legs tight against my chest to try and calm my breathing.

"You should have taken the chance to get out when you could," Haley says.

"I'm not getting out. I'm going to play."

"Don't be silly. It's called seniority. I've put in my time, it's my turn to play. One of you girls will stick around, and it will probably be Brit."

"I don't accept that." I turn back to watching the field.

"Whatever." Haley goes back to sunbathing.

Whatever is right. Even if I give my all these last two days of camp, I'll still get cut. I'm just postponing the inevitable right now.

I take a deep breath. I'm not going to quit. I'm going to keep fighting. I owe it to Mom to make this team. This is my scholarship.

* * *

I toss the plush ball back to Brit, aiming it right at her face. She plucks it out of the air midsentence and keeps talking—like a fly she just shooed away.

"I'm serious. Now that he's gone, I really am happy we broke up."

The ball flies back toward me. "That's what all girls say after being dumped. It doesn't mean it's true, though. Tell me one thing you hate about him."

Brit laughs. "That's easy."

"Then say it."

"He was always talking about extraterrestrial worlds. He believed that aliens came from other places and settled in America a long time ago."

"Really?" I'm not sure this is something Brit hated about her ex-boyfriend, but having never had a boyfriend, I'm doing my best to relate.

"Yeah."

"Okay, maybe you really are happier without him." Brit's throw is a little high, and I miss it. I walk around the bed and reach around the office chair to grab it.

"He said the aliens all had this mark of a blue flower," Brit says. "Based on some story from the Revolutionary War. And he really thought that there were people with this mark."

"A blue flower?" I don't throw the ball back. Other worlds and blue flowers. Blue, like the light that was on the trail when the man found me.

"Uh huh. Stupid, huh?"

The only thing stupid here is how my hands are clammy and my throat is dry.

I pull my shirt off over my head. "Like this?"

Brit stares at my chest. The blue flower peaks out from beneath my bra, just as real-looking as always. A puzzled look crosses her face. "Yeah. Exactly like that. He has a poster of that exact flower in his bedroom."

"Exactly like it?" My voice is a little shaky.

Brit nods.

This is really weird. I slip my shirt on and toss the ball back to Brit. "Maybe he wasn't as crazy as you think."

Brit catches the ball, but she's still looking at me strangely. "Where did you get that?"

"I don't know." I wish I knew. And I wish I knew why I felt so weird to learn about it being on Brit's crazy boyfriend's poster.

A knock at the door ends the conversation. Brit is closer to the door, so she swings it open.

"May I come in?" Coach Fant asks.

Neither of us dare say no.

Coach crosses the room and sits at the small desk in the corner. The desk is littered with plays. I've scribbled notes on most of them. Coach picks them up and flips through them.

"You've been working hard."

We both nod.

"And you've become friends."

We nod again.

Coach takes a deep breath and sets the plays down.

"I've asked Haley to leave the team," Coach says. "Her heart isn't in it, not as much as you girls. Neither of you have her skill, but you have more grit than she ever will."

We stare at her in shock. I bite my lip to stop a smile.

"I thought..."

"I know," Coach interrupts. "I know. I thought you were another Haley. But this afternoon you proved me wrong. One of the other girls told me about your dad after dinner tonight. We have our first game in two weeks. Miller, will you be ready to start?"

Several seconds tick by before I remember to speak. "Yes, Coach." My voice is barely audible.

"Sorenson, you'll be the backup."

"Yes, Coach." Brit is beaming. She doesn't feel the same need to suppress her emotion.

Coach nods. She looks tired, but as strict as ever. "We have a lot of work to do this year. We'll make it happen. Work hard, or I'll cut you anyway."

We don't start screaming until the door latches shut behind her. I don't know why we bother. Our screams are so loud I'm sure she hears us all the way back to her room.

11 Roommates

Lydia

We won the season opener at the University of Michigan. I had several key stops and Joana scored the winning goal with under ten minutes left.

We're on the plane flying back to Seattle now, and I'm sitting next to Brit. We picked seats as far away from Joana as possible—which means we're sitting at the very back of the plane. It'll take us longer to deplane, and we'll get similarly poor seats on the bus, but we don't care.

"How is school treating you?" Brit asks.

I shrug and look up from the book I'm only pretending to read. "First day was okay. Second day wasn't. You?"

"I really like my classes a lot so far."

"Really?"

Brit doesn't strike me as someone who would be that into school, but she nods.

"What are you studying?" I ask, trying to picture my demure friend as a nerd.

"Chemistry."

"Nerdy! I can't stand chemistry. Something about studying things you can't see drives me crazy."

Brit laughs. "A lot of people complain that chemistry has too much memorization. But, how are you supposed to understand the world if you don't know what's in it? What are you studying?"

I sigh and lean back in my chair. I'm not a nerd about anything. "I don't know. I'm not good at anything but soccer. I probably need to figure out what I want to do with my life before I make any decisions about what I want to study."

"You're really good at soccer," Brit says, and she squeezes my hand. "I would have felt so much pressure out there, under the lights for the first time, but you played like you couldn't feel it."

"I did."

"I love watching you," Brit says, her eyes looking down at her lap as she blushes, but she continues her adulation. "That was such a great stop you had there in the tenth minute. Maybe when I grow up, I'll play like you."

"And maybe when I grow up, I'll study like you." I laugh and look down at the novel in my hand and the textbook on Brit's lap. Even though Brit would never believe it, she's the better player. The only thing I have on her is confidence. And, the only one I can thank for that is Mom. I was raised on the soccer field. How many girls are lucky enough to say that?

"I'm fine with the way things are right now." Brit smiles. "By the end of the season, I'll be able to tell you about every stadium in the PAC 12, and who has the most comfortable benches."

I laugh. Brit is happier now than when I first met her at camp. I wish I could say the same for myself.

"Have you met any new friends?"

She turns bright red.

"A boy?"

"Yeah, I met this really cute guy from San Jose. I've seen him every day since I moved into my dorm." She looks down at her hands and smiles.

"No way!"

"Yeah, he's really cute and really smart."

"That's fun." I hope Brit's right and this guy really is nice. Brit deserves someone good. Someone who will take care of her, not take advantage of her.

"Have you met any boys, Lydia?"

Boys? I shake my head. The only guys I've met so far are obsessed about beer, video games, and sex. Not that any of them have tried to talk to me, of course.

"Is there something bothering you?" Brit asks.

I shrug and look back at my novel. I hate it when I'm so transparent.

"You don't have to tell me if you don't want to. I just want you to know I'm here for you."

I shake my head. How can I tell her that I don't belong? That the only place I'm at home is on the soccer field? And, that I'm going crazy thinking about some strange connection to a blue flower and another world.

* * *

Cool air from the AC makes me shiver when I walk into our room. I set the basket of clothes on Maria's bed, next to the other five baskets. It's going to take her a long time to unpack.

I brought my stuff from the house, but I unpacked one box and left the other in the corner of the closet. That box holds a lot of mementos, but very few clothes. I put a picture of me and Mom on the wall, and my old cell phone rests on the dresser. That's all I need out.

"I'm finally here!" Maria walks in behind me holding another large basket of clothes. Her parents made her go through two weeks of school before they finally decided to give her permission to move down here. She arrived late last night and

63

then left for a party without even unloading her car, which means that we're spending the morning doing that.

Which, of course, is fine.

"I heard about another party tonight," Maria finds a huge pack of bubble gum in one of her many baskets and pulls it out. "After your soccer game. Is there any way I can convince you to come?"

"No."

"There will be lots of boys there." She winks.

It would be fun to meet some guys and actually talk to them. And if I was with Maria, they probably would talk to me. But, I'm not going. Not when all the guys will be drinking. I can still smell Dad's breath that night he hit me. Besides, all the boys would think I'm the ugliest girl they've ever seen, and if they're drunk, they're more likely to tell me straight up.

"I'm not going to go." In just a few minutes, Maria will slip into a bright summer dress, add sunglasses and red lipstick, and head out to the party. And then tonight will be just like the last two weeks. I'll slip into some comfy pajamas and spend the evening by myself. I'm like a mom who sends her kindergartener off to school each day, curling up in bed with a novel as soon as the house quiets down.

We put clothes on hangers for a few minutes in awkward silence.

It isn't that I don't want a social life like Maria. I want to be liked, and I want to know what it feels like to have a nice guy. But, the last thing I need is to find a guy who seems nice on the surface, but who is really like my dad.

And, I really don't want to be around alcohol.

So, since I'm a freshman in college, I don't have a social life.

"Have you heard anything about your Dad?" Maria asks.

I shake my head.

"My dad told me that sometimes jail time mends relationships."

Not our relationship. Too much was said that night. I keep my eyes down and put another armful of Maria's clothes in the dresser.

Maria sighs. "This unpacking stuff stinks. Let's go for a bike ride."

That sounds fine to me. I grab my old cell phone and we head downstairs to where Maria's two bikes are locked up. We rope the bikes to the back of Maria's car and drive through Seattle to the I-90 bridge, park, and ride over Lake Washington and around Mercer Island. The breeze is cool, the scenery green, the air fresh.

The fresh air off the lake and the light drizzle soaking through my clothes lightens my mood more than I expected. Being in nature beats sitting around talking about parties and what a loser I am. Go figure.

On the way back across the bridge, I stop my bike to look out over the lake. Green mountains surround the lake, beautiful in contrast to the deep blue of the water. Without much morning traffic, we can hear the water as it churns and licks the side of the bridge beneath us.

I told Brit the only place I belong is on the soccer field. I may have to take that back.

Maria pulls her bike up next to mine and leans against the railing next to me.

"How was your party last night? Did you find a date for tomorrow night?" I ask.

Maria responds with an exaggerated sigh. "No. Nothing but bad luck. I thought I was getting something going with this guy, but he was too dense to get the hint and ask me to go to your game with him."

"Maybe he had a lot on his mind."

"He should have had me on his mind. Guy's brains are supposed to only have one track, and that track should have been me. I was standing right in front of him."

"I think you're the one with the one-track mind. Forget the stereotypes, it turns out girls aren't that complicated after all."

"Yeah right," Maria laughs. "He's probably at home playing a video game right now. He's so missing out."

"Maybe you need to brush up on your hints. Maybe he didn't realize you were trying to get him to ask you out."

"Not good!" Maria puts her hands on her hips in mock shock. "Lydia Miller, you're looking at the best hint giver in all of Seattle."

"Honored," I say, and I give her a mock bow. I laugh. Maria can make me laugh sometimes. It feels good. For a minute. As long as I don't say anything too dumb after I laugh. "I haven't had a date since homecoming our junior year of high school, so if you are the best hint giver maybe you can teach me something. Or, does skill not translate to being able to teach?"

"I could teach anyone, Lydia, even people more hopeless than you. Ok. It goes like this."

She undoes her hair so that it falls over her shoulders. She's wearing a sleek black and pink biking outfit, and she looks snazzy—especially for an early morning bike ride. She shakes her head to fluff her hair, and she steps back at the exact moment a young man in a purple U-dub sweatshirt runs by her. He trips over her and falls into the railing along the pedestrian path.

"Oh!" She falls forward and lands on her hands and knees.

The jogger manages to catch himself on the railing. He looks pretty upset until he looks at Maria.

"Are you okay?" he asks. If she had been a guy, he probably would have pushed her over the rail into the lake. Instead, he reaches out and gently helps her stand.

"Yeah," Maria says, standing slowly and brushing herself off with exaggerated effort. "And you? I didn't know anyone was behind me."

I bite my lip to stop myself from smiling.

"Yeah," the man says. "Sorry!" He turns to run away. Well, everything but his eyes turn, anyway. They stay glued on Maria.

"Do you run for U dub?" Maria asks, taking a step toward him. I'm embarrassed for her, she looks so desperate, but it works for her. The man stops and leans against the fence, no longer in a hurry to continue his run.

"Oh no. Just for fun. I got this shirt at an orientation meeting. I think it's important to stay in shape, you know. Exercise and all that."

"So you're a freshman at U-dub, then, just like us!"

He smiles, and his smile is cute. "No, but I was one last year."

"Really?" Maria says, feigning surprise. "It isn't often you find a guy who is so good looking and still gets good enough grades to pass all his classes."

The guy laughs. The wind blows through his hair. "I didn't say I passed all of them." He offers Maria his hand. She takes it with a small curtsy.

"I'm Brian."

"Maria. And this is my friend Lydia."

Brian looks at me and smiles. His smile makes my knees go weak. I try to think of something to say, but before anything comes to mind, his eyes go back to Maria. I'm in a sweatshirt and shorts. Hardly boy-catching material next to Maria. She should have thought of that before she decided to try and teach me anything.

Though, Maria's outfit does look incredibly uncomfortable. I would never wear that thing on a leisure trip bike riding. Maybe that's my problem.

"Brian," Maria says in an exaggerated voice. "This Miss Lydia is not just any friend, she's also a star on the university soccer team."

Brian's eyes flit back to me. "You're Lydia Miller, then." And he smiles.

He knows my name! I blush stupidly. "Do I know you?"

He laughs. Maybe he doesn't think I'm completely stupid. Or maybe he does. "Oh no, I saw one of the women's soccer ads on campus." Then he blushes. "I don't really follow soccer that much, but I remembered your name. You have a, uh, distinctive look. I remember it from the ad."

A distinctive look? What in the world does that mean? I look to Maria, but for the first time in this whole exchange, she, too was caught off guard. And she's not going to bail me out.

"You should come to our game tomorrow night," I mumble, fighting embarrassment. If the lake water wasn't so cold, maybe I'd jump over the side of the bridge and go for a swim right now.

"I don't think I'd know what was going on," Brian says. "I actually don't watch soccer."

"You should ask someone to go with you," Maria says. "Someone who has an inside connection to the game who could explain some things to you." She looks back at me and winks, her spunk is apparently back.

Brian laughs. I'm surprised Maria is still going for the date. Well, I guess she's not the one with the distinctive look. I shouldn't take it personally. Everyone thinks like that.

"Now, where would I find a girl like that?" Brian rolls his eyes.

"Hmmm..." Maria says, rolling her eyes right back at him.

I can't believe how forward she is.

Brian smiles. "Ok, you got me. What time does the game start?"

"7."

"Would you meet me out in front of the field, around 6:45?"

As we ride back into the city, Maria glows with triumph. "I told you it was easy," she says. "You really should get out more."

"I'd have to take my distinctive look with me. Even you didn't know what to say when he brought that up."

Maria's face grows serious. "I think you're pretty, Lydia. Just because you have a unique look doesn't mean you're ugly. Just different. It takes people some time to get used to different. Besides, your facial features may be a bit different, but your curves are drop-dead sexy. I'd give anything for your hips. Don't pay attention to what Brian said. I'll set him straight tomorrow night."

"Sure, you will. I'm sure you'll talk about me plenty."

"Well, maybe not. After he sees you playing soccer, he'll probably dump me and start chasing you."

"Right, and you just let that happen?"

Maria blows a bubble with her gum. She giggles. "Not a chance. He seemed way to cute to give up that easily. Besides, Lydia, I don't want a boy to ruin you. You have your head on straight, and you're going places. I appreciate that you spend time with me."

"Even when it takes you away from boys?"

"Even then."

12 Rain

Lydia

The next evening, I put my old cell phone into my locker and join my teammates outside the locker room. The sounds of the crowd and the smell of the early-autumn rainstorm rush into the hall each time the door opens. I review the plays in my head and shift my feet. Brit stands nearby, but we don't talk. Finally, Coach appears and it's time to go.

Our cleats echo on the hard floor. With each step the sounds of the crowd grows louder. A staff member holds the door open, and we jog onto the field as the crowd cheers. A lot of people are here tonight.

The drizzle of the rain hits my face. The bright lights shine against my gold Huskies uniform.

It's the home opener.

Warm-ups fly by, and I run onto the field with the starters. Even Joana looks nervous.

Stanford. They looked really good on tape.

I find my place near the goalie and survey the field. The field scattered with collegiate athletes is as beautiful a sight as the lake this morning. I'm home. The crowd roars as the referee steps to midfield.

Game time. I smile and dig my cleats into the turf.

I hope Brian actually showed up and is up there somewhere with Maria. Maybe from up in the stands, he'll decide my distinctive look isn't as ugly as his original impression. Especially if Maria is right and my figure is attractive.

I'm such an idiot. He's with Maria and therefore not thinking about me.

The whistle blows, and the game is underway.

It doesn't take long to decide that as good as the Cardinals look on tape, they're even better on the field. It takes all my concentration to stay in the game, but I stay in it. And so does the team.

Where would Mom be sitting in this stadium if she were here? Whenever we traveled to watch soccer games, she was always religious about where we would sit.

Each stadium she had her own unique seat that had her name on it. If the seat was already taken, we wouldn't buy the tickets.

I don't remember where her seat was in Husky Soccer Stadium, but I'm sure she had one. If she were here today, that's where she'd be, and she would be loving this. This is what she wanted for me. Watching me play on the same field she played on. I run, I kick, the girls push, I fight for the ball. And the time flies by.

I'm exhausted by half time, but exhilarated. The game is going well, and it's still scoreless. We're in this thing. We're keeping up with Stanford, the defending champions.

On her way off the field for the half-time break, I notice Joana run over to talk with a girl on Stanford's team—a girl who played soccer at Issaquah. I frown at the breach in protocol, but Coach is up ahead and no one else seems to notice. Joana hugs the girl, whispers something in her ear, and then rejoins us, bumping me rudely on the way to the front of the line.

Everyone knows you're not allowed to talk to the other team during the game. Even at halftime. Even if you're friends.

The second half starts promising with several Husky possessions that result in shots on goal. I make a few stops, and the minutes tick by. Still, no points.

During the 70th minute, the action moves to our side of the field. I'm on the left side of the field covering Stanford's forward when the ball sails towards us. The forward fields the ball and jukes me out of position. I fall for the juke, but I recover enough to kick the ball out of bounds before she gets past me.

Corner kick.

A girl grabs the ball and runs over to the corner. I man up with a tall Stanford girl on the far side of the goal as the field fills up with girls from both teams.

Stanford's forward approaches, and the ball flies to us, aimed to give the taller girl a chance for a headshot to put the ball in. I jump as high as I can, too, but the ball sails over both of our heads. I look down as a second Stanford girl, who is running at a full tilt towards me, trips on the wet grass and falls.

I'm suspended in the air, helpless as flying bodies come at me.

And then the contact. The falling forward crashes into me on the side of my left knee just before I hit the ground. At the same time, the tall girl lands against me on the right. I hear a snap and my knee buckles backward as I hit the wet ground and collapse. My hands sink into the sodden turf, and I scream, my leg awkwardly bent from the weight of the girl on it. I gasp when she rolls off my leg and jogs away. Through my pain, I see her face—the girl from Issaquah.

I lie on the wet grass, writhing. I'm not screaming anymore, but I grab the wet turf with both hands and clutch it. I grind my teeth. Pain shoots up my leg, but I can't seem to move my body around to even look down.

69

A young man kneels next to me. My teammates surround me. The man palpates my knee. It hurts. "We've got to stabilize this and get her to the doctor right away," he says.

I shake my head, which is fuzzy from the pain. I let my face fall into the wet turf and scream into it. I look up to see a blur of people all around me. Amidst the chaos, my eyes focus on Brit. She's kneeling the grass next to me, huge tears coursing down her cheeks.

"You can't do this, Lydia! I can't go in there."

"I'll keep playing," but I gasp when I try to move, and my leg doesn't respond.

"You've done a number to your knee," the trainer says. "Stay still. We're going to roll you over."

The crowd cheers as the trainers help me onto a stretcher and wheel me off the field. I squint though the bright lights to see Brit still standing where I fell. The lights reflect off her face.

"You can do this Brit," I yell, hoping my voice doesn't get drowned out with the crowd.

She waves weakly back and slowly disappears along with the field. The lights, the crowd, the game, it all fades away until I'm put in an ambulance.

"When will I play again?" I ask.

"Not this season. Your knee was bent the wrong way—most injuries like this require surgery. You're in for a long and painful recovery before you get back on the field. Which is a shame, because you're really good. That stop you had after the Stanford girl beat you was amazing."

Without soccer, what am I going to do?

13 Reunited

Karl

Palm trees, saguaro cactus, open space, brilliant sunrise colors.

I've missed the desert. After my red-eye flight, I'm in Phoenix. Home. Just a few hours away from picking up Pearl in Flagstaff.

I roll down my windows and breathe in the air. It's dry—crisp and clean. The sight of the cacti against the horizon, a wide-open sky. Suddenly, the four years in Pittsburgh fade away into a dream. As the sun breaks into the sky, I feel a freedom that I haven't felt in years.

Tara was actually right. I needed to come here.

And I was right to not bring her with me, even though she threw a fit about it.

An exit sign reminds me of Andrea, and I'm glad that I'm not staying in Phoenix. I'm going to pick up Pearl and we're going to Arches National Park in Moab, Utah.

And from that point on, freedom, frustration, and loneliness battle inside me until the Phoenix desert disappears behind me. I turn on the radio and drive numbly until I find myself at some apartments near the main NAU campus in Flagstaff. I park the rental car, stretch, and follow Pearl's instructions to her apartment on the third floor of Building 2B.

Can you ignore your family for years and then show up with an expectation that everything will be like it was before you left? If she doesn't answer the door, it would serve me right.

If Tara hadn't talked to her, I wouldn't be here. If I had the courage to call her back, I wouldn't be here.

But I didn't call back. And now I'm here. And I think I'm happy about it.

I take a deep breath and knock.

Footsteps behind the door. The bolt unlocks. The door opens, and I look expectantly into the face of a girl in pajamas with long black hair, accented with pink streaks.

Not Pearl. I recheck the apartment number.

She yawns and rubs her eyes. "Hello! What can I do for you?"

The number of the door is definitely correct. I followed Pearl's directions exactly.

"Umm...I'm looking for Pearl Stapp."

The girl nods. "Pearl," she calls behind her. "You have a hot guy here to see you."

That's the first time I've been called hot in years. But, then again, maybe she's referring to the fact that carrying around so much extra insulation tends to make me hot and tired.

I take a deep breath and let it out slowly. Of course Pearl has a roommate. It's normal that Pearl's roommate's hair would have pink streaks—streaks like that are ubiquitous on college campuses, including Pittsburgh campus. Tara might have pink streaks in her red hair by the time I get back.

Pearl's head pokes out of the back room. A smile splits her face. "Karl," she says in a voice that barely makes it to my ears. "You really came." She walks over to me, and I stand still, watching her approach. I can't believe I'm looking at my sister. She has grown up; she's a woman now.

We embrace, and she feels real. She smells like Pearl.

"You look great!" I say. She wears blue jeans and a white T-shirt. Her hair is pulled back, and she looks as in-shape as I'm out of shape. We haven't talked in forever, yet it feels like just yesterday we were kids together. Regret, excitement, love. I'm not sure how to describe all the emotions that rush through me.

Pearl laughs, and she wipes at her eyes. "Wish I could say the same thing to you. You've put on a ton of weight."

"Yeah."

"And when was the last time that you shaved?"

"I'm a scientist." I was going to shower before the plane ride, but things got really busy.

"Einstein didn't have a beard," she laughs again. I love hearing her laugh. "And he wasn't nearly so fat! How do you have a girlfriend?"

"That's a long story." And a question I wonder about, too.

"Good—we have a long trip coming up."

We stand looking at each other for a few more minutes. Eventually, we simultaneously notice the girl with the pink hair smirking at us.

"This has to be the strangest family reunion I've ever seen," she says.

"I'm almost ready." Pearl sounds just like Mom as she takes charge of a situation. "Why don't you chat with Kat here for a minute while I finish getting my things together?"

I look over at Kat and she looks back at me. Then we sit down across the room from each other and study the vein patterns on the back of our hands while Pearl finishes getting ready.

* * *

The drive to Moab flies by, and it isn't long before Pearl and I are sitting across from each other at a Pizza Hut off the main road.

"So, you want to be an elementary school teacher?" I ask after the waiter takes our order.

"I enjoy it," Pearl says with a small laugh. "But, if the opportunity presents itself, I would rather get married and have a family of my own. Maybe I could teach after I raise children."

"You sound like Mom," I say, and it's true. Her expression and her words are just like Mom.

Pearl looks away and wipes a tear from her cheek. "I miss her a lot sometimes," she says quietly.

I nod, and I look down at the table, stroking my beard with my hand. Has it already been four and a half years since Mom died?

Pearl reaches out and squeezes my hand. Fortunately, it is then that the waiter brings out the pizza.

"It's been too long!" I bite into a big piece, anxious to put the moment of weakness behind us.

Pearl laughs. "Do you not eat pizza often? I still eat pizza at least three times a week."

"I don't believe it. You would be chubbier by now if you did."

"There is an important secret I know."

"What's that?"

"I don't know if you'll even know what the word means." Pearl laughs and it's contagious. She finds joy in everything. How can she laugh and talk with me like this when I've ignored her for four years?

She leans forward to whisper: "Exercise. It's this thing where you leave your computer on the desk and you move your body around. That's a secret you should learn more about, whether you eat pizza or not."

She laughs so sincerely that I have to laugh with her. "How do you know that I'm not exercising regularly?" I grin and rest my hands on my large belly.

"Just a hunch. Mom stayed thin all those years through good exercise. I think you should consider it. You need to start eating pizza again."

"I end up eating with my officemate for most meals, and that usually isn't pizza."

"Well, I think that's just silly," Pearls says before stuffing another large slice of pizza in her mouth. "Give me your officemate's phone number, so I can call him up and let him know what I think about your lack of pizza."

The word "she" gets caught on my tongue just in time. I've avoided talking about Tara since the apartment, and I mean to keep it that way.

* * *

The next two days fly by. The weather is cool, but nice with a light jacket. Pearl and I enjoy exploring the different arches and marveling at the beauty of the park.

The next thing I know, I'm lying in bed on the final morning of our stay. Pearl sleeps peacefully on the other side of the room. I grab a blanket and tiptoe quietly onto the small deck. The air is cold, but I huddle down into a lounge chair and watch the sunrise, letting the light warm me as the sun slowly blankets the red landscape. I love the fresh air and the openness of the desert.

For a moment, I consider going back into the room and turning on my computer to check on the processing jobs I kicked off before I left. Surprisingly, I don't want to check on them. I tell myself I don't want to disturb Pearl, but I also know that I don't want the magic of the past few days to end. I will go back to reality soon enough.

Over the past two days, I've enjoyed life as it once was, as it could have been had things turned out differently. Pearl and I haven't talked about the past. Still, being out here together brings back so many memories.

My earliest memories of Pearl are when we were children. When I was ten, she was four, and she always tried to come out and play with the neighborhood children. I spent a lot of time outside with the other kids.

Andrea was there, of course. I met Andrea when I was five and our family moved to the neighborhood. She lived across the street, and as kids we played together under the large orange trees in Andrea's backyard. We'd climb up and drop oranges on Pearl as she ran around underneath.

Eventually Pearl stopped playing with us, and we recruited more kids, mostly boys. Andrea was a tomboy back then, and she was the leader of our little gang. We played war and had water balloon fights. We did that for years until she stopped playing with us. It happened so fast, I don't think I even realized it happened.

Until that night. I was 15 and walking home from flag football practice when I noticed Andrea sitting out on her porch. Instead of turning into my house, I went on an impulse to talk to her, still in my bright purple uniform.

"You don't hang out with us anymore." Something about her was different that night. Her hair was down, and she had make-up on. For the first time, I realized that she was a girl. And that she was beautiful.

"I've grown up," she said.

I remember how red my face felt as I lied, "I've noticed."

"I've got the worst crush on you."

I sat down on her porch, she took my hand, we started talking, and just like that, we were high-school sweethearts.

A couple weeks later, I decided we should prove that it is possible to fry eggs on Phoenix sidewalks. We spent a long time sweating outside in the heat of the day, watching the egg dry out on the cement behind the house.

I had just checked on the egg and was ready to give up. "This was such a dumb idea!" Andrea stepped forward and kissed me for the first time. I was so surprised that I jumped into the cactus that was growing by the porch.

A kiss like that is one that you never forget.

Neither did Pearl or Mom. Andrea was so embarrassed that she ran home, and I had to endure nearly an hour of teasing from Mom and Pearl while they pulled cactus needles out of my back.

Things had been so good. After high school Andrea went to college in Tucson at the University of Arizona, and I went to Arizona State. I got to know the drive from ASU to the U of A very well, and we always spent our summers together.

Everything was going to work out. I would graduate from ASU, marry Andrea, take over Dad's business, and raise a family.

Except for the fact that I wasn't excited about Dad's business. I should have been. Ever since I was a boy, I knew that I would take over his business. It would stay in the family. Dad sent me to ASU, and I worked hard, pursuing an accounting degree.

And I hated accounting. I counted down the days until graduation, even though I had three years left. Everything changed when I took a chemistry class for one of my general education credits. The professor was amazing. His nonpareil lecture style captivated my attention, and I found myself enjoying school—well, enjoying chemistry.

Office hours became my second home. Near the end of the semester, the professor called me to his office and suggested that I consider a career in science. "With your bright mind, you will make a difference for good in this world," he told me. The words echoed in my mind.

My life changed forever.

As if he knew what had just happened, Dad called me home that weekend for Sunday dinner. I still remember the tension in the house that day. Dad met me at the door and took me to his office.

"Thanks for being here, son."

"I'm going to change my major to a scientific field," I blurted. "Something like bioinformatics or chemistry."

Dad didn't react. Not how I had expected. He set the book he had been holding down on the table. He stared at me over his reading glasses. "Why would you do something like that?"

I shrugged. "I love it."

Dad shook his head and paused as if he were about to disagree. But the only thing he said was, "I guess you'll learn everything you need to know once you start working with me."

I opened my mouth to respond, but Dad had some news of his own to tell me. "Your mother was just diagnosed with an advanced breast cancer."

Those words hit me harder than a cation hits an anion. I had been prepared for a battle with him about my major, but not this. Mom? Cancer?

"The doctors don't know if they will be able to help her or not. Will you move back home?"

I remember nodding.

Mom was in the kitchen, preparing my favorite meal. We hugged, and we cried.

It wasn't long before I got into the Bioinformatics program. I excelled in school, and I loved every minute of it. I knew that I could never go work for Dad after experiencing it. I loved the science—it would consume me, and I would lie awake at night trying to figure things out, putting the pieces together.

The situation at home got worse, and I found myself working extra hours at school to avoid the high stress and raging emotions at home. The fall of my senior year I sent out applications for graduate school. I was going to tell Dad, but then he asked me to quit school. "Mom is getting progressively worse. You need to stop spending so much time with school and spend time with the family. Maybe you can go back later."

I didn't do it, I couldn't do it, and Dad was upset about my choice. I couldn't throw away my future—not when it meant that I would be stuck with the future that he wanted for me. Dad was hurt, and Mom was too sick to smooth things over.

Even when I got into the PhD program at Carnegie Mellon, I didn't tell anyone. I didn't know how to broach the subject with Dad, and we barely spoke by then anyway. Mom was tired, and I only saw her occasionally. Her best hours were usually at times that I was at school, which was intense the last two semesters before graduation.

And then it came. March 18th: the day that is forever etched in my memory. I came home from a long afternoon in the lab to find Dad sitting on a chair in the front room, staring blankly into space.

"It's nice for you to finally get home," he said. "Go see your mother."

I took my time putting my things away, fuming at how rude Dad was. Finally, I did go and see Mom. I knocked lightly on the door, and she called me in.

She looked awful.

"My dear Karl." I can still hear those words and how she said them. "I love you, son."

I knew at that moment that this was the end. That she didn't beat the cancer. She knew it, too, and tears fell onto her face as I came over and cried next to her bedside.

"My dear sweet boy." Her voice was so soft. "How I love you! I want to be here to see you marry that dear girl of yours. But, I'm afraid God has other plans for me."

She couldn't go. I needed her to explain to Dad about my PhD. I needed her to be there when I married Andrea.

"There is something I need to tell you," she said. "These days people think that they need to have a grand career to make something of themselves. When I was young, I was tempted to think that as well. But then you came, and I found greater purpose in being your mother than I ever did in my career.

"Please remember that. There are many things that you can do with your life. There are great successes out there waiting for you. But now, as my life comes to a close, the decision to be your mother stands out as the best decision I ever made. Promise me, that you will put your focus on your family? Don't get so caught up in your work and leave poor Andrea out in the cold."

"I will Mom. I will." I tried to say more, but the words didn't come.

We looked at each other, and Mom held my hand. "I'm tired now. Come talk to me more after dinner."

"I will. I love you Mom."

"I love you too, son." Her hand dropped and she smiled. I walked out of the room and never saw her alive again.

I jump as the door opens and Pearl joins me on the porch.

"Karl!" she says. "Are you crying?"

I force a laugh. "Hi Pearl. I guess I was just remembering the last time I saw Mom." I don't tell her it's the first time I've thought of that day since it happened.

The surprised look on Pearl's face vanishes and she smiles. She knows. She understands.

"Having you here brings back a lot of memories for me, too."

She sits down next to me and helps herself to some of my blanket. "I have a question for you, if you don't mind me asking."

"Go for it."

"What happened between you and Andrea? I've always wondered."

The question is so sincere that I decide to answer.

"I was really busy my last semester of college. Between Mom's funeral, graduate school interviews—which I hid from Dad—and trying to finish all my classes, I didn't have much time to spend with Andrea. I saw her briefly at the funeral, and I was such a wreck then that I didn't even talk to her much.

"I was tired of being separated, and I wanted to marry her before we went to Pittsburgh. So, shortly after graduation I took her up to Prescott to propose."

Pearl gasps. "That is so romantic! You took her there all the time." She laughs. "I thought that it must be the most romantic place in the world."

I smile. "Yeah, Andrea loved hiking, and it's nice up there. We had a beautiful day, hiking around and enjoying nature. We climbed up a ridge and looked over the mountains. I kissed her and told her I wanted to marry her."

"So cute! You two were always so proper. I used to sit in the front room and watch you kiss her. You were always so gentle and considerate."

Heat creeps into my face. "I never realized you were watching."

Pearl just laughs. "You were always proper. Nothing to be embarrassed about. I'm still hoping a guy kisses me like that someday."

My face reddens even more. But, I'm not thinking about Andrea this time. I'm thinking about Tara, and the good feelings are all gone. There wasn't anything proper about the kiss we had just a few days ago when she dropped me off at the airport. I'm glad Pearl wasn't across the street watching then. I blush, suddenly naked in front of my sister.

"Please, continue." Pearl slaps my arm playfully. "At Prescott, kissing?"

"Okay. I tried to go in for another kiss, but she asked me if I was really going to go to graduate school, and she was really upset when I said yes. I told her that I wanted to marry her first, and that I would take her with me."

"And she didn't like that?"

"She told me that professors never have time for families. I told her that wasn't true, that I would always put her first, but she started crying.

"She said something like 'I don't want to move away from my family, and I don't want to sit at home by myself with kids while you spend all hours of the day off in school for years and years.'

"'We can work through all that!' I told her, 'We don't have to have kids for a while. Not until we're ready.'"

Suddenly I can't go on. The pain is deep; the betrayal smarts like it just happened. Pearl reaches out and grabs my hand. I'm there again, standing with Andrea on that mountaintop.

Pearl doesn't press me, and I battle the hurt inside me for a long time before speaking.

"That was when she told me she was pregnant," I finally manage to say.

Pearl gasps. "With Vince's baby?"

I nod, and the shame of it hurts me more than I expected. Now my sister knows what happened. That my girl slept with another guy and left me behind.

"It was a shotgun wedding," Pearl says, shaking her head. "I can't believe it. And you still had to get her home. How did that work? What did you say?"

"She ran away and called a friend. I sat there on that rock, stunned. I got home really late."

"Do you ever wish you had run after her?"

"Sometimes. But most of the time not."

Pearl puts her hand on my arm. "I'm sorry," she says.

We sit in silence for a long time, until the sun makes its way over to us and I take the blanket off. Pearl stands up and opens the door to the hotel room.

78

"That was the night you told Dad that you were going to Pittsburgh."

We both know how that went. Anger. Unkind words. A slammed door. A son that never returned.

Pearl sighs. "Thanks for talking to me." I stand, and she gives me a long hug. "Let me shower, and I bet we can see a few more arches before we have to head back to Flagstaff."

14 Reflection

Karl

By the time we leave the hotel, we only have a couple hours before we need to start our way south again.

"Is it worth going back into the park?" I ask Pearl.

"You know"—she laughs shyly—"I would love to visit Double Arch again. The hike is short, and it's so cool in there. I bet it looks even better with the clouds that are racing through the sky today."

"We have enough time for that." And so we drive through the park, past the Windows and Balanced Rock and to the Double Arch parking lot. Only one other car in the lot breaks the view of the red rock. I step out of the car and shiver; it is colder now than it was this morning. We may not want to stay long, in case a storm shows up.

"I intend to enjoy this, even if I freeze to death," Pearl says as I park the car.

"Phoenix girl."

She laughs. "I don't carry five extra layers of fat."

Touché.

We get out of the car and make the short hike to the arch, watching the incoming storm blow the clouds in. We don't hike very fast; these are our last hours together and I find myself savoring each step.

Once we get close to the arches, we stop, and I put my arm around Pearl. The view is spectacular with the clouds racing above the towering arches. Two girls, about our same age, are also here. One of them is a tall, pretty blonde with short pink shorts and a bright purple University of Washington sweatshirt. She's climbing on the steep rocks between the arches while other girl watches, her back to us. The watching girl has brown curly hair, and she wears blue pants and a gray sweatshirt. A set of discarded crutches is propped up on the rock next to her.

Eventually, the blonde calls to us. Her "Good morning" echoes around the cavern that the two arches create.

"Hello!" Pearl yells back. "Sorry to interrupt your view. Wow! It's pretty today." She steps away from me and starts to hike up the arch.

The blonde scrambles down the rocks while she yells at Pearl some more. "We've been here for a while now, and you're the first people we've seen. I've only been here once before, and it was packed! This is the time to come. I'm never coming in summer again!"

Pearl gets close enough that they stop yelling, though they keep talking. I wander aimlessly toward the arch.

You can't appreciate Double Arch until you stand under it. That's when you realize just how small you are. The two arches tower over me, 40-50 feet off the ground, with bright red rock accented by darker red lines marbled throughout. The space between them reveals an even greater sky above. I climb up the slope, leaving the trail. The entire entrance feels open, like the main floor of the Cathedral of Learning on Pitt campus, but with a different kind of beauty; it is a main hall of a grand palace.

The girl with brown hair stands as I approach and pick up her crutches. When she turns, I'm surprised at how pretty she is. Her hair is curly, and her features are soft and unique. Really unique. Her nose is small, and she doesn't have ear lobes. I wonder if she speaks English, though I'm not sure I've ever seen anyone who looks like her, or what part of the world she might come from. But even though she looks strange, she's pretty.

And my eyes have lingered on her for longer than is polite.

"Maria," she calls to her friend. "Why don't we head back and let these people enjoy the arch?"

"Okay," the girl calls back. "I just want one more look out of the second arch." She and Pearl scramble up the rock to the top to the great view out over a large valley. I looked through it yesterday when we were here, and the height of it scared me to death. I don't need to go again.

The pretty girl puts her weight on her crutches and starts back down to the trail. A large cast covers most of her left leg. The hike here isn't difficult or too sandy, but I'm impressed that she made it all the way on crutches. I watch her, still fascinated by her foreign features.

The ledge at the base of the arches isn't too far off the trail back to the cars, but several large rocks need to be maneuvered to get to it. The girl cautiously maneuvers through the rocks and moves surprisingly adroitly until she's almost to me. Then, her crutch hits a rock and gets caught. She loses her balance. I jump forward and catch her by the elbow.

Upon contact, a strange blue light starts to seep through the cracks of the red arch. I blink, trying unsuccessfully to clear the glare out of my eyes.

"Are you okay?" I ask. The red arch is glowing blue. What is wrong with my eyes?

"Yeah." The girl smiles. She has a pretty smile. She pushes herself up, away from me and the arch. I keep my hand on her elbow for support.

As she steps, whatever light is shining in my eyes explodes. It pours out of the arch like a tidal wave and drenches me and the girl as if it were water. The whirlpool of light spins around us. All I can see is light. Bright blue light. I'm screaming, but I can't hear it. The only thing I can feel is my grip on the girl's elbow.

And then, as quickly as it appeared, the blue light is gone.

I blink and try to clear my vision. I see me, and I see the girl. I no longer see the arches or the red rock or the girl's cast. I see myself standing in a bright, sunny meadow full of wild flowers. The sun is low in the sky, as if it's the end of an early summer's day. I hear birds chirping.

I feel my pants starting to slip down, and I reach down with my free hand and pull them up. My zipper and belt buckle are gone! I look at the girl, and her crutches have also disappeared.

The girl looks around at the meadow with wide eyes, her free hand reaches up to touch her chest just above her right breast. If I didn't know better, I'd say that it looks like blue light is glowing underneath her shirt.

I take a step back. As I do, I notice blue light shimmering above me. The girl hops backward toward me to keep her balance. The same blue light floods around us again, and seconds later the illusion is gone. My pants are zipped up, and the girl has her cast. Her crutches have fallen to the ground, but I still have her, so she hasn't fallen.

I let go of the girl and blink a few times. No lights in my eyes. Everything is normal.

"Okay," the blonde calls. "I'm coming." She starts the climb down the arch.

I bend over and hand the girl her crutches.

"Thank you." The look in her eyes matches how I feel right now. Shock. Disbelief. Worry. I just had a major hallucination, and I don't know why. The girl opens her mouth, but then closes it when nothing comes out.

"What's going on?" the blonde asks, stepping next to the girl.

"I slipped and this boy caught me and..." Her voice trails off.

"And your friend lost her crutches," I say. "It's a bit slippery here, and a little hard to maneuver."

I don't know what I saw. What I thought I saw. I try to clear my brain, but it feels clear already. What happened to me? Blue light? A meadow? Is it possible the girl saw the same thing?

Impossible.

Just a weird reflection of the light or an ugly reaction to breakfast. It has been an emotional time I've spent here with Pearl.

The girl on crutches is still looking at me.

I look back at her warily.

Maria breaks the awkward silence. "Yeah, she forced me to come out here. I'll take her the rest of the way back." She pushes the girl on crutches forward.

"What is your name?" the girl asks as she starts to step away.

I'm not sure why I answer honestly, but I do. "I'm Karl. I'm from Pittsburgh."

"Pittsburgh," she repeats.

"Come-on Lydia," the blonde sighs. "Pittsburgh is really far away from Seattle."

"Thanks for catching me," the girl says. Lydia says.

"What was that all about?" Pearl asks after I climb up to join her on the slope between arches.

"She tripped when she went by me, and I caught her."

"No, why was she looking at you so intently like that? Did something happen when she tripped?"

"I don't think so. We got a weird glare of the sun in our eyes for a second."

Pearl nods and starts talking about something else.

It was a just a weird glare. That's all it was.

15 Rivals

Cadah

"It's time for you to leave," Ore says. She grabs my fuma skin from the corner and tosses it into the center of the room.

I open my mouth and close it again. I knew it was a bad idea to bring up her father again, but I had to do it. She needs to know the truth. Why does she not believe me?

Ore glares at me. "I'm serious. You keep bringing this up. I don't know why, or what you're hoping for, but I'm sick of it. Arujan said he fell. I saw where he fell from."

"But Ore, I saw Arujan hit him! I saw Arujan knock him off the trail."

"From so far down the mountain? How do you know he wasn't trying to save him? You bring this up all the time! Why? I'm done, Cadah. I'm done with you."

"Where am I going to go? You're my best friend." I bite my lip to stop it from trembling. I don't ask my real questions. *Who will be your friend, Ore, after I leave? Who is going to listen to you talk about men and plan the harvest? Who will you find to fill your days, if not me?*

"Ask your new boyfriend," Ore says, and she grabs my pack of clothes and tosses it onto the fuma skin. "I'm sure he can find a place for you to live."

She reaches for my dad's wood carving, a rendition of the Blue Princess fighting to save the mountains. It was his greatest work, and the only thing I've kept from him. The carving shows the princess emerging from a cave, wind blows her curly hair behind her as she raises her hand, which has fire shooting from it.

"No," I say. "Don't touch that. I'll take it. I'll leave. I'll talk to Ler and find a new place."

Ore's face hardens at the mention of Ler. She picks up my dad's statue. Before I can get to her, she swings it over her head and smashes it on the ground. The princess's head flies across the room and into the fire, her hand breaks off and the wood cracks down the middle.

I stare at her, shocked. "Ore," I manage to say.

"Don't talk to me!" she shouts. "Get your things and get out. There is no blue princess. We are not friends. Don't come back here. Ever."

I move around the room and gather my things: my extra tunic, my fuma skin, an old necklace from my mother. Ore doesn't look at me again.

It's not Ore's fault. She's suffering from the loss of her father. I've been there. I am there. At the loss of my father's gift, I feel like I've lost him all over again. And it hurts. A lot.

* * *

I lean into Ler, taking solace in his strong arm around my shoulder. "Sometimes I just think she might be right," I say. "Her and that strange man. Maybe there is no Blue Princess. Maybe Wynn isn't real."

"Why would you say that?" he asks patiently. This isn't the first time we've had this conversation.

"Two hundred years? That's a long time for someone to be alive. And an even longer time for two people to be alive."

"Both of them are Azureans, Cadah. Powerful people. They can heal, they can avoid aging. That's why they're so dangerous."

"Okay, but if the Blue Princess is dangerous, how do we know we can trust her? What makes one Azurean good and another bad? How can we wait for centuries, without knowing if we may just be replacing one monster for another?"

"What other choice do we have?"

I shrug. "I just don't know if she's going to come, anyway. And maybe it doesn't matter. Maybe we can be happy here. Or maybe we can be happy in the valley."

Ler's arm tightens around me. That means he's thinking, taking all my thoughts and emotions seriously before responding. I wait and let his warmth soothe my fears. Eventually, his arm relaxes. "I had a friend from Keeper who wasn't there this year when I went to visit," he says.

"You have friends in Keeper?"

"I've been going to Keeper since I was small. The girl there, Sharue, has been determined to marry me since my first visit when we were five." Ler laughs.

I sit up a little straighter.

"Don't worry, Cadah. I'm not interested." Ler laughs again.

I don't join in. I'm not sure why he just told me that.

"Seriously," he says. "But I had another friend, too. His name was Anu. He snuck out of the mountains regularly when we were young. A funny habit of his, I suppose. He found people down there, a village a lot like ours. People there had seen Wynn, and according to Anu, Wynn was every bit as terrible as the legends say. But this time when I visited Keeper, Anu wasn't there. He was gone, and no one knew where he was."

"You think he decided to stay in the valley?"

Ler shrugs. "Either that, or he was killed. He never told me he wanted to stay in the valley. He always said the opposite."

I don't know what to say, so I put my arm around Ler's back and rub it softly. We sit like that for a minute before Ler speaks again.

"Cadah, I don't know for certain that the Blue Princess is really out there, but I believe she is. I don't think Togan would really leave all his friends up here to die. I think she will come, and I think there is a better life for us than this one."

"I hope you're right." My cheeks warm at the mention of a life for us. How fast things have changed! I want that life for us. A life with Ler, whatever it is.

Ler laughs again. "Me, too."

He looks down at me, and I look up at him, wishing he would have given me another moment for my heart to slow. His face lowers slightly, his lips approaching mine. My breath catches, and I close my eyes as my heart beats even faster. My skin tingles with the anticipation.

I can feel his breath on my lips when we hear crunching on the trail. Ler pulls away, leaving me feeling cold and disappointed. He stands, and I follow, brushing myself off. I'm glad it's almost dark now, and so Ler can't see how giddy, despite my disappointment, I am from the moment.

And then the person approaching calls out in a high-pitched voice and the smile disappears from my face.

"Ho there! I'm looking for a place to stay in Watch."

I don't need to look to know who that voice belongs to. It's Arujan.

16 Rousseau

Lydia

I crack open my text book, which is an awkward thing to do with my leg elevated.

I hate having my leg elevated.

The doctors say it must be up six hours a day. Minimum. They clearly have never tried to do anything with their leg in this position. Yet, I do everything, aka midterms, midterms, and more midterms, with my leg up. Apparently healing a torn LCL is more miserable than tearing it in the first place.

I flip the pages of the book until I get to the right page. Page 281. *The French Revolution.*

Yuck.

Is this really going to be on the exam? I look longingly at Maria's empty desk. It would be nice to have someone to talk to, but I haven't seen much of Maria since we got back from Moab. She's been attending a string of homework dates Brian has set up. Talk about cute! It turns out that Brian is a better influence on Maria than her parents hoped I would be.

Not that I can complain about her too much—I owe her a lot. And not just for helping me through the summer. The trip to Utah was just what I needed to get out of the funk I was in after the injury. I'm studying again, and my grades will be okay by the end of the semester.

Still, I can't help but wish it were me making eyes with Brian over my textbook right now.

The only guy I can see right now is a picture of Jacque Rousseau. Nope. Not making eyes with him. I shudder and put the book down.

With Jacque out of the way, my thoughts turn, as they do all the time now, to the meadow. I pick up my phone, open and close it, and twirl it in my hands. What would Mom think about my trip to the meadow? She would believe me, I know that. I've replayed that day in my mind hundreds of times. I fell, Karl grabbed my arm, and Arches was gone. We were gone. No red rock, no Maria, no cold.

I felt something strong there. Like the pull of a magnet on my chest. I belonged there; I needed to stay there. I haven't felt so at home since Mom died. But, it's weird, because I'm sure the pull pulsed from the flower on my chest. I haven't ever felt anything from that flower.

I may be going crazy.

Still, whether I'm supposed to be studying Jacque or Newton, I can't stop thinking of that meadow. Was it on earth? Did we travel through time?

And the most important question of all: How am I going to get back there?

The only thing that competes with thoughts of the meadow is how much I miss soccer. Thoughts of the meadow are less painful, so that's where I tend to direct my thoughts. At least I try to, though it's harder when my leg hurts.

Another strange thing, every night over the past few weeks, I dream about going back to the meadow, and every night Carl stands in the meadow with me. Always Carl, and only Carl. And I remember a lot about the meadow—the details are minute and beautiful. It doesn't make sense. We were only there for a moment; I shouldn't remember as much as I do. In each dream I even see a trail across the meadow. I know I'm supposed to go down that trail.

Maria thinks the memories and the obsession are love.

I may be obsessed, but I'm not in love. That guy was nice, but I only touched him for a minute, and we only spoke enough to exchange names. Still, when he walked away, I can't help but thinking that he took my key to returning to the meadow with him.

Why couldn't I have been brave enough to say more to Carl before we left? What is he thinking about the meadow? Would he go back with me?

I slip the phone into my pocket and lean awkwardly over my computer.

Carl Pittsburgh.

Google returns millions of irrelevant results.

Karl Pittsburgh.

A different set of nothing.

I don't know anything else about Carl. At least not in real life. Though, in my dreams, he's always a student. I google the list of colleges in Pittsburgh. It's long, Carnegie Mellon, Pittsburgh, Duquesne, Point Park, Chatham, Carlow, and many more. Talk about tedious, but it's either this or Jacque.

As if that was even a choice.

Karl Carnegie Mellon. Carl Carlow. Karl Point Park. I type in search after search. I look through pages of photos. Nothing, but at least most of the guys aren't as scary-looking as Jacque.

If only I had one more piece of information about him.

Like last night, in my dream, he told me he was studying biology.

Ten more searches, and then I'll do something else.

Karl student Carnegie Mellon biology.

I looked at the results and gasp.

It's him, I'm sure of it, though the picture shows a much thinner Karl than the one I met at the arch. I click through the picture to a LinkedIn page for a Karl Stapp, a graduate student in computational biology at Carnegie Mellon University.

I laugh out loud. No way! It's only been a half hour, and I found him.

Karl stares back at me, his sandy brown hair and bright blue eyes are confident.

I have to call him. But not right now.

The door slams open and Maria walks in, giggling as she tells Brian something before slamming the door closed behind her. She throws her backpack on the bed and walks to her closet.

"Hey Lydia!"

"Hi Maria. How was studying this afternoon?"

"Strong biceps, well-shaped shoulder muscles, irresistible lips. I'm ready for the final," she shrugs, glancing back at me. "Hey! Isn't that the guy from Arches?"

I blush at her expression and nod.

"How in the world did you find him?"

"I was trying to figure that out when you came in. I only looked for a few minutes."

"No way." She pulls a stick of gum out of her pocket and joins me at my computer.

I shrug.

"When are you going to Pittsburgh?"

"I'm going to call him."

"That's not exciting. Will he even remember you? You need to go out there, silly. You need to dress up cute—not overdone—but nice. That way he'll be willing to talk to you. You have a nice voice, but guys are visual. If you're dressed right, he won't say no."

"Maybe." I don't tell Maria that some guys don't talk to cute girls, and sometimes guys talk to girls that they don't think are cute. That would ruin her worldview.

"I'll help you pick your outfit."

"It's got be something that goes well with crutches. And I don't do jeans."

"A skirt. It will show off your legs."

"Leg. Just one leg." And one big cast.

"I wish I could go with you, but my parents say I'm not allowed any more trips until my grades improve."

"I'm calling, not going."

"You have to go. Love's spell doesn't last forever."

Love has nothing to do with this. But, Maria is probably right. He probably doesn't even want to talk to me.

* * *

Four days, four phone calls. Maria was right. Of course, it's easy to tell someone to travel across the country when you have means to do so, aka a car.

Since I sold my car, I have no means to get to Pittsburgh. I can barely get to the soccer field to watch the team practice.

They're almost done by the time I get there. I stand by the entrance, watching the girls run through the drizzle in the distance.

The cold rain slowly seeps through my sweatshirt.

I should be over there with them, but I don't move close enough for them to see me. I can't run anymore. I can't play. It doesn't matter how hard I worked to make the team. I'm hurt. I'm out. Forgotten.

The team finishes, and a few girls run past me. They don't stop or even say hi.

Brit trudges off the field in my direction. Her head is down, and her shoulders are slumped. She almost walks right by me, but I reach out and grab her arm.

"Oh! Hi Lydia." Brit's eyes are blotchy.

"Rough practice?"

Her body droops even more, like a wilting plant finally sinking to the ground after a week without rain. "My brother died this morning." The words choke in her throat and she starts crying. I try to maneuver my crutches so I can put my arms around her. I hate these crutches almost as much as I hate the pit forming in my stomach. I close my eyes, but all I can see is the face of the police officer who told me Mom was dead.

I pull one of my arms back and reach into my pocket and clutch my phone. I shouldn't have called my mom that night. I shouldn't have done it.

Her sobs continue. I take deep breaths and my panic slowly subsides.

Finally, still a little dizzy, I step back and balance myself on my crutches. "How did it happen?"

"A car crash."

Oh no. I close my eyes and take a deep breath. Hold, two, three. Breathe.

"I'm such a baby." Brit looks at me for the first time and I force a smile. "Of all people, you know about losing someone you love. I suppose you dealt with it better than I'm doing. I can barely do anything."

"That's not true." Even my voice is quivering. "I still miss my mom." If I grip any harder, I'm going to crush the phone in my pocket. I lean heavily on the crutches.

Brit nods and looks away. I don't tell her that she will feel the loss everyday of her life. That she will see her brother every day in the faces of others. I don't tell of the anger or the depression that will be her new companions.

"When are you heading out to Wisconsin?"

"Next week, right after our second game with Stanford."

"You're going to play?"

"I have to keep my scholarship Lydia, I have to!"

They have special arrangements for these kinds of things, but Brit doesn't need advice. She needs love. And someone who knows what will help her. I'm sure I'm not the right person for either. Not if I'm going to have a panic attack every five minutes just at the thought of what she's going through.

"Is your boyfriend going to drive back with you?"

Something other than grief flashes through her eyes. "Oh no. He can't make it."

"What a dud of a boyfriend." That was the wrong thing to say. Brit starts crying again.

And then I realize how close Wisconsin is to Pittsburgh. Is Maria right? Should I really visit Karl?

Calling certainly isn't working. If I have any hope of seeing Karl again, I need to go to Pittsburgh. I think he's the one to take me back to Arches, just like he does in my dreams.

And Brit needs my help.

"Can I take you?"

"I can't ask that of you," Brit sniffs and wipes her face with her hand. "I'll be fine."

"I really want to. I actually really need to get to Pittsburgh. Soon. If it isn't too much, could I take you and then borrow your car to visit Pittsburgh?"

Brit looks at me skeptically.

"I'm serious, I really do need to go to Pittsburgh. And I want to help you. I know what you're going through." What I'm going through.

Skepticism morphs into relief. "Thank you, Lydia! I'm sorry I'm such a mess. Of course you can borrow the car."

We hug again, and the light, drizzly rain turns into a downpour. With a quick goodbye, we part ways—Brit to change and me to drop a few books at the library.

I decide to wait out the rain in the library. I don't want to be walking around on crutches in a river running down the sidewalk.

I wander the aisles of the library aimlessly, shivering in my damp clothes. Not really in the mood for reading, I crack open a few old books and smell the hundred-year-old pages. There are probably books in here that have never been opened.

A large book on the shelf catches my eye, and I pull it down. *Things You Never Knew About History.* It's heavy and dusty. Its spine creaks as I open it. The pages are yellowed and beautiful. I flip through the pages, and then start to close it when I notice the headline on the last chapter.

Visitors from another world come through magic portal.

I lean the book against the bookshelves and keep reading.

Believe it or not, early American history holds several accounts of visitors from other worlds. Most notable is the record of Lovina Hurt, who wrote a brief history about how she fell in love with one of these visitors and had a child with him before he disappeared.

This hard-to-find record is found in a small library in Washington DC. It seems that historians have not given enough clout to the story to ensure its preservation.

However, there is more to this story than meets the eye. Three independent accounts mention meeting the people Lovina included in her biography. Although these accounts disagree on some details, each refers to a forgotten world and the order of the blue flower.

My free hand slides under my shirt and fingers the texture of my flower tattoo. A blue flower. I turn the page and nearly drop the book when I see an old photograph of Lovina's diary. A blue flower is on the cover. It matches the mark on my chest.

Is there something in Lovina's history that could help me get back to that meadow?

I push the book into my shoulder bag, and I move to the computers to find out.

17 Revolutionary

Lydia

It isn't long before I find the full text of the journal. I settle into the seat and read.

I am Lovina Hurt. Knowing that I will soon die, today I sit down to write my unique story. Perhaps future generations will discount what I write, but I know that it is true, and I want my descendants to know it.

I was born in Philadelphia in 1770, right before the war that separated us from Britain. My father was a passionate man, believing in the cause of freedom. He died in that war, leaving my mother to survive by herself with three living children, of which I was the third.

My brothers were both sent off to apprenticeships when they were 11, but I stayed with Mother. We worked hard and life was tolerable.

Despite the great victory in the war, it did little to improve our lives in the new country. And so we struggled on.

It was during the summer of my 17th year that a large convention came upon Philadelphia. Delegates from each state descended on the city, and despite the heat, they stayed all summer. The influx of guests provided many opportunities for work, for which Mother and I were grateful.

At the time, though I was older, I continued to live with my mother because of my inability to find a proper suitor. My station, dowry-less, with a mother to support as well, left young men estranged from me. I was often lonely, and although Mother often called me pretty, potential suitors did not agree.

It was during this time that one night I was hurrying home late in the evening. I had helped prepare a large meal for a social gathering. After the meal, I had stayed, hiding in the back and watching the ladies and gentlemen as they listened to a fine chamber orchestra and dancing. The food was a success, and I had been invited to return the following day to help with the cooking again. Fortunately, I hadn't been caught in my spying, or I would have lost the job.

As I hurried down the street that evening, I was stopped by the most peculiar of people that I had ever seen. Two men approached me, dressed in strange attire, and although they held themselves as if they were noblemen, they were not wearing wigs.

As I approached, the larger man hailed me. It was dark, and I feared to oblige. I was not a whore. But there was nowhere to run, and so I stopped.

"I'm King Togan," he said in my language, "and this is Kinni."

For a moment, I thought he was jesting, but I could see from his expression that he thought himself serious.

"We have no kings here," I said, marveling at the man's strange attire. The clothes were nothing like I had ever seen. My heart jumped when I looked at the man he called Kinni. He had to have been the most handsome man I had ever seen. Even in the darkened street, I could see his strong features and his confidence.

"What! No kings, then how are you governed?"

"We are governed by the people," I said, acting with boldness, unbecoming for a lady of my station. I repeated words that I had often heard the strangers from the convention say to each other, not sure what they meant. The man said he was a king, and I surely thought myself very important conversing with him in such a manner as this.

"By the people? Then surely you have anarchy."

"Indeed no, sir. The people choose who governs them."

Taking my eyes off of his companion, I could see that what I said interested the young king. "I must understand this better. Young lady, can you tell me more?"

"No, sir. I do not understand the ways of men. However, fortune has smiled on you, as here in Philadelphia this summer, reside some of the greatest political minds of our time."

"Then you must introduce me to them."

"You cannot go around dressed as you are, for others will see you as traitors and foreigners. You will not be safe."

I didn't want anyone to hurt the man called Kinni. He smiled at me, and I blushed, grateful for the darkness to hide the redness of my cheeks.

The king nodded and commanded that I take him and Kinni to my home. I dared not resist the will of a king, despite living in the land of no kings, and so I led them to our home. Mother was nervous at the appearance of the strangers, but they did not hurt us. That night, Mother procured gentlemen's clothing for them through the maid of one of the delegates from North Carolina.

The next day, I pointed out delegates to the king, not daring to approach them myself. The king spent the day in great discussions with many of them, Kinni always at his side. Every chance I got, I would sneak to the main square and watch him, concealed among the crowds. The man was quiet, and he obediently followed his king. I was in love with him.

As I watched them depart the next morning, Kinni left his master and approached me.

"Lady Lovina," he said, "Thank you for your kindness."

Never before had a man spoken to me with such respect. I blushed from head to foot, and despite myself, I returned his kind gesture with a lady-like curtsey. I looked into Kinni's eyes. I will never forget those eyes. His eyes were of a brighter blue than I had ever seen before, and despite his piercing gaze, they were full of kindness.

They left then, and life threatened to go on as before. I could not stop thinking about the kind young man, Kinni. I dreamed about him constantly, that he would one day return and take me with him back to his own land.

A year passed, and although the delegates left our town, the memory of the man named Kinni did not fade.

At length, at the same time of summer that following year, we heard a knock at our door early one morning. I opened the door and was delighted to see the king with his servant Kinni at his side.

Kinni stepped forward and bowed to me saying, "Kind Lady Lovina, King Togan of the Order of the Blue Flower requests lodging at your place once again." He handed me a flower, which I dried and have kept to this day.

I let them in and we served them our finest meal. They were pleased with the food, especially Kinni. Although I told them that the delegates had finished their work and departed, the king insisted that he had come to speak with the people about their new government.

"If the government is truly by the people, then I must understand how it works for the people," he said.

After breakfast, Mother departed for work and the king and Kinni went out to meet with the people. I cleaned up the remnants of breakfast and was about to leave myself when Kinni walked into the house.

"Did you forget something kind sir?" I asked, my heart beating faster at the sight of him.

"No ma'am," he responded, "I have returned here alone. My master is not in need of my assistance today."

"What business do you have here, then?" I asked, not daring to hope that he had indeed returned to see me.

"Only the business of my heart." Kinni stepped forward and looked at me with love in his eyes. Feeling the happiest feelings of a young girl first blessed by love, I impulsively rushed to Kinni and kissed him. We spent the day together blissfully ignoring the harsh reality of our pending separation.

The next morning Kinni and the king prepared again to leave to return to their own land. Not standing the thought of losing Kinni after only one day, I boldly approached him while he made final preparations to depart.

"My kind sir, I implore you to take me with you to your own land." I was shocked at my own boldness, but unable to restrain the words.

"My lady," he responded. "I come from a distant land, one where a magic portal lets two pass from land to land. Those that go through the portal must be from my land, and no stranger can pass through. Only those who have come here through the portal may go back."

"Then stay here with me," I inveighed, losing all sense of propriety.

"Ah, this I also cannot do," Kinni said with sadness in his eyes. "The only way to get through the portal is with two, hands joined. I cannot keep my master here. But I think there must be a way. I will try to find a way to come back to you."

At that moment the king entered the room and we said no more to each other. Kinni left with his master that morning, taking my heart with him.

He never returned, but he left me a gift besides the flower. Kinni's son is strong like his father, his complexion and facial features just as foreign and handsome. Most blessed of all, the babe was born with Kinni's bright blue eyes. Many have ridiculed me for my child, but I have never confessed to anyone until now the father of my child. Despite the disdain that has followed me since his conception, I have stayed here in this, my childhood home, to await Kinni's return.

I'm old and will die soon. My son has grown and bought a farm. He has a goodly family and has cared for me in my old age. He has entreated me many times to move with him and his family to the land they call Ohio, but I'm waiting for Kinni.

I will always wait for Kinni.

I close the webpage and look around the library, barely recognizing anything. I push my hand against my collarbone and feel the skin where my tattoo hides underneath my clothes. Then I stand up and wander back to my dorm room.

18 Romance

Karl

I trudge up Dithridge, my head down, my eyes scanning both sides of the street. Pearl told me to find a church building here. For some reason, I'm doing it.

Eventually a large red-brick building comes into view on the opposite side of the street. The lights on the building reflect bright against a white steeple, which stands out in sharp contrast to the sky behind it. I stop under a tree and shiver. Snowflakes drift around me. Light snow falls on the sidewalk, and the cold of the night leaks through my old jacket.

The large gate to the church parking lot is open, so whatever information Pearl found online seems to be right. A single's activity is supposed to start here in five minutes, though the parking lot is nearly empty. Only one car, a blue Honda, is parked under a street light next to the building's doors.

I shiver and blow a snowflake off my eyelash.

The bare tree I'm standing under, combined with the darkness of the evening, gives me an appropriate hiding place, out of view from the church. The minutes tick by and other pedestrians walk by me on the sidewalk. They don't pay attention, but I feel subconscious anyway. Eventually, others show up and go into the church. Some of them drive. Some walk.

I stay in my secluded spot.

In the weeks since my trip to Moab, I've talked to Pearl every few days. I've enjoyed it for the most part, and the conversations have been safe. Until yesterday when she brought up my love life.

Not wanting to talk about Tara, I resorted to complaining. With my position, it's impossible to meet a girl I could consider dating, marrying, and raising a family with.

It was the wrong approach. Instead of understanding and moving on, Pearl took my complaint as a challenge.

"You have to start going to the places where those women are," she told me. "I'll help you do that."

Her help is the last thing I need.

Next thing I know, she calls me this afternoon with the address of this church, just up the street from where I work. She wouldn't take no for an answer, and I promised to come here this evening.

Here I am.

It seemed simple at the time. I'd come, go in, and tell Pearl it was awful. But now I'm standing outside, hiding in the darkness, freezing in the cold, and watching a bunch of happy, strange people. Who are they? Are they doing anything meaningful with their lives? Are they worth associating with? Why am I here?

I know one thing. I don't want to go into that building.

According to Pearl, these are the people who are getting married and having babies. The people whose lives mean more than just a name on a paper.

I picture myself walking into the church—I haven't been in one since Mom's funeral.

This is insane.

I walk up the sidewalk, past the church and away from campus. The wind blows against my face, and the wind blows flakes under my hood to sting my cheeks. After two blocks, I turn around and walk back to my hiding place. It's ten after the hour now. The activity has surely started.

I hide under my tree again in time to watch as an old car turns into the parking lot. A girl with straight blonde hair and a slender figure steps out of the car. She's pretty.

I imagine myself walking across the street. I walk into the building, find the activity, and I see that girl sitting by herself on the back row. I sit down, and we start talking.

Which is about as likely as a meteor shower. I don't belong with these people. I'm not going to wander in and meet an attractive girl. If I go in now, no one will notice me, and those that do will keep talking to their friends. Anything they say about me will be about my scruffy beard and ill-kept clothes. All the cute girls are in groups flirting with men who are thinner, more attractive, and better-groomed.

I'm not the person they're looking for.

Promise or no promise, it's time to go. I don't know what I'll tell Pearl, but I'm not going in there.

I try to hold on to anger, but as I start back down the street, I feel despair more than anything else. Will I ever fulfill my promise to Mom? Am I stuck with girls like Tara from now on?

This is Andrea's fault. I shouldn't be here, standing alone in the cold. I should be home, with her.

"Karl!"

I freeze at the sound of Tara's voice. How did she find me here?

She jogs down the sidewalk toward me. That's when I remember that she lives somewhere around here, but I'm not sure where. Hopefully her apartment is far enough away that she's just seeing me now.

She's dressed provocatively, as per norm, very different from the girls I've been watching. Tonight she's wearing spandex tights and a short skirt; her coat is unbuttoned enough to show cleavage. I let my eyes hang there—it feels better than looking at the church. She throws out her arms and steps into a tight embrace. I like feeling her against me.

"Hey stranger," she whispers in my ear.

I let the cold and confusion of the evening dissipate in the warmth of Tara's body against mine. All those hoity-toity kids across the street can think what they want; Tara likes me.

"What are you doing here?" She steps away. I like looking at her.

"Just walking. I was turning around when I saw you."

She doesn't think twice about my story, even though we both know that I never go walking.

"Good, because I'm headed down to campus now. Will you accompany me?"

She takes my hand, and we start to campus.

"What's at campus tonight?" I ask.

"I'm going to a study party for a big exam tomorrow."

"You're pretty dressed up for a study party."

She giggles. "There are some cute boys in my class."

My face gets warm. Who are the guys in her class?

Tara smiles as she watches my reaction, and I feel my face warm again. Tonight, of all nights, I'd like Tara to accept me as I am and not who I'm supposed to be. I don't want her to go flirt with other guys. I want her to stay with me.

"How are your runs coming?" I ask. I've been helping her set up experiments all week.

"Finished just before I left my apartment," she says coyly. But, her voice gets a little squeaky, like it does when she's excited. We both know that these are the runs that should generate publication-ready results.

"And?"

"You got it!" she says, and I can't keep a silly grin off my face. Anytime work creates something good, it's worth smiling about. Tara stops walking, puts her arms around my neck, and kisses me.

"Congratulations sir," she whispers.

And she kisses me again.

We stand under the light of the street lamp kissing in a way that Pearl would never call "proper." I let myself forget all about why I came out here in the first place and instead disappear into the warmth of Tara's body.

She pulls back, and we are both breathing fast. "Will you come back to my apartment with me?" she asks. "I can skip my study party."

Snowflakes fall onto her face and melt. Her body presses against me, pushing away the loneliness. This is what I want right now. I want to be with her. I don't want her to go flirt with her study group.

But it isn't really what I want. I let my arms fall and step away. If I do sleep with Tara someday, it won't be because of jealousy or loneliness.

"I don't want you to fail your exam tomorrow," I say, even though I don't care about her exam at all. I feel confused and rejected, even though I'm the one who said no.

We're on campus before either of us speak again. I walk her to the building where her study group is and stop.

"It's in the Cytochrome C Oxidase complex," Tara says. "The signal is pretty strong."

"That's a Nature paper."

"You'll help me write it, right?"

She kisses me again. I kiss her softly and push her away. She's late for her study group by now, if there is such a thing.

After she's out of sight, I walk slowly back to the office. I've spent so much time working on Tara's project, that all of mine are falling behind. I have a few hours I can spend on them before going home for the evening. Or maybe I can outline the Nature paper.

* * *

The next morning Tara is waiting for me when I get into the office. She's there the next morning, and the next, and the next. We work all day, taking occasional breaks for food, making out, or hurrying through her homework. I even take a shower now and then, though Tara rarely says anything about it anymore.

Writing a paper is no easy task, but we are motivated. And Tara is a good writer. I'm glad she's letting me be a part of this paper. This is much bigger than any of my research. After this gets published, I can probably convince a committee to let me graduate, and that keeps me motivated. We spend time agonizing over each paragraph, scrutinizing every sentence until it's just the way we want it. This paper will give us an amaranthine existence in this program, a reputation that will live on for decades. Generations of future students will come here and read this paper, talk about it, and marvel that it was written right here in this office by me and Tara. No one will remember me as the student whose advisor got murdered. No one will feel sorry for me anymore.

We spend every waking moment for the next week on the paper. That means, unfortunately, I don't have time to contact Pearl. She tries to follow-up with me about my trip to the church, but I ignore her. The timing works out great, anyway. I don't know what to tell her, but once the paper is out, I'll talk to her again, and she'll have forgotten about that wild errand.

* * *

Finally, at the end of nearly two weeks, I sit at my desk with Tara on my lap. My heart pounds as I stare over her bare shoulder at my computer screen. Midnight passed a long time ago, but I'm alert as ever as Tara moves her mouse to hover over the Submit button.

"Do it," I whisper.

She smiles at me, and I let myself get distracted by what I see under her loose-fitting sweater.

"I'm about to submit a paper to Nature," she says, and she waits until I force my eyes up to look into hers. We are both tired. And giddy. This is huge.

"Not just any old Nature paper," I say as she kisses my ear, "but real ground-breaking research!"

"I'm just happy to be seen with you."

I laugh. "Who sees you with me? We're alone in this office all the time."

"I see me with you, and that is all I need." She points at the submission screen. Indeed, she's right next to me on the author list: Tara Howell, Karl Stapp, Hienrich Melzer. Thousands of people will see her next to me.

Click.

The submission form is replaced with a spinning wheel. After two minutes, the page loads with the proofs of the manuscript.

"We did it!"

Tara keeps her arms around me as we stand. "Hooray!" she says, and she kisses me hard. I taste a little alcohol on her breath. When did she sneak away for a drink?

I kiss her for a few minutes, and then for a few minutes more. Finally, I pull back and smile jubilantly. The grandeur of the moment competes with the utter exhaustion I feel, but it comes out on top.

"What time is it?"

"I think we just passed 3:00 AM," Tara giggles. "I guess we need to sleep together in the office, or you'll have to walk me home."

"I'll take you home, and then I'll come back and sleep here."

Tomorrow morning, I really need to get back to my work. Maybe I'll call Pearl. Maybe I won't. Maybe I'll sleep all day. Maybe I'll even draft up a graduation proposal for Khanh.

Tara and I bundle up and venture out into the dark, cold streets of Oakland. We laugh about dumb things as we walk. I'm glad all the lights are out when we pass the church on Ditheridge. By the time we get to Tara's apartment, the cold has seeped through my coat and my teeth are chattering. I need to buy a better coat— one that fits around my belly.

"You look cold," Tara pushes the door open and flips the lights on inside her apartment. The warm air rushes out the door, and it feels nice.

"Why don't you come in and have a cup of coffee?"

"Okay." I step into her apartment. "Though if you have hot chocolate, I'd prefer that this late in the night." I've told myself I wouldn't come in here, but it's cold outside, and I'll only stay a few minutes.

Tara closes the door behind me and bolts it with two bolts.

It's a one-bedroom apartment, with a large front room and a door to the bedroom in the back. Tara has a small table and desk in the front room, with a small area for cooking. All-in-all, the room is a nicer version of her office. The colors are mostly blacks and golds, with some splashes of bright pink to accent.

My body relaxes in the warm air, and my eyelids start to droop. "Your place looks really nice. Where do you find time to design your apartment?"

"Are you saying your apartment looks like your office?"

"Worse," I say as I wander around the room to study the strange artwork she has on the walls.

She shakes her head. "I don't even want to know about it. It's a wonder that men survive without a woman around."

She motions for me to sit, and having completed my tour of the room, I sit at the small black table near the kitchen area. Tara takes my coat and goes back into her bedroom. The warmth of the apartment is really getting to me. My eyes glaze over. I'm in the middle of a yawn when Tara comes back into the room.

She, too, has taken off her coat, and her sweater. She's wearing a tight-fitting navy tank top, and a pair of short denim shorts. The navy looks great against her white skin; the yawn doesn't come, and I sit up straighter. I feel more alert.

Warning bells go off in my tired mind.

Tara works in the kitchen for a few minutes. I like the sound of her bare feet as they pad around the floor. Something seems right about this somehow, despite the nagging feeling that I should leave. Was this how Andrea felt that night with Vince? I shudder at the thought. I should go soon.

Once the chocolate is hot, Tara puts a large helping of pink and yellow marshmallows on top and joins me at the table. "I love the flavor of the colored marshmallows," she giggles.

The warm liquid sooths my cold throat. Biology makes sure that I don't feel tired, not while I'm looking at Tara in the low light of the apartment. Words like commitment and promises float through my mind, and some other thoughts as well. I keep shoving thoughts of Andrea out of my head, but she keeps coming back.

As I near the bottom of my cup, the rational side of my brain takes momentary control. I set my mug down. "I better go. Thanks for everything."

Tara frowns and stands up, too. "Leaving already?" She moves in for a kiss.

The rational side of my mind surrenders, and I put my arms around her and kiss her, my resolve dissolving as fast as the marshmallows did.

"You really want to leave?" Tara asks, pressing herself up next to me.

No.

"Yes."

"Why?" she asks. "Don't you like me?"

She kisses me again. Slowly. I want to stay. Is this what Andrea felt? That she didn't want to feel lonely anymore? That it couldn't hurt for just one night?

What would Mom say if she could see me now?

"Do you love me, Tara?"

The question startles her. "What do you mean?"

"If I graduated and got a job, would you still want to be with me?"

"You don't need to graduate yet!" She snuggles up to kiss my neck. I didn't expect her to answer my question, but I'm annoyed at her answer. I hold on to the annoyance and pull back.

"Let's say I wanted to. And then what about us?"

Tara stops smiling. "Karl. You're taking this all too seriously. Relax. We just submitted a Nature paper. Don't go all serious, talking about love and the future. Can I get you a drink or something? I have some hard liquors. Or a beer."

I shake my head. "Love is an important thing to me. I think I want to go."

"Don't be ridiculous, Karl. Stay here. Move in with me. You have another two years until the program makes you graduate. That's time to write another paper together, don't you think?" She reaches up to kiss me, but I put my hands on her shoulders and stop her.

"I want to be with someone I love, and, well, I've never known why you like me."

For some reason, my statement strikes Tara as funny. "You're talking like you've never slept with anyone before." She laughs. "This isn't the time to talk about stuff like this. You're ruining the moment!"

"I haven't."

"You haven't what?"

"Slept with anyone before."

"What are you waiting for? Love?" She stops laughing. Her voice is challenging now, like a professor talking down to an insolent student.

"Yes, love."

"Come on Karl, be real. You're overweight, you never shower, and you work too much. You'll never find anyone who *loves* you—you've met plenty of professors just like you to know that by now. You're going to spend the rest of your life alone in an office, and that's how your life is going to be. Alone."

She's right. I've had all the same thoughts in the few months that we've been together. Mom asked me to never let my career get in the way of a family and marriage. I promised her I wouldn't. But that's exactly what I've done.

Tara smiles and kisses my neck again. "So, stop being so serious and take advantage of what you have," she whispers. "We're good for each other. Tonight."

Is she right? The fantasies start in my brain—after being with me a couple years, Tara will consider marriage. In thirty years we'll think back to this moment and laugh at how we thought it was only temporary.

I shake my head. I'm not so dumb that I think things will work.

I hate the thought of leaving and being lonely again. Is being with someone who doesn't love you worth avoiding loneliness?

"Come on, Karl." Tara puts her hands under my shirt and slides them up.

My hands respond, but I stop them and push them down.

"No." I step away. "No."

"If you leave now"—her voice has an edge now—"we're done. You know that, right?"

"Oh, because the paper is in now, and so you don't need me anymore?"

Tara's eyes narrow. "You know I have a term paper due next week."

I scoff. "So, you do need me?" Is she serious? I almost stayed? "Well, you'll have to find someone else to help you with it." I unlock the first bolt on the door.

"You're an idiot." Tara laughs. "I give you the setup of a lifetime and you're just going to walk out?"

I unlock the second bolt. "This isn't the setup of a lifetime. This is a shallow business deal where you get good grades and I get a prostitute."

She slaps me across the face. Hard. It stings. Her arms are strong. I guess that's another benefit of working out as much as she does. "You'll never have anything else, you idiot." The venom from her words sting as hard as her slap. "Good luck with your life of loneliness. Hope you enjoy being fat, alone, and overworked for the rest of your life. Let me know if you ever talk to a woman again."

She slaps me again, this time on the other cheek. That one hurts, too.

I remember watching Andrea run down the mountain, away from me, away from us. I've hated her for years for that.

I was stupid not to follow her.

"Good bye, Tara." I step into the cold and slam the door. The cold is even more brittle without my coat, but I don't stop at the office. I walk all three miles to my house.

By the time I get to my apartment, my entire body is numb. I'm not sure if I'll ever feel some parts of my body ever again.

But I do feel something inside.

Pride. Maybe I'm not as shallow as I thought.

And I'm going to call Pearl tomorrow.

Just as I'm drifting off to sleep, I remember how the doctors said that Sam was poisoned. Tara was there, right when it happened. Coincidence? I shudder at the thought, and I have a tough time believing that Tara would do such a thing. But, is that reality talking, or is biology getting in my way of rational thought again?

19 Road Trip

Lydia

28 hours at the wheel in two days. I yawn and roll my neck. The small screen on my phone says the exit to Waunakee, Wisconsin is still ten minutes away.

Might as well be an eternity. An eternity of looking at miles and miles of empty cornfields.

But, I'm glad I'm here. Brit is a mess; she hasn't touched the steering wheel once since we left Seattle. It's been up to me, and Brit will make it home before her brother's funeral.

My left leg throbs. It ached last night at that Podunk hotel, and the pain has increased throughout today. Brit might need a stretcher to bring me into her house. If she manages to get out of the car. Anything I say drives her further into her shell. She's withered like an etiolated plant, just a shell of the vivacious young lady, the girl who has been instrumental in Washington's first place standing in the PAC-12. I wonder if I was the same way after Mom died. At least Brit didn't head to the pub like Dad.

Right now, she's curled into a ball with a blanket over her head.

Hopefully, being home will help her recover. At least she told me she did okay on her midterms. Nothing can stop that girl from keeping her scholarship.

"You have arrived," the GPS announces as I pull up next to a small blue house. A huge tree obscures most the house from view. Snow covers the ground and the sidewalk leading around the tree to the house.

"We're here." I touch Brit's shoulder.

She stirs and the blanket lifts up as she looks dumbly out the window. There is only one Waunakee in the world; I know we're in the right place. She finally mumbles, "We're the next house up," and slumps back under the blanket and into her seat.

She said something. Progress.

I reignite the engine, and the car rolls forward 50 feet. I stop in front of a small, two-story house, white, and similarly covered in snow. I kill the car again, and Brit wanders out with her blanket around her shoulders. I pop the trunk. She opens it and starts pulling out suitcases. Gently, I open the car door and slowly maneuver my left knee onto the road. Even the slightest bend sends pain up and down my leg. I take short breaths while pain subsides, and then I stand up slowly, using the car for balance.

A door slams behind me and a woman, presumably Brit's mother, runs out of the house.

"Brit! You're home!" The lady has short, curly black and gray hair. Her face looks like an older version of Brit.

After a long embrace with her daughter, she approaches me. "You must be Lydia! I'm so grateful that you would help Brit. I'm Beth."

Before I can reply, I'm enveloped in a hug from the large woman. I can't remember the last time I got a real hug from anyone, and after two long, lonely days it's more than I can do. Tears splash onto my cheeks. Beth smells like baking bread. Safe and inviting.

"I'm happy to help," I whisper.

"Do you need help getting in? Brit told me what a number you did on your knee."

I can barely move, but I shake my head. "I can manage." I wipe the tears off my face and motion to Brit. Beth smiles knowingly and returns to the trunk to guide Brit into the house.

It takes a few minutes, but I make my way on crutches to the door. Every muscle in my body fights me every step. Pain sucks.

* * *

I plunge my hands into the warm water. In the cold of Wisconsin winters, washing dishes warms up a body better than anything else I've found to do here. I've helped with the dishes for all three meals since I got here, and I don't intend to stop until I leave.

Despite the cold outside, the warmth inside Beth's home has gradually broken through Brit's dazed stupor. Beth has the magic that only mothers have. Mom had it, too. Watching Beth has deepened the ache I feel for Mom, and I know I can't stand to stay here too much longer.

Beth joins me and rinses the dishes I've washed so far.

"Thanks for doing this. Again."

"I'm happy to help."

"On one leg, no less." Beth has a cheery way she talks that makes it easy to smile when I'm around her.

"Your other daughter arrives tomorrow morning?"

"Yes. She called me a few minutes ago to say she was stopping for the night in Springfield. I don't know why she doesn't just come the rest of the way tonight, but her baby has been screaming for the past two hours."

107

"I'd have given up an hour and fifty minutes ago."

"I just want her home. Having Brit here has done wonders for me. It keeps my mind off Jacob and on her."

I stop washing for a few minutes and dry the dishes Beth has rinsed. Once I get caught up, I go back to washing the last few pans.

"It was so awful with Jacob," Beth says. "Your mother died, right?"

I freeze, the water suddenly turns to ice, and I'm drowning.

"It was a car accident," I finally get out.

Beth sighs. "What a tragedy. I sat there in the hospital for hours with Jacob, watching the life go right out of him. I hope"—she stops and wipes tears away with the back of her wet hand—"you didn't watch your mother die like that."

"She was dead when the police came to my house." Even though my phone has been dead for years, I don't want to take it out when my hands are wet. I remember the screams. I remember the silence.

"I don't know if that is better or not," Beth tries to laugh, but instead she sobs. She hugs me—something I've gotten used to—and she cries. I feel the tears build up behind my own eyes, and suddenly years of pent up emotion run down my cheeks. I squeeze Beth, and she holds me tight. She's warm. I'm safe.

Too soon, Beth pulls back.

"You're really going to leave tomorrow after the funeral?"

"Yeah, I need this trip, and I want you to have time with your family. My leg has finally loosened up, so I should drive somewhere and get it all stiff again before I get used to it."

* * *

I pull up in front of the Mellon Institute in Oakland, PA just after dark. It doesn't seem real that I'm here, a world away from Seattle—I've never been this far away from home before.

Unless you count the meadow. And I have no idea how far away that is.

I put the car in park and grab a copy of Lovina's history. I've also made a copy of Lovina's sketch of the blue flower. Karl's a biologist, maybe he'll be able to make sense of it.

What if Lovina's history is true? If so, it partially explains my story. If I'm from the forgotten world. But how did I get here without a traveling companion? Is Karl also from the other world? Does he know it?

He has to be connected. His bright blue eyes are just like Kinni's. Karl couldn't have been more than six years old when I showed up, so it seems unlikely he's the traveling companion who brought me here. Still, according to my dreams, he's the only one who can take me back.

I need to talk to Karl, and I need to go back to that meadow. I felt something there that I've never felt before. If I go there, I'll find out who I am and where I came from. I know it.

The institute is a large building with a lot of steps that ascend to a set of double glass doors. The entire face of the building is lined with columns. Half black and half white; each column is stained on the side that points toward Pittsburgh. Is there that much pollution here? I hold my breath for a minute, but then I decide I won't make it to the top without the oxygen in the air—clean or not.

I put some quarters in the parking meter and look around hopefully for another entrance. I don't see one anywhere in sight, and traveling around the building to look for one is definitely out of the option. So, I spend ten minutes maneuvering my way up the steps. Finally, I make it to the top and move over to the large glass door and pull. It doesn't budge.

Locked.

That would have been nice to know before I came all the way up here.

My light Seattle jacket is made to repel water, not the cold that seeps through it now. I don't really want to go down all those steps.

But, after a few seconds of shivering outside at the top of the steps, I'm convinced that I want to go back to my car. I carefully put my crutches onto the first stair. Then the doors open behind me.

I whirl around as two students leave the building. They're so busy talking to each other they don't notice me as I awkwardly scramble past them and get my crutch into the door before it locks shut again.

Inside the building, I find more columns, these located inside a tall, marble hall. These columns are a dark gray and unstained. A carving on the far side of high ceiling displays a bunch of ancient looking men and a dove. *The beginning of scientific knowledge*, it says. Weird. My crutches echo around the entryway as I make my way through.

It feels eerie, as if I'm sneaking into a museum after hours instead. It doesn't feel anything like the academic buildings back in Seattle.

But I know I've found the right place when I find signs pointing to Karl's department and then find his name listed under room 104 in the directory. This is it. Will he remember me? Will he take me back to the meadow?

Of course, the door to room 104 is closed, as is every other door in the office.

I should have thought this through better. It's Friday evening, what did I expect? If I really wanted to find Karl today, I shouldn't have stayed for the lunch after the funeral.

I knock on the door just in case. I hear scuffling inside. I hold my breath.

A red-headed girl swings the door open, her hair pulled back in a pony. Boxes line the room. She doesn't look happy to see me.

"Can I help you?" she asks in an English accent.

"Yes, I'm looking for Karl Stapp. Is he here?" I try to look around her into the room, but she closes the door so all I can see is her face.

She eyes me up and down, her face is drawn into a tight scowl.

"No."

Okay. This is awkward.

"Do you know when he'll be back? I mean, is he out for the weekend?"

The girl's eyes narrow into slits. "How do you know Karl? I've never seen you before." Her voice is soft and venomous.

"I, uh, met him a couple months ago. Down in Moab. I don't know if he remembers me, but I have some things I need to talk to him about."

The girl gasps. The door is now open just a crack—I can only see one of her eyes now.

But I don't need to see more than that to sense her inexplicable hatred radiating at me. "And are you a graduate student? A professor?"

"A student," I say. I don't think that this girl is going to help me find Karl. "We just bumped into each other in Moab," I say. "I was in the area today and hoped to see him."

"Oh! I'm sure you bumped into each other," the girl says. "He told me he was going out to 'see his sister'." She slams the door.

Okay. I will try again on Monday. In the late morning. Hopefully more people will be here. Other people.

As I reach the end of the hall the door opens again, and the girl steps out into the hallway.

"I didn't lose to you," she shouts. My mind flashes back to the night Dad knocked me over. This girl won't do that to me. I'm stronger than she is. But maybe not as desperate. However, I'm on crutches. I round the corner and try to move faster.

"He was with me—the whole time. You're a worthless nobody. He's a fool, and I hope you have another place to stay because I don't think he's straight. Unless you've slept with him already."

I keep going, and I don't say anything. I don't have any idea whether Karl is straight or gay, and it really doesn't matter to me.

The door slams, and the echoes reverberate down the hallway.

What did I just step into?

* * *

Despite the rude welcome, Pittsburgh turns out to be a fun city with plenty to see. The next morning, I find a 48 Hours in Pittsburgh website and spend a couple hours planning a weekend that takes me around to the best parts of the city, and to a second-hand store to purchase a winter coat.

Saturday, I visit the Pittsburgh zoo and aquarium (fortunately they have little carts I can ride around in) and ride the Mt. Washington incline. On Sunday, I hit the Cathedral of Learning on Pittsburgh campus. Since all the students are away for the holidays, the area around campus is quiet, cold, and not nearly as rainy as U-dub's campus. It's fun to see the sun in the middle of winter. Not that I'd want that all the time, but it's nice for a day.

Aside from my adventures, I spend time taking warm baths and nursing my sore knee. I try to feel confident, traveling alone and exploring the city by myself. Mom and I went on so many trips together to watch soccer games, but I haven't traveled since she died. I think she would be proud if she saw me handling myself like a grown woman in a strange city. I haven't found the best soccer facilities yet, but other than that, this trip is just as good as any I took with her.

I wake before my alarm on Monday morning, anxious about my next trip to Carnegie Mellon. Though it seems like it can't go worse than my first trip, I don't have a compelling reason to believe that Karl will help me. I'm just operating on hope.

After a bath, I stare for a long time at the fancy outfit Maria bought for me to meet Karl in. I put it on and walk by the mirror a few times, but then decide I can't do it. Today, I'm just going to go as me. I'm limping in a knee brace, and I'm wearing a warm blue sweater with black stretchy pants. I'm comfortable, and besides, if Karl is gay, it doesn't matter what I'm wearing anyway.

When I get back to the institute, I drive around and manage to find another entrance with a door that isn't locked. When I get to the hallway, most of the doors are open, and one of them is Karl's. I stand at the end of the hallway and review what I'm going to say again, taking deep breaths to calm my nerves. I should have followed Maria's dad's advice and memorized this testimony as well.

Then I start the long hobble.

Karl's desk is against the same wall as the doorway, and so it isn't more than a few hobbles before I see him sitting hunched over a laptop. It's him. He's here. I take another breath and force myself to keep moving forward.

At least I don't see any sign of the angry girl. One thing has gone right so far.

Karl looks up as I approach, and my breath catches. But, his fingers don't miss a beat in their typing, and his eyes go right back to his computer screen.

Not a good sign.

I put on my best smile, thinking about Maria meeting Brian. Yeah, that's not going to happen. I tap lightly on the door.

"Are you Karl Stapp?" What a dumb question! Would I be there if he wasn't?

He looks over his computer screen at me. Does he recognize me? His eyes flit back to his computer screen without the slightest signal of recognition. I'm not sure he even looked at me.

111

"Yes," he says, as his fingers start to fly again.

"I'm Lydia Miller," I begin. "From Seattle. We..."

"I don't have the midterms graded yet," Karl says. "And no, you can't influence your grade at this point. What's done is done."

He stops typing and makes a few clicks with his mouse.

"I'm not here about a midterm." Is he going to pay any attention to me? Maybe I should have worn that outfit Maria picked out.

He keeps his eyes glued on his computer. "I'm really busy right now," he says. "I have a paper that I need to get done by midnight." I wish he would look at me. Everyone recognizes me.

"For school?" I ask. Maybe if I'm friendly he'll look at me.

And he does. He looks at me like I'm the dumbest human he ever set eyes on. Then his expression changes, and he looks startled. Finally! He looked at me long enough to recognize me.

The look of recognition changes to something that looks a little more like panic. His eyes move away from me and then dart around the wall in front of him.

"For research," he finally says. "My time taking classes ended a few years ago."

Perhaps I'm as dumb as he thinks I am. What was I thinking, driving across the entire country for this?

"I came here from Seattle to see you." Time for another approach. "You haven't answered any of my calls."

"Huh?" Karl leans back in his chair. He finally meets my gaze.

"I'm not a student here. I go to the University of Washington. We met at Arches last month. In Utah." I'm feeling a more than a little desperate, and it comes out in my voice.

"Right. You were on crutches."

"Yes!" I lift up one of my crutches triumphantly. I'm such a dork. "I want to talk to you about the light at the arch. And the meadow. I want to go back there with you. There's something important there, I know it. I think I may have even come from there originally. Maybe you do, too. Were you adopted?"

The words bubble out of me, and I'm not sure they're sensible at all. Karl stares at me blankly.

Yeah, should have written down my lines and memorized them.

"You saw the same thing I did. The blue light, the mountain..."

"How did you find me?" he asks suddenly.

"Online. I found you online."

Karl's eyebrows raise.

"You're the only one who can take me back. The portal only takes those to the forgotten world who come from there." Assuming Lovina's journal entry can be trusted, but what else do I have?

"You're saying I come from another world?" Karl rolls his eyes. His bright blue eyes—just like I remember, and just like Lovina's book. "Actually, I was born on Earth."

My heart drops.

"Unless you call Arizona another world," he says with a small laugh. "Which you might, coming from Seattle."

"But your blue eyes?" I ask.

"Are my mother's."

"Oh."

"You really came all this way to see me?"

"Yes. Um, no. My friend had a brother die in a car accident, and so I was out here already."

"I'm under a lot of pressure right now, and so I'm really busy," Karl says. "We got some light in our eyes at the arch, and that was pretty weird, but I can't take a break. Not right now. I really have to get some of my research done."

"Don't you think...Could you spare just a few minutes?"

He holds up his hand to stop me. "Really, I'm not interested."

He thinks I'm stupid. Can I start over?

He stands to close the office door, but I have one last hope left. I grab a pen from his desk and write my name and number on the top of Lovina's history.

"Will you at least read this? And call me?"

"Sure." Karl takes the paper without looking at it. He puts it on a big stack of other papers and stands up to close the door. I maneuver my crutches backward as he closes it in my face.

"It was nice to see you again."

Click.

That was it. I feel even worse than I did after meeting the angry girl. I'm not sure if I want to cry or yell. The chances that I will ever hear back from Karl are zero.

But what did I expect? I showed up as a complete stranger. Should he have taken me into his arms and kissed me? Promised to run away with me?

I walk out of the building and down the steps to the car. I came so far; I found Karl. I accomplished nothing.

Karl is from Arizona. He has a mom and a dad, and he's proven it. He isn't my traveling companion. He doesn't feel connected to the forgotten world like I do. He's happy and busy and not alone.

But I'm alone, and I don't have family and I don't have soccer.

And I don't have a clue what to do next.

20 Ruined

Karl

It isn't until the second or third knock that I finally accept the fact that the knock on my office door isn't going away. I write three more sentences to finish my thought, stretch, and get out of my chair to open the door.

"Hi Candice."

She walks into the room without being invited and pushes the door closed behind her. Today she wears a ridiculous purple shirt draped over her body. Her glasses are just as purple as the shirt and her hair is tied back.

I'm not sure what to make of the ridiculous grin she gives me as she sits in the empty chair at the desk across the room. The desk that used to be Tara's.

"Hello young man." She can't be that much older than me, but I smile back anyway.

"Hi Candice," I say again.

"What you workin' on?"

"A paper. I'm pretty under the gun to get something out soon."

"Sit down." I'm still standing by the closed door. I walk back to my desk and sit down. It's weird, sitting here with Candice, talking across the room like I used to do with Tara. For a moment, I miss it. I miss her and her outfits and the ridiculous way she coaxed me into helping her with everything.

Candice laughs. "Not sure what you're thinking about, but I got some things I want to say to you that I don't want nobody else to hear. Just wanted to congratulate ya, 'bout getting your head on straight."

"Excuse me?"

"Why, with kickin' Tara out of your office like you done."

It was Tara who left of her own accord, and I miss having her in here.

Candice laughs and shakes her head. I smile awkwardly, but I'm not sure I get the joke.

"Now don't you repeat these words to nobody," she whispers, "but I don't like that girl. I hate to see her takin' advantage of nice guys like you. She's got a flair for attractin', as far as I can see, and she certainly got a lot out of you.

"Now, I need some info. She told me that it all fell apart because of some girl you met in Utah," she pauses, and then she laughs. "Well, those aren't exactly the words that she used."

"Utah?" I have no idea what she's talking about.

"You going to tell me that there wasn't no Utah girl? After all that?"

"Utah girl?"

There was a girl who stopped by my office a few weeks ago, but I thought that was after Tara moved out.

"Come on, Karl. Think for a minute. Why would Tara tell me about some fling you had in Utah if there wasn't no girl?"

"I guess I did meet one girl while I was visiting my sister."

"Guess! My lands boy, are you telling me that you got this girl pregnant and you don't even know her name?"

Something in my expression strikes Candice as funny because she really laughs this time. "I'm just repeatin' what I heard," she says, struggling to regain control. "Your expression says it all. The rumor mill is churning, and this is all about Tara saving face for why a bright young man like you would turn down the 'gorgeous' Miss Howell."

My face starts to go red. I'm struggling to find the same humor in the situation. "I can't believe she's saying that about me." And I was distracted thinking she might try and poison me.

"All right. I need more facts. She's got to have this based on something. You found a girl? Is she good for ya?"

The papers the girl gave me are still uncovered, sitting on the corner of my desk.

"She stopped by a week or two ago." I pick the papers up. "I didn't have time to talk to her, but she gave me this packet to read. Yeah—it says her name is Lydia, right here at the top."

Candice stares at me with her mouth hanging open.

"I'm gonna take everything I said right back. About you havin' got your head on straight. A nice girl shows up serendipitously at your door, from God knows where, and you turn her away? My lands boy! You a helpless cause. I'd tell you to call that girl, but I reckon I'd be wastin' my breath."

She shakes her head and stands up to leave. I stare blankly at Lydia's name and phone number. Candice is right. A nice girl serendipitously showed up, and I sent her away. I think back to my conversation with Pearl, and I realize what a fool I am.

"At least you got rid of the viper." With her hand on the knob, Candice smiles and looks at me through her big purple frames.

"Somewheres you got yourself a mama, and I know she's mighty glad you ain't with Tara no more. A fine boy like you, I'd bet she's mighty proud about ya."

My eyes drop. "She passed away a few years ago."

"Well, that don't mean that she's not proud. Mamas care too much about their little boys to stop a carin' when they're back with God. Now, before you get back to work, you read that document that girl's left you and you give her a call. But, if she turns out bad, you remember what you learned from ol' Candice."

She laughs at her own joke and leaves me staring at the closed door.

I must be the stupidest man who ever lived. That Lydia girl, she was even pretty. Exotic, really. Why didn't I talk to her?

Maybe my problem isn't my job or the people I meet. Maybe it's me.

I look at the document in my hands. The Journal of Lovina Hurt.

Hurt. Mom's maiden name. The document isn't very long.

* * *

For months, I've been telling myself it was just a strange glare of the light, that there was no meadow or strange place.

Maybe I'm tired of lying to myself, or maybe I'm still reeling from Candice chewing me out, but I've read the story five times now. It doesn't make any sense, but there are so many similarities to my family history. The bright blue eyes, Mom's maiden name, Lydia thinking I came from the other side of the portal.

That guy Bob saying he was looking for a way to get to another world.

When I wake up my computer, it isn't my dissertation that I go to. I find an old email with some family history files from Mom. It doesn't take long before I find her: Lovina Hurt is my 4th great grandmother.

There isn't a father listed for Lovina's son, and he took his mother's surname. I stare blankly at the screen.

Where did Lydia get this document? I know my bright blue eyes come down the Hurt line. I have them, Mom had them, my grandpa had them.

My thoughts are interrupted by another knock on the door.

It's Candice again. "Dr. High-and-Mighty Program director needs to see you." She smiles when she sees the document rolled up in my hands. "Why he can't walk twenty feet and tell you himself is beyond me."

"Thanks Candice." I walk down the hall to Khanh's office, still holding the papers from Lydia.

I knock on the door to Khanh's office and go in.

A large, ostentatious desk stands prominently in the middle of the room, and Khanh sits directly behind it, scowling at me as I enter. I approach the desk and stand next to a six-foot-tall DNA double-helix model that is awkwardly placed right where a chair should be.

"You wanted to see me?"

Khanh nods and his eyes narrow. "I have interviewed Miss Howell," he says, "and I've talked with Heinrich. It's obvious that the decision to use fabricated data

116

was yours, and that you successfully hid your plan from your colleagues, who thought that they could trust you."

I stare blankly at him. "I don't know what you're talking about."

"Miss Howell's paper. Her discovery. It was all based on fabricated data. Fabricated data she received from you. On your phony website. And then you tried to publish it in Nature. I got a call from the journal this morning, and from the school. There will be a complete investigation on this. You will likely be expelled."

Fabricated data? The data was all from Tara.

"Sir," I say, "Tara provided the data."

"That's not what she says," Khanh spits back at me. "And we've already confirmed that the website she pulled it from was set up under your name. How do you explain that?"

Impossible. I stare back at Khanh in shock. First poison, then rumor, and now this.

"I just don't understand it," Khanh says. "A bright student like you didn't need this. You never applied yourself. You could have excelled in this program. You would have had a distinguished career. Instead, you threw this all away so you could get a paper with Miss Howell. I'm already getting calls from reporters. The bad press from this is going to consume my time for weeks. Can you tell me why?"

"Sir, I didn't do anything wrong. I'm being set up. I'm innocent. The data was Tara's."

Khanh shakes his head. "The longer you persist in your flagrant lies, the harsher the consequences will be. The university has started its investigation already. I've told you once already that they've already confirmed that Miss Howell's data traces right back to you. That means you are guilty, Karl. We've found out. It's time to accept the truth."

I turn to leave. I need to go somewhere; I need to think this through, figure out what is going on.

"Don't go anywhere. You'll need to stay here. There are some university investigators that will want to talk with you. Let me just say that I'm very disappointed."

Khanh's words barely register in my brain. I'm not going to talk to anyone else. I close the door to Khanh's office as quietly as I can, and then I see him sitting in the foyer. Bob. The man with the ponytail. The man with the gun.

Yeah. I'm leaving.

I run down the hallway to the other exit door.

Bob runs after me. He's fit and I'm not. But I know the Mellon Institute better than anyone. I go through a couple doors and duck into a broom closet. He races by me, and I sneak out a back way. Once outside, I hurry to a bus stop and jump on the first bus that shows up.

117

Now what?

I try and think. Tara clearly set me up. That was her plan from the start. She needed me in case people realized the data she was using was false.

She used me.

This is bad.

The bus I hopped on is heading downtown. Where do I go from there?

I take the bus all the way to Point State Park. I wander through the park, and finally stop at the Point, where the Allegheny and Monongahela Rivers intersect to create the Ohio. Pittsburgh ends here in a great arrow pointing west. The rivers push downstream relentlessly—nothing in the world can stop the flow of that water.

I'm the water. The current pushes me, but I don't know my destination or why I'm being pushed. All I know is that it's taking me somewhere, and it may not be where I want to be.

I need to escape, I need somewhere to hide. Somewhere to think. Somewhere to figure out how I can prove myself innocent.

I look down at the ground. In my left hand, I'm still holding the paper from Lydia. On the top of the first page is her phone number.

Is the meadow real?

She picks up on the second ring.

"Hello?"

"This is Karl."

"Uh...hi, what's up?"

"I need to go through that portal with you. As soon as possible."

21 Restless

Cadah

"You're fools. All of you," Arujan says. His beady eyes smolder with rage.

But the rage isn't new. Since he's shown up, I'm not sure anyone in a position of authority hasn't smoldered under his glare. Except for Ore, of course.

Ziru's response is not calm. "It is you who are the fool!" His deep voice echoes through the small house. I push myself against the wall and wish I had picked a different time to come and visit this evening. Ler hasn't returned from the day's work gathering food, and Arujan showed up just minutes after I did. To talk to Ziru, of course.

Ziru towers over the smaller man. Arujan doesn't flinch. His beady eyes glare up at Ziru.

He could kill him, I realize. Break his neck and we'd be done with him.

But Ziru isn't a murderer. After 40 years of handling petty disputes as the village shepherd, he can control his anger. Better than I could if I were standing there.

Arujan looks at me, and I wonder if he sees how much I despise him.

"You say you have come to lure us out of the mountains," Ziru says in a voice that is now surprisingly calm. "You know full well that if we leave, we will all be slaughtered by Wynn. Don't pretend you don't know it to be true!"

"No one knows that to be true." Arujan's lips curl into a cruel smile. How can he be so calm? "No one knows what the Great Wynn will do to your people. But, I'm not depending on his grace. He will never know they left the mountain."

Great Wynn? In all my life I have never heard anyone call Wynn anything but a monster. One more reason not to trust this man.

Like we needed any more reasons.

I finally speak up, unable to hold back my own anger any longer. "Now you're talking complete foolishness. We have waited on this mountain for over 200 years. All who have left, have been killed."

"Not true. I left the mountain, and I returned."

"Liar!" Ziru shouts before I can say anything more. "And even if it were true, you are one man. How can you expect to deracinate thousands of people without someone noticing? People will die because of the false hope you're giving them."

"False hope? You're the one who believes in the false traditions. A princess? We all know no princess is going to save these people. It's been 220 years. She's dead. She didn't come."

Ziru is quiet. So am I. Our greatest fear isn't one we say aloud.

Arujan laughs. "You know it's true. These mountains are not a place for people. There isn't enough food, not to mention a great deal of unrest."

"The unrest is your doing."

But Arujan ignores Ziru. "These people will not be contained for much longer. I'm going to lead them to safety—off this mountain. Are you with me?"

"No." Ziru's voice is flat. "I'm not afraid to fight you."

"Oh, I don't fight." Arujan's expression changes from hatred to mocking. "But I don't lose either."

"I don't want you in my village."

"You don't have a choice."

Ziru? Not have a choice? The man has been loved in the village from the time I was a little girl. The statement is preposterous. But somehow, as I think about it, I realize it's true. Arujan has the upper hand. He's cunning, and yet everyone likes him. Everyone, that is, but the village leadership. The people don't see him for what he is, and not one of them will turn him away.

"I'll make a deal." Arujan chuckles. "Take me to see the portal, and I'll leave your village before the snow starts to fall."

I gasp at the audacity of the request! Ziru stares at Arujan in stunned silence. Arujan repeats his request again.

"See the portal? I thought you didn't believe the princess would return?" Ziru finally says in a whisper.

"Oh, she's not going to. But I'd like to see it."

Nothing Arujan does makes sense. The portal is sacred. Only a handful of villagers have ever been there, and even then, only on sacred occasions. I've never gone.

"If we go, the town loses our efforts for a full day. Winter is approaching—how can I leave my people in this time of need?"

"I don't just want you," Arujan smirks. "I want four or five others to come."

"The location of the portal has been a sacred secret for over two hundred years. We don't just take people up there. Especially not when it would require losing an entire day's work!"

"I never said you had to take me. Just that I would leave if you did."

120

Ziru looks at me and then back at Arujan. "I don't see the difference," he finally says.

22 Reassured

Lydia

The blast of frigid air hits me harder than that girl from Stanford did as I step out of the rental car at the trailhead to Double Arch. I pull my coat around me and slam the door, and Karl follows suit on the other side of the car. I wonder how long the car will sit here before they tow it away. How much will they charge me for it?

I laugh at the thought. We may only be here a few minutes.

The drive through the park this morning was glorious. Brilliant white snow clings to the red rocks, and the white and red stand out in stark contrast with the blue sky and bright sun overhead. Arches was beautiful in the fall, but it's amazing in the winter. Any other day, we would need to stop, bask in the beauty, and take pictures.

Not today. I don't need a camera to remember this.

I hobble away from the car and squint against the light reflecting off the snow. I only see one thing; Double Arch looms just ahead.

It's time to get to that arch.

The wind whips my hair back and around my shoulders. The cold air bites at my cheeks. But I keep walking. I don't know how this arch works, but I try to will it to work. If there is any such thing as ESP, I send out signals, telling it where I need to go.

Footsteps crunch on the trail beside me.

Karl's hair is disheveled, more so than the other times I've seen him, and his clothes are dirty and wrinkled from his long bus ride. He walks stiffly. I think he's gained even more weight since the last time I saw him, if that is possible.

He hasn't said a word since I picked him up this morning from the shuttle at Green River. At least we're out of the car now, mitigating the smell of his large body.

Karl isn't the guy I want to take with me on a magical journey. He looks more like a bum I picked up on the side of the road to take to a homeless shelter. I should consider myself lucky he didn't mug me and steal the car.

Why couldn't someone else take me through the portal? Someone like Brian. Only Maria could be so fortunate.

I wish I could move faster. I wish I could get to that portal sooner and escape my nagging doubts and fears. I stumble, and Karl's hand shoots out and catches me.

"Why don't you steady yourself against me?" His kind voice is at odds with his wild appearance. "It's a long trail for a weak knee."

I'm grateful for his help and repulsed by his odor and touch. He's right though, I don't want to mess up my knee any worse than it already is.

Still, I grimace as Karl's fingers close around mine. His hand is chubby, like a marshmallow. I'm surprised it isn't sticky and gooey, too. Dad's hands were coarse from years of hard, manual labor. Tough, firm. Not like this.

I take a step and suddenly shimmering blue light augments the scenery. It streaks out of the snow and swirls around my feet.

We're not to the arch yet. Why can we see the light already?

But the light means this is real. I take a breath and put my hand in my pocket. Mom would approve of this. She would want me to go.

Then, Karl takes a step too, and the light explodes around us. If light can be sensed with touch, this light is warm, like slipping into a bath after a long day of soccer in the rain. Light swirls around us, entirely envelops us, and within seconds, it's gone.

We stand together in the mountain meadow. I pull my hand away from the marshmallow. He's not taking me back this time.

Fresh spring scents greet us. Sunshine dances across my face, its warmth as strong as the bitter wind that chapped my cheeks only seconds ago. Bees buzz around me in a sea of flowers—red, blue, orange, yellow, and even green.

At my feet I find a cluster of small blue flowers. I know these flowers; I've wondered about them every day of my life. I reach down to pick one but find that the stem is unnaturally strong. It doesn't bend at all. I put more pressure on it and it snaps in my hand. The flower matches the tattoo on my breast. Exactly. It's the same size, too.

I'm from here. I feel it—the same sense of belonging I felt last time we were here. This is my home. I want to find out how. I need to find out why.

Karl moves away, poking around the meadow. We hadn't made it to the arch. Was it just about him the whole time? Could we have gone through the portal back in Pittsburgh?

Not with the way that he treated me!

I turn away. Being here isn't about him. I hope he feels at peace, but I'm here for me.

I shrug, and my coat slips off without unzipping.

All the metal I was wearing when I came through the portal is gone. My knee brace has fallen off my leg.

My phone! It's gone.

Mom!

Only the cloth from my clothes is here. Fortunately, my stretchy pants are still hugging my legs.

But the phone. Mom. She's gone.

I twist to look back at the portal, and feel my bra get totally messed up under my shirt.

Is it possible to feel like you belong somewhere, and to be really uncomfortable at the same time?

I duck down so that I'm nearly invisible in the grass and flowers. I slip my hands into my T-shirt and manage to get my bra off. There is no reason to keep it without the metal clasps. I don't like how my shirt feels against my chest, but I'll have to deal with it. At least my T-shirt is cotton. I shove the bra underneath my coat.

Karl clears his throat behind me and I nearly jump to Mars. How long has he been there?

I stand, and I force myself to look at him. At least his face is a little red, too.

But then I notice his eyes. Blue light, just like the light from the arch. Karl's eyes are glowing.

"Your eyes," I say.

"Excuse me?"

"Your eyes," I say, louder this time. "They're glowing. Neon blue. I've never seen anything like it! They didn't look like that on Earth."

He looks at me strangely. He doesn't believe me. "I'm not sure what to do here," he finally says. "Maybe we should call it a day."

I'm too surprised to say anything.

"We could come back," he says. "But let's move the car. Let's find out what clothes will make it through the portal, so we can both be comfortable. Then we can come back. I'm worried about your knee without a brace. If you get hurt, I'll have to take care of you."

I start to smile, as if it's a joke, but the smile catches before it happens. He's serious.

I'm not going back. Not yet. What if we can't come back here?

"I'm okay." I stand up and try to look strong and confident. My knee does hurt a little, but he doesn't have to know that. "We haven't been here long, and I'd like to look around."

"I don't know if that's wise. We don't know where we are. We could be right in the middle of a war zone, and we wouldn't know it."

He's lying—he isn't going to bring me back. I've waited months to get here, and I'm not going to leave now.

"I'm really want to head down that trail." I point across the meadow. I can't see the trail, but I remember it from my dreams about this place. I think it slopes into the pine forest away from the meadow.

Karl's eyes narrow. "Look. We should be careful. The plants are strange. I don't know what we'll find. We don't know what is poisonous or if this place is even habitable by humans."

I can see fear in his eyes, through the glowing blue light. I take a step away from the blue flowers, away from the portal. I don't want to be sensible or think things through right now. Besides, I'm from here. Of course, it's habitable by humans.

"I'm not leaving."

"You *athletes* think you are invincible," he calls after me. "You're about to hike down a trail with an unbound, injured leg without a second thought."

He spits out the word athlete like it's a swear word. As if we're all the same. He didn't know my Mom. She knew soccer better than anything. And she was amazing. Smart, happy, and cool.

"What proof do you have that there is any danger?" I call back over my shoulder as I push through the flowers, annoyed by his fear.

"What proof do you have that there is not?"

"I feel good about going."

For some reason that strikes him as funny. "Just think about what you are saying! Anyone knows that feeling has nothing to do with reality. Now is a time to think logically."

I stop dead in my tracks and turn around to face him. He isn't too many steps behind me. "Think logically? Like how you call me out of the blue and make me drive down here on an instant's notice. Or, how as soon as we get here you're ready to go?"

He opens his mouth to say something, but he closes it again and looks at the ground.

"I just want to be safe," he finally mumbles.

Why would he need to find a safe place? But, he doesn't say anything else. He continues to stare at the ground, and even though I start to feel sorry for him, I decide I don't really care. I walk away from him and find the trailhead right where I expected it. My knee is stronger than it was a few weeks ago, but I can't go too long without the brace. I'll see some of the trail and then turn back before it gives out. Hopefully I'll find something interesting before that happens.

Karl grabs my hand from behind. Before I can stop myself, I take a step forward. So does he.

Nothing happens, except that I'm extremely annoyed. I yank my hand away.

"The portal must be more specific here," I say.

"I'm coming with you," Karl says. "I can't get back through the portal by myself."

He doesn't want to give me any reason to trust him, does he?

I should probably be nervous, too. But, I'm excited. And curious. And annoyed at Karl.

I start down the trail. This part of the mountain wasn't in any of my dreams. This is all new.

Karl hikes behind me. In silence. The plants here look a lot like plants on earth. As if we know we aren't on earth right now. But, if this place wasn't safe, why would it feel so familiar?

23 Relaxed

Lydia

After about an hour hiking, we run into a small river. We haven't seen anything particularly interesting, or dangerous on our hike so far, although the forest has been incredible. It reminds me of Mount Rainier with its tall trees and soft trails.

The river's water runs down the mountainside, shimmering in the sunlight as it glides over the rocks. My tongue sticks to the roof of my mouth, sweat trickles down my back, and my knee aches.

"Let stop and rest for a few minutes," I say. It's the first thing either of us have said since the meadow.

"I don't think we should drink that water," Karl says. Does he think that everything in this world is going to kill him? He sits down on the bank of the river and looks around like a nervous animal.

I feel strangely safe in this world, albeit a little discouraged. The afternoon hike through the forest has been nice, but it hasn't taught me anything about myself. There are tons of great hikes in Seattle, and Mom and I have been on almost all of them. Hiking was always second only to work and soccer. Even Dad would go on hikes with us once in a while.

The water is too tempting, and Karl's warning too paranoid. I hobble to the side of the creek and sit, careful not to tweak my knee as I find a comfortable place next to the water. I plunge my hands into the stream and raise them to my mouth. Water trickles down my arms and drips off my elbows, and some of it makes it to my mouth. It's cool against my parched lips and throat. I dip my hands into the water again and again.

"You really should try some of this," I tell Karl.

"You won't be saying that once you get giardia," he tells me.

Whatever. "What makes you think there is giardia here?"

He shrugs. "I don't have any way of knowing what microbes are here. We could already be dying. You could have just poisoned yourself. We don't know where we are. Or when we are."

He's right. We could be on earth, or the portal could be a time travel thing. Or, maybe we're across the galaxy on some other planet. Is time moving the same across worlds? The plants look mostly like earth plants, but I'm not sure if that is relevant.

But, I don't think we're dying of anything.

When I finish drinking, I untie my shoes, roll up my pants, and slip my bare feet into the cool water. I gasp at the cold on my skin. It feels good, though the movement hurts my knee. I can't hike too much longer. My knee is already throbbing from not wearing my brace. I hope I haven't pushed it too far already.

Frustrated, I watch the river as it rushes by me, the clear water broken every so often with a leaf or a bug along for the ride. I see a small fish swim into an alcove at the opposite end of the river.

I want to talk to someone. About the peace here, about my disappointment at finding nothing, about my confusion of what to do next. I need to talk so I can make sense of what is going on.

But I don't say anything to Karl. He's so grumpy! His head twitches nervously; he jumps at every sound. Has he never been in the woods?

I push the thought that I'm forcing him to be here against his will out of my mind for the hundredth time. He called me. He told me he wanted to come here.

But, I don't know what to do next. Nothing makes sense. Why did I want to come here so badly? Should I have waited until my knee was stronger? Did I really come from here? Where are the people? Is it really time to go back to my world? Was this my only opportunity to be here?

If I leave with Karl now, coming back doesn't seem likely. Not that we can go back; I'm not sure if Karl will make it back up the trail to the portal without having a heart attack.

Karl's eyes catch mine—panic shining in the glowing blue light. He looks wild. Coming here with a complete stranger probably wasn't the smartest thing I've ever done.

Maybe it's time to go.

I sigh and lean my head down on my hands. I feel so confused; I wish someone would decide what to do for me.

I pull my feet out of the water and set them on a rock to dry. The sun feels good on my bare skin.

A loud crash and shout startles me and my feet fall back in the water. Karl jumps up, spinning around wildly.

"Ratoiqk, Hgiqou'ui!" a voice demands.

Men wielding sharp knives pop up out of the bushes. They surround us. Eight men, clean shaven, with long, braided hair. They wear black tights and brown leather boots. On top, they wear brown, animal-skin tunics that go down to their thighs.

People. Finally. We found them. Their faces are set in scowls; the sunlight reflects off the blades of the knives.

And they look like me. Flat noses, no earlobes.

Karl crouches next to the stream like a cornered animal. His eyes dart from side to side, searching for a way to escape.

He isn't going to find one. We didn't hear them, and they surrounded us. Besides, I can't run. Though, Karl might be the kind of person who leaves me behind if he gets scared.

I stand up slowly, careful not to move too suddenly or tweak my knee. Unfortunately, since my feet fell back in the water, they're wet and collect dirt quickly. I hope I don't have to put my shoes on soon—they will be especially uncomfortable with dirt caked to my wet feet.

The largest man steps forward. "Ratoiqk Hgiquoui," he says. The same words as last time. He bares his teeth, yellow teeth, peppered with cavities. His eyes stare out at me from behind his braids of hair. I think of the early Americans who were skinned alive by the Natives, and for the first time I feel nervous. Is that my fate, to die here, to have the sun bake my bare muscles and bones while I scream in anguish?

He repeats himself a third time, and I realize I understand the meaning of the man's words. "Who are you?"

No, those aren't the words you shout at someone before skinning them alive.

No one moves as I try to figure out what to do next.

The men's faces seem more curious than malicious. I turn my gaze back to the man who asked me who I was. Did I really understand him? Can I speak back to him? My voice comes out timid, reflecting my diffidence, "We are strangers here."

But those are English words and the man's face tightens as I say them. The other men shift anxiously.

A man behind me grumbles, and I understand his words, "Our leader hesitates in our time of greatest need."

I don't understand the words the people are saying, but I understand their meaning. Will speaking work the same way? I close my eyes and think of what I want to say to the men. I hear strange words come out of my mouth, "Yturiqa ooupu noit."

We are strangers here.

A smile tugs at the large man's lips, and the grumbling voice behind me swears. I keep my gaze focused on the large man in front of me. The leader.

"We have you surrounded, but we mean you no harm. We wish to understand your purpose here."

129

Karl shuffles over to me and whispers frantically in my ear. "What are you doing?"

I shake my head and try to concentrate, but he nudges me again, nearly knocking me over.

"I can understand them, and apparently they can understand me. Now be quiet and let me concentrate," I say.

And then I scream as a fair-skinned man tackles Karl from behind. He pins Karl quickly, his knife menacingly set against the skin of Karl's neck. I jump away, into one of the other men. He pushes me back into the middle of the circle and my knee buckles. I fall hard on the ground, scraping my hands as I catch my fall. I land next Karl and the man with the knife.

Even though Karl is twice the size of his attacker, his weak body is helpless against him. He lies face first in the dirt with his arms pinned behind him, not putting up any kind of fight.

"Let me go!" he moans.

"Arujan!" The big man takes a step forward.

"Don't you stop me," the little man, Arujan, says with a snarl. "We know Sapphiri cannot be trusted. They are killed on sight—your own laws demand it."

"You do not instruct me on our law," the large man says.

"Please don't hurt him," I say to the large man.

"You would leave the traitor man alive?"

"He's not a traitor. He's my, uh," I nearly say friend, but he really isn't my friend. Hardly that, we've barely spoken to each other. Even to save his life, I'm not ready for that kind of commitment. "He's come to help me here." That is mostly right.

"If he has come with you, then we will do him no harm," the large man says. "We will only kill him when you say."

I shudder. I can't imagine telling them to kill someone. Not even after he's been a jerk to me all day.

"You give him a chance to deceive us with his lies," Arujan yells in a squeaky voice. "He will betray you and you will all rue the day that you didn't leave his body to rot here atop the mountain. We must kill him now, and the girl, too. I will do it."

I stare at the men, and even though they're talking about killing Karl, I can't help but smile. I understand them! I was right—I do belong here.

"No," the large man says. "Lower your knife, or it will be your body that is left to rot here today."

The other men grumble their agreement.

The small man may be able to fight Karl, but he's no match for the other men. The knife comes away from Karl's neck, and the man steps on him to walk back to his place in the circle. Karl doesn't move. He curls into a ball and puts his hands over his head.

Pathetic.

"Lower your weapons men," the large man commands.

I walk toward the man, trying to hide my limp, but failing badly. "Hello," I say, and I can tell that I'm starting to get a bit better at communicating through thoughts and emotion instead of words. "I'm Lydia." I stretch my hand out.

The large man stares at my hand warily for a moment. Then he bows his head. "I'm Ziru," he says. "Where have you come from, Lydia?"

"Me and this man." I'm still not sure what my relationship is to him. "We've come through a magic portal that brought us here. We were surrounded by blue light and taken from our world to yours."

My words set off a ripple of conversation among the men. "It's the blue princess," I hear one of them say. A couple of the men drop to their knees.

"Is this true?" Ziru asks. "Are you the blue princess?"

I stare back at him. "I don't know who I am. I was found alone when I was a baby."

Ziru nods.

The fair-skinned man snarls behind me; he's the only one still brandishing a knife. "See! They're imposters. She's not the blue princess. We must kill them now."

"Do not speak again, Arujan," Ziru says. "And put that knife away."

Arujan doesn't move, but Ziru ignores him.

"Now child." Ziru's voice is kind. "Do you have the mark of the blue flower over your right breast?"

"Yes." He knows about my tattoo. Does everyone here have them? Does that mean that I belong with these people? Does that make me their enemy?

"Impossible!" Arujan yells. Two men step over to him and pull out their knives. He glares at them, but he finally stops talking once the knives are in his face.

"Will you show us?" Ziru asks kindly.

I pull hard on my T-shirt to get the collar down, and it stretches far enough to uncover most of the tattoo. The men gasp. Ziru drops to his knees. Within seconds, seven men are on their knees with their heads bowed, though Arujan doesn't follow suit.

"I don't know what's going on," I say.

Ziru lifts his head slowly and meets my eyes. "Your friend has the eyes of a traitor, yet you're the long-awaited for princess."

He doesn't offer any further explanation.

At least I don't think that they will kill us.

"Will you come with us to our village?" Ziru asks. "We will find suitable clothes for you, and we can talk more about the strange events that brought you here."

I look at Karl. He wants to go home, and I was about to take him. But now we've found people, and they have a village, and they might know something about me. I find myself liking Karl less and less every minute. If only I could let him go back home and continue on without him.

But, I can't, and that means I have to take him with me. If I'm going to go, and I really want to go.

"We have to go with them now. They have decided not to kill you, but they're taking us to their village."

Karl uncurls and stands slowly. He's completely covered in dirt.

"I don't want to go with them," he says.

"I'm not surprised." What if he doesn't come? These men want to kill him—I'm not sure he's even safe here.

"You can really understand them?"

I nod. He looks at the men; every one of them watch him suspiciously.

"You can't convince them to let us go back?"

I'm not going to try. I shake my head.

He has no choice. The guilt for lying to him hurts more than each step with my bad knee, but I really want to see this village. I'll take him back home soon, once I've learned something.

24 Ravine

Karl

We round yet another turn in the trail, and I squint down yet another ravine. Finally. A small collection of houses huddle together against the slopes ahead. It isn't much, but I bet this is where we are going.

It better be.

It looks like the middle of nowhere. But, at this point I'll take anything to stop this interminable hike.

Not that getting there means anything.

I'm in trouble. Captured. Nearly killed.

At first, being here was a breath of fresh air; I stopped looking over my shoulder every five minutes. The strange plants and weird looking insects intrigued me.

The intrigue only lasted ten minutes.

If there's one thing I learned in my many years of post-secondary education, it's that biology kills what doesn't belong.

I don't belong here. We don't belong here. I've never been so scared in my life.

We should have never come—I should have realized there are worse enemies than Tara and Bob. The microbes and bacteria on my world are things I can fight, things my body understands. There is nothing but strangeness here. Nothing but a new biology that is going to kill me.

I should have forced the svelte soccer girl to go back the minute I realized the danger. Why did I follow her down the trail? Life shouldn't venture out of the environment it evolved to survive in.

But I did. I turned my fate over to an athlete. All body, no brain. I probably trusted her because she's pretty. You'd think that after Tara I wouldn't be so stupid. Maybe this time I'll learn my lesson. From now on I should only talk to ugly girls.

The sun disappears behind the mountains as we enter the village, which is a generous word for the small collection of scattered houses, people bustling about, and children yelling in the streets. The trail we followed all day splits up, winding through the trees and the rocks to connect the houses.

How quaint.

People notice us as soon as we get close. Their eyes grow wide when they see me. They gather, they point, they talk. I can't understand anything, but I'm guessing the language they speak doesn't always sound so anxious and angry.

They're pointing at me.

A hand slips into mine. The athlete's hand. I pull back, but she has a strong grip.

"Don't fight me," she says through gritted teeth.

"What do you think you're doing? We can't be transported back to Earth from here. We've already tried, remember?"

She laughs as if I said something funny. "Oh Karl," she says with exaggerated sweetness. "I'm not trying to get back to Earth right now."

What a jerk. I tug again, but she holds firm.

"You need to understand something," she says. "And you need to stop pulling your hand away."

"Okay." It's embarrassing how much stronger this girl is than me. *Athletes.*

"These people hate you."

"Oh, is that why they all look like they want to kill me?"

"Because of your eyes. They usually kill anyone with eyes like yours on first contact. However, they spared your life because you're here with me."

"They like you?"

"Yeah, they think I'm a princess." She smiles and waves at the people. No one waves back, but they smile at her. Since I started holding her hand, their expressions have softened. A little. Maybe.

I thought she said we had to go with them.

"What happens once they realize you're not a princess?"

She shrugs. And smiles. She's been lying to me.

"Let's bolt right now."

"With my bad leg?" She winces as she takes her next step. How much of that is an act?

"We have to trust these people." All body and no brain.

"Trust them, huh? Didn't you just say they wanted to kill me?"

This girl has spent her life chasing a ball. That's what dogs do. And then, in soccer, you spend considerable amounts of time hitting the ball with your head. She probably has sustained permanent brain damage.

"Ziru promised you would be safe."

"What's a Ziru?"

"He's a who. The leader. Behind me."

We stop walking suddenly; the crowd watching us has grown large now. How many people live here? More than I thought, given the number of dwellings. They stand together, jabbering away. I stand stupidly next to the girl, my hand stuck in hers. The man she calls Ziru steps in front of us to address the crowd.

134

Hundreds of people. Maybe thousands. And they all hate me.

Ziru starts talking and he keeps talking. It gets boring really quick.

Eventually, the athlete lets my hand drop and steps forward. She pulls down her shirt collar to show off a strange tattoo over her right breast. The people gasp and fall to the ground on their knees.

Just when you thought things couldn't get any stranger!

I don't kneel. I stand there and watch the moths swirl around the lanterns. They fly in erratic patterns, eventually diving into the flames so the fire can consume them. And that is how their lives end. I end my life by taking a pretty girl through a portal. For all the schooling and training I've had, it turns out my intelligence is on the same level as a moth.

* * *

The athlete takes me to a small house in the center of town. We sit on a porch and eat some nasty tasting root vegetables. They're probably poisonous. Oh well, I'm starving, and we might as well die and get that over with.

"They asked if we were married," the athlete says. I'm so used to not understanding anything that it takes me a few chews to realize that she's speaking English. I offer a grunt in response. I'm not ever telling anyone I'm married to this empty-headed pretty girl.

She laughs. "Don't worry, I told them no. So, they're going to separate us."

I drop my food. They can't do that. How are we going to get back if we're separated?

"Don't freak out. I think we'll be okay for a while, but we'll find a way to get back to the portal eventually."

"Don't freak out!? That's easy for you to say. You, who are loved by a bunch of strangers because of your gorgeous body and your funny mark. You aren't risking your life, and so you don't mind throwing mine away." The words that have been rattling around in my head all day feel good on delivery.

Lydia looks away quickly. "I talked to Ziru, Karl. He says his son Ler will take care of you. I think you'll be okay."

"Oh, and I'm guessing that Ler is another really nice guy, who hates me for my eyes, but he can see past all that because of how pretty you are."

She stiffens—I'm starting to get through. "I don't think it's like that," she says.

"You have no right to sentence me to death."

"How can you say that? When you called me, you said you wanted to come here. Here we are. We'll go home eventually."

"I needed to go somewhere to think. I'm thinking now, and this place is death. Maybe you should try thinking for a minute." I know I'm being rude, but I'm scared and want out of here. All the pent-up emotion from the day seems to have removed all my sensibility filters.

Lydia stands up and walks to the other end of the porch.

Too many whacks of a soccer ball to her head say I'm not going anywhere. Ziru joins her and says something. She trudges back over to me, her eyes downcast.

"Ler will keep you safe," she says, her eyes on her feet. "He's a respected worker in the village, and he's Ziru's son. As long as you stay with him, no one will hurt you. I trust Ziru. I think you should, too, and we'll both stay alive."

By the time I come up with a retort, she's gone. A large man walks over. He does look like Ziru. Genetics.

The man called Ler claps me on the shoulder and speaks loudly. He has a huge, stupid smile. I call him some nasty names and follow him onto a trail leading away from the village center. As angry as I was at Lydia, I panic now at not having her here with me. The connection to my world is gone now. I look back, but don't see her anywhere. Footsteps move away, and I hurry to keep up with Ler.

The moon lights a well-worn path that we follow through the village down to a small house that sits just feet away from a cliff.

Hopefully there won't be an earthquake tonight.

It's dark inside the house, except for a few coals in a fireplace in the corner. Ler steps in behind me and stirs up the coals. Smoke fills the house, but it's replaced by light and warmth after a few minutes. It's nice to be warm—I was getting cold outside, which is a feat given my layers upon layers of fat.

With the light from the fire, I see that I was wrong to call this a house. It's a shack. I stand on a dirt floor; the walls are made of clay, and there is a single window near the fire pit. The room is mostly empty. There are no beds, no chairs, and no decorations except two large white animal skins that hang in the corner.

Ler finishes stirring the fire and says something to me.

I tell him he's the offspring of Tara sent to torture me for trying to run away.

He laughs and walks over to the animal skins. He hands one to me. It's soft, and huge. I could fit my entire body inside this thing. Is this how we sleep?

Ler takes the other skin off the wall. He throws it out with the inside of the skin against the floor and the soft part facing up. He motions for me to do the same.

It takes three or four throws, but I get it eventually.

I look back at Ler. He's completely naked.

No way.

Ler gestures for me to follow suit but I don't move. Undeterred, he steps forward to help.

Nope, that's going too far. I shake my head, and then I strip quickly, keeping an eye on Ler, who looks away.

I grunt when I'm finished. My bare white body practically glows next to Ler's tanned body. I watch as he lays down at the edge of the skin, grabs it, and rolls over twice. Just like that, he's completely enveloped by the skin and I'm left standing naked next to a huge white slug.

Cold wind blows through the window, and I shiver. Who can see into the shack? Impossibly, I wonder what the athlete would think if she was looking. I look at the rolls of fat on my body and sigh. Something serious is wrong with me.

Shivering against the cool night air, I lie awkwardly on the skin and manage to roll over like Ler did.

The skin is soft. And warm. Wrapped up, I'm actually comfortable. Not only does the fur keep me at a perfect temperature, it takes away the shock of the hard, rocky floor. Although I was feeling irritable when I laid down, I'm overcome by sleep within seconds.

* * *

I wake up with a bolt of energy early the next morning—as soon as sunlight makes its way into the room. I close my eyes and try to go back to sleep, but I've never felt so awake in the early morning in my life.

"Where are my clothes?" The place where I left them is empty. I don't see them anywhere. Ler comes into the house, already clothed. He smiles and gestures toward a small washroom outside. I shake my head and point to where I left my clothes.

Ler points at the fire.

"You burned my clothes!?"

He laughs and gestures to the washroom again. I follow him outside, freezing and still naked. He shows me a large basin of water, where to stand, and how to wash myself. Then, he leaves me shivering in the small room, which has too many ventilation windows for me to have any privacy.

The rocks on the floor are sharp and the air is cold. I pick up the bowl, fill it with water from the bucket, and pour it over my head.

And scream. The water is colder than the air.

Ler is back within seconds. He laughs when he sees me, shivering buck-naked on the rocks with freezing water dripping down my body, which is now turning pink. I shake myself dry and glare at Ler.

That was the worst shower of my life.

And apparently, the funniest thing Ler has ever seen in his.

Next thing I know, I'm wearing a pair of tights, a tunic, and a strange looking pair of boots.

The tights are uncomfortable. They hug my legs tighter than Khanh runs his lab. The only nice thing about these tights is that I have some breathing room around my crotch, so I'm not strapped in like a male ballerina. The tunic fits me loosely, and my stomach pokes out at the bottom.

I've never worn tights in my life, but I do now. I've never gone outside naked, but I do now. I've never slept on the floor, but I do now.

137

This is my new life—do what others say and don't complain. They won't listen or understand anyway. And they might kill me, or they might not.

I can only imagine what Tara would say if she saw me here. She was right; I should have never broken up with her. Everything in my life has fallen apart since then.

Though, she still would have blamed me when they found out about her fake data, so it doesn't really matter.

* * *

Ler doesn't seem to notice the cloud of negativity that follows us through the village. He waves at everyone and greets them with a smile. This guy is seriously happy, but he's big and others seem to stay away from me when I'm by him.

We pick up a bland breakfast of eggs and root vegetables. Only my extraordinary hunger makes the meal palatable. We eat it as we hike back through the village and its sneers and glares.

As we near the edge of the village, Ler puts his big, sturdy arm around me. He says something, but I shake my head and shrug his arm off. I'm not going to get buddy-buddy with my foreign captor, especially if he's a large, stupid oaf.

"Karu, Karu, Karu," Ler says.

He sounds like a howling dog. What happened to the "l" at the end?

"It's Karl."

"Eez Karu," he says. And then he laughs. I hate not knowing what people are saying.

I follow Ler to pick up a couple large carts, and then we hike a well-worn trail for three or four miles, most of them straight up hill.

Yeah. Pretty much miserable. Where is Lydia? Did they capture her? Torture her? I was so mean to her last night, I wouldn't blame her if she was avoiding me. But, I need her now. I'm ready to apologize and make up. And then I can leave this nightmarish hike behind and go back to the world where I belong. And I'll call Pearl and tell her about Bob and she'll know what to do.

Eventually we come out of the forest into a large meadow, like the one Lydia and I started in yesterday.

Ler pulls out a few gunnysacks and a couple small shovels from the cart. He dances around to show me the different plants in the meadow. Some are good and some are not good. Our job is to find good plants, dig up the roots, remove the tops, and place the bulbs in the bag. And that is how we get the disgusting food we eat for every meal.

Have these guys ever heard of agriculture?

Once Ler is sure I understand what to do, he hands me a shovel and we get to work. He's about four times faster than me, even when I try.

Sweat drips down my back. My hands blister. Sunlight heats up the fabric against my legs. And I keep digging.

25 Rumors

Lydia

I have a hard time keeping the smile off my face as Cadah, my guide, leads me through the village.

The mountain peaks surrounding the village tower above us into the sky, trees cling to them until they become so steep that only snow and rock can hold on to the surface. The air is clear—amazingly so, and the sky was so full of stars at night. I can't think of anywhere on Earth that could compare.

But as much as I love the scenery, the clothes are even more amazing. Clothes from Earth never fit so well! These clothes were made to fit my body in a way that clothes at home never were. And, they're not too hot, nor too cold. Comfortable. The best description I can think of is stretchy pants on steroids.

I belong here. Sure, I'm missing class and homework and my knee hurts like crazy. But I love it here. The people have the same skin tone I do, the same odd facial features, the same body types.

If only my phone had made it through the portal. I've felt for it again and again, finding nothing but empty pockets. It's the first time I've been without that phone since the night Mom died.

"I think I've shown you the entire village." We've arrived back at the village center. People hurry around us with carts of roots and berries.

"Thank you."

I've warmed quickly to Cadah, which isn't like me. She has been patient with me this morning. My leg isn't as sore today, but that hasn't stopped me from walking slowly. Avoiding reinjury is difficult on these rocky paths, and my knee is stiff from all the walking I did yesterday.

From what Cadah showed me this morning, there are probably about 500 houses in the village with a population of maybe 1500. Most of the people are middle aged, which Cadah says is due to some particularly harsh winters over the past few years.

That is a harrowing thought. This place is beautiful, but it's destructive, too. Not as destructive as Karl thinks, but still dangerous.

"The people all seem anxious," I say as Cadah and I sit down on the front steps of the large, unoccupied building that is the village center. It's the same building where we ate dinner last night.

"Yes," Cadah says. "This has been a stressful summer."

"Why?"

"The winters have been harsh lately, and unrest spreads across all the mountain villages. Food is scarcer than it used to be. And many are stirring up rebellions. Some say you have arrived a hundred years too late, but even last year would have been better than now. The problems are much worse farther up the mountain where they're overcrowded and have even more problems with snow."

The princess thing again. No one has told me what they expect me to do about it, only that I'm supposed to do something.

"If the winters are so severe, why don't you move? Perhaps if you moved farther down the mountain you'd find a milder climate."

"Moving into the valley would be certain death."

"Why?"

Cadah shakes her head sadly. "You don't know anything about us?"

"How would I know?"

"And Wynn, do you know about Wynn?"

"Wynn? Is that a person?"

Cadah looks puzzled, but she nods. "It doesn't make sense," she says. "The legends say that you would come out of the portal, posed to strike down Wynn and free us from these mountains. You would have fire in your hair and throw darts from your eyes. Everyone would fear you, and the armies of Wynn would fall before you. We would be free, and you would be our ruler. I thought some of it might be exaggerated, but it's still disappointing to see you show up and have it not be true."

I raise my eyebrows. Darts from my eyes? No wonder everyone is acting disappointed. It was fun to think of myself as a princess for a while, but if I've walked into a badly exaggerated legend, I should starting listening to Karl. Even though he was so mean to me yesterday. He was scared, but that doesn't make the things he said to me hurt any less. I push the pain out of my thoughts.

"Do people still think I'm the blue princess, even though I can't do those things?"

"Yes. You have the mark, impossible to replicate, in the exact right spot. You must be the princess. We will take you to Keeper, and then you will have the weapon you need to defeat evil and return the mountain people to the valley. You really don't know any of this?"

I shake my head again. I have no idea who I am. What does she mean that I'm hundreds of years late?

Cadah looks away. "You come, having the mark of the flower, but you can barely walk. Many of us expected you to stand over Wynn's body within a few hours of arrival. Instead, you can barely get across the village in that time."

Maybe she hasn't been as patient with my slow steps as I thought. My heart drops as I realize how much I want this girl to like me. But, if I'm being held up to an impossible standard, that probably won't happen.

"If nothing is how you thought, how do you know I can defeat this Wynn person?" I'm not a killer; I'm a soccer player.

"You have blue blood; you're an Azurean like he is—the only one who can defeat him."

Blue blood? What in the world does that mean?

"I don't have blue blood." The good feelings from this morning are fading fast. I love it here, but things are so strange. Maybe they will kill us when they realize I'm not what they think I am.

"I'm sure you do," Cadah says confidently. I open my mouth to protest—I've seen lots of my own blood through my soccer days—but I stop myself. Is it smart to discredit myself when doing so might leave me dead?

For a second, I find myself doubting the color of my own blood.

Cadah is quiet now, and I don't say anything else. I'm a mess, trying to put my thoughts together. The thought of getting caught up in a war with a group of desperate people scares me. I don't feel like I'm understanding anything that is going on. The physical similarities, the mark of the flower, the feeling of belonging. There is so much to love here.

But, I want to find out who I am, not get involved in saving people from a crisis.

I hear a sound and look up to see a group of three men and two women walking toward the building. Ziru leads the group, and I recognize the other men from yesterday. Arujan is not with them.

Ziru leads us inside the building. My clothes, which have been comfortable all morning, apparently don't do as well in stuffy rooms. No climate control. I'm used to outside heat—I've played soccer for years—but suffocating inside a hot building doesn't seem fun. Hopefully we won't be in here long.

I sit across from Ziru, who smiles at me. The men sit on one side of the building, and the women sit on the other, facing the men. The building is small; the seven of us fill all the floor space. At least I can cross my legs without hitting anyone.

"Let us begin," Ziru says.

"We need to discuss Arujan," an older man across from Cadah says.

"Arujan will cause us no harm," the woman next to Cadah counters. She looks like she's about the same age as Cadah, and she has long blonde hair.

My head darts from side to side, trying to keep up with the conversation. No one introduces themselves, and no one tells me what we are doing here. I wonder if I should stop everything and ask, but one look at Ziru is enough of an answer for me. I might be a princess, but he's in charge here. Maybe I'm more of a figure than a ruler.

I sit up straight, keep my mouth shut, and try to handle myself with aplomb. If they think I'm a princess, whatever that means, I might as well try and act like one. Hopefully my preconceived ideas of what a princess should act like, matches their preconceived notions.

A young man is speaking. "No harm? Have you heard the rumors about what he did in the north?"

"Rumors," the younger woman is not fazed by the younger man's mocking tone. I'm glad he isn't talking to me; he doesn't seem very nice.

"He balkanized them!" he shouts in her face. "Ousted their leader Dynd and created a bunch of warring factions. There might not be anyone left up there."

"You don't know that." Her look stays as calm as drizzle on a windowpane. "That report was given to our scouts from the scouts at Keeper. Surely it is exaggerated. Arujan had to flee Keeper to come here."

Cadah speaks up next. "Ore, it is strange that you would defend Arujan like this. We all know Arujan did not flee from Keeper. The rest of the council is intent on getting Arujan out of our city, and yet it seems that your defense of this man grows stronger each day."

"We need to make sure we are fair," she says, narrowing her eyes at Cadah.

"Young love is a strange thing," the other woman, farthest from me, says. She looks like she's at least in her 70s, if not older. The girl called Ore blushes.

"Love?" she stammers.

"It's no secret that you and Arujan have spent a lot of time together," Cadah says. "There are rumors you slept with him."

Ore's expression darkens.

"Now child," Ziru says. "You were always wild, and you're young and impulsive. But, your father was a dedicated member of this council for many years. As his only living child, you're entitled to the position you have on this council. Now, let's forgive your indiscretion and move on."

"What?" Ore shouts.

"You have been giving information from our meetings to Arujan," the man next to Ziru says.

"How can you say that?" Ore's eyes dart from person to person until her gaze finally settles on Cadah.

"We all know how much time you spend with him," Cadah says. Her voice is calm, in contrast to Ore's, which is getting louder and higher each time she speaks.

"He has to get all of his information from somewhere," the man next to Ziru says. "And you have been overheard by someone here."

"Enough of this," Ziru says. "Ore will not betray us again. In the meantime, having won the affections of Arujan may allow her to play a pivotal role in a plot to get him out of here."

Several in the room nod their consent, but Ore's glare stays fixed on Cadah.

The younger man interrupts the silence. "We have other things to discuss beside Arujan. He's causing trouble, but is he not a symptom of all our greater problems?"

"There is less food this year," the older woman agrees. "Many of the younger generation do not recognize how much we have to skimp. Nor do they see how skinny they all look compared to what we looked like when we were their age."

"Yes," the man next to Ziru says, "but now the Blue Princess has arrived."

"Arrived, but she's worthless!" Ore says, her shrill voice startling everyone. She turns her glare to me. I don't know how Cadah acted so calm under a glare like that. "She has the mark of the blue flower, but she can't do one thing to help us. At least Arujan can walk and is trying to solve our problems."

"She has never been here before," Cadah says.

"Exactly!" Ore shouts. "Why not? We've waited for generations. Where has she been? She looks younger than me." Anger burns in her eyes. It's the same look Dad had when he hit me. I fight the impulse to run.

"Where have you been?" Ore says in barely a whisper. "Where were you when my father died?"

I don't know what to say. I don't know who her father is or why she would blame me for his death. I see Dad's fist swinging toward me, and I close my eyes.

"That is enough, Ore," Ziru says. "The legends never said the princess would save us overnight. Every legend I have heard says that when the Blue Princess comes, we must take her to Keeper."

"Keeper has the secrets of the blue blood," the older woman agrees.

"I thought Keeper had the weapon the princess would use to defeat Wynn," Ore says with a smirk. "This girl can't do anything. What would she do with a secret weapon? Grow wings so she can get around?"

"You're planning to take her to Keeper?" the older man asks.

"Yes, Hattak." Ziru nods.

Ore interrupts again. It isn't hard to see why no one seems to like her. "I don't see why we need to spend time on a worthless quest when we have real problems. Our time with warm weather is already too short."

"When do we leave for Keeper?" Hattak asks, completely ignoring Ore.

"Some of us will leave," Ziru says. "I will take Tran, Cadah, and Lydia. Hattak, I need you to stay here and watch the village. Ler will be busy protecting Karu."

"I don't know why the traitor is still alive," Hattak says. "You expect me to keep order in the village with the traitor and Arujan still here?"

"Yes," Ziru says.

"Impossible!"

"That is why I leave it in your hands. Netta will also be here."

"And Ore?" Tran asks with a smirk on his face. "I'm guessing that she will be put in charge of keeping an eye on Arujan?"

Cadah giggles, but Ziru doesn't appreciate the quip. "Enough! We are all friends here, and Ore is a trusted member of this council. That is exactly what I had in mind."

Cadah looks at me behind Ore's back and rolls her eyes.

"How far away is Keeper?" I ask. I feel like a little girl, sitting here while this committee decides my future. Maybe I want to go, but maybe I don't. There are other things to consider, like how I told Karl that he would be okay. I'm a girl trying to figure out where she came from, not a warrior wanting to get involved in a war.

"One hundred miles," Netta responded. "A week's journey."

A week. That is a long way, but maybe it will be okay. And after we go, I could take Karl back home. A week's journey would give me a sense of what is here in this world, and then I can stop my selfishness and take care of Karl.

"Could we take Karl with us?" That way I would know he's safe.

"We can't afford to lose the manpower," Ziru says. "And besides, we don't know how friendly the people of Keeper would be to a traitor. He's safe with Ler."

"Perhaps," Hattak says. "But maybe not. And you must be careful. Although the people in Keeper gave reports to our spies a few months ago about Arujan, we don't know if they have sided with him in the meantime. We have always had a good relationship with Keeper, but Arujan is cunning. He broke up the Northern Alliance, perhaps he has put some kind of political pressure on Keeper to break the traditional leadership."

"We need to be careful," Tran agrees. "And that means that we can't take Karu. Keeping Karu with Ler is the best plan. Besides, who cares if he dies?"

"I do," I say quietly. My dislike for Tran is increasing as well.

"And so do we," Ziru says and puts a hand on my knee. "It's decided. We leave the day after tomorrow."

Everyone stands and embraces each other. I stay on the ground. I feel confused. I barely understand what's going on here. Is this okay with me? It seems like it is, and I want to go on this trip more than I want to go home and back to school. I think I trust these people.

This is my one chance to be here. Mom would want me to stay, to figure something out before I gave up.

Cadah helps me up, and I'm pulled into an embrace with each of the other council members. Everyone hugs everyone, although Ziru is the only one who is not reserved in his hug with Ore. I'm reserved in my hugs to everyone, though I feel like

I'm on an emotional roller coaster as I touch each person. Maybe the heat is getting to me.

How am I going to break the news to Karl?

* * *

The sunset in the mountains is majestic. The jagged peaks let some light stream in, creating silhouettes surrounded by the color of the setting sun. Should I have grown up here, surrounded by color and mountains? Would I trade the beauty here for the time playing soccer with Mom?

I'm on the edge of town walking with Cadah. The walk was my idea; I was tired of Karl trying to catch my eye during dinner.

I don't want to talk to him right now. I don't know what I would say that won't make him angry again. And I don't want him to be angry and yell at me. I'll take care of him. Later. I will.

He's probably figured out I'm avoiding him. In just another day I'm going to leave for Keeper. I'm leaving, but I'm not abandoning him. I'll be back, and we'll go home.

He's not going to like it. I wish I had come through the portal with someone cool, someone who could speak the language, someone everyone liked. But that's not what happened.

At least the night is beautiful. If only it was enough to lift my spirits. Would I be happier if we just went home tonight? Called this an adventure and got me to a doctor?

I look over at Cadah and try to think of something to say that will distract me from my thoughts.

"Cadah," I ask. "Who is Arujan?"

"Why do you ask? I know that you have met him."

"Yes, I've met him. Where is he from?" Crickets chirp. We slow and then stop. We need to head back before it gets too dark.

"He says he's from the North."

"Where is the North? What does that mean?"

Cadah gives me a puzzled look.

"Okay," I say. "I've figured out that we are in a village called Watch. There is another village 100 miles away called Keeper, and we'll be going there. I'm guessing there is another village called North?"

Cadah laughs. "No, of course not! The North is a series of villages, the Northern Alliance. People moved up there when Watch and Keeper got overcrowded. We were all united until recently when the alliance fell apart, probably because of Arujan. Now, with supplies dwindling, tensions are high and most of them have started fighting each other."

"Was it Arujan's doing?"

146

Cadah shrugs. "He's trying to get people to go off the mountain." She laughs at the idea. "Terrible, evil man!"

"I don't understand why that would be so bad. It doesn't seem to be too great up here."

"Wynn."

"It seems like he should be dead by now—didn't you say that he's had you stuck here for hundreds of years?"

"He's an Azurean."

What in the world is an Azurean?

Is it a real threat that keeps these people on this mountain? Trapped for hundreds of years, they have faced starvation, mutiny, and overcrowding. Through it all, they stayed on the mountain, not leaving no matter the cost. Are they trapped by myth? Or is there real threat in the valley?

A light off to the side of the trail catches my attention.

"What's that over there?"

"Mara."

"What?"

"She claims to be from the world off the mountain."

Well, there you go! Maybe "Mara" can help me sort this all out. Maybe these mountain people are trapped in a lie.

"People live off the mountain? Besides Wynn?"

"Of course! Wynn's people live down there."

"So, you don't go down there, but they come up here?"

"The border is blocked by hemazury," Cadah says. I don't understand half of what she says. "Only those who are descendants of the great King Togan's closest friends can come up here. And they all did, hundreds of years ago."

I stare at her, wishing the words she was saying could make more sense to me. All I hear is more myth and more fantasy. And, she's not explaining Mara's presence here.

"You're saying that you can cross the border to go back? But they can't follow you here?"

"Right," Cadah says. "Except for Sapphiri. They can cross the border, and many have come to help Wynn. That is why we kill every one that we find. Well, every one until Karu."

"Sapphiri are the people who have the glowing eyes."

Cadah nods.

"Why didn't you kill Mara? Doesn't she have blue eyes?"

"No, she doesn't. No one knows why she could cross the border. Hattak wanted to kill her, but he made the mistake of taking her to Ziru first. Ziru opens his heart too wide, which is why so many people are listening to Arujan. If Ziru had killed Mara and her baby, I don't think they would listen to Aurjan."

She has a baby?

As if on cue, a soft cry fills the darkening sky. I turn away from Cadah and follow the trail to the small hut. I need to get away from Cadah, her cold words are making me sick. You don't kill babies. That's just not right.

"Where are you going?" Cadah calls after me.

I ignore her, my eyes focused on the path in front of me so I don't hurt my leg. How can she be so ruthless? Kill, kill, kill. This society kills anyone that isn't like them. No wonder there is unrest.

I slow my steps as I approach the light at the end of the trail. Three sticks are propped up with a ragged cloth barely attached, blowing in the wind. Cadah didn't follow me.

"Hello?"

"Come," a timid voice responds. She speaks differently than the other people I've talked to, but it's the same language, I think. In any case, I understand her the same way.

I pek around the cloth and discover a topless woman reclined against a rock nursing a small baby. The woman's face is gaunt, her hair matted, and her eyes drooping. A tattered dress droops around her hips, different from the clothes the mountain people wear. The dress is covered in blood. Red blood, like mine. She sits in the light of a single candle, tear marks wet on her face.

"How old is that baby?" A small, naked baby sucks on the woman's breast. The scene is like something you'd see in a refugee movie.

"Just a few days," Mara says softly. "Just a few days."

"Do you have food?" I try to make my voice sweet, trying to cover my disgust at the situation. The nights are cold! This lean-to isn't a place for a new baby.

"The man they call Tran brings food every third day. I seem to have enough for Jarra."

"Will you come with me?"

"I'm happy to be alive." Mara lets me help her up stand, which makes my knee ache. Traitor or no traitor, she won't die out here with a newborn. If they don't let me help her, I'm leaving. This is wrong.

Mara moans as she leans against me as we walk up the trail, which puts another strain on my knee. Having her lean on me makes me feel strangely depressed, and my courage falters.

I see Cadah shift in the light of the rising moon up ahead. "Mara is going to move in with us," I say. "She will die out here otherwise."

"She will betray us to Wynn." Cadah's voice is soft, hesitant.

"It isn't right to leave her to die out here."

Take us to the village, Cadah. Don't kill this woman! How can you think that she will betray you? Just look at her.

Cadah doesn't move.

I don't move, either. I stare Cadah down like I would a forward moving up the field toward me.

The baby starts to cry.

Cadah turns.

I take a deep breath and follow her back toward the village.

26 Reckless

Karl

I sit at the table, nibbling the food, if you can call it that.

Lydia disappeared. She was sitting just across the way a few minutes ago and now she's gone. Both her and the girl that she's always with.

She didn't say anything to me. Not a word all day.

Was this her plan all along? To use me to get here and then to abandon me while she lives the life of a princess?

I gag on the food and spit out whatever I was chewing. No, that can't be it. The food is too awful, and she's injured. It's only a matter of time before we go back. The real question is how much more I can endure before we do.

A woman passing by the table stops abruptly. I give her a feeble smile—the look on her face isn't friendly, but I have only seen one friendly face the entire time I've been here, and that's Ler.

She draws a knife and points it at me.

"Hey," I put my hands up. "I never did anything to you."

She speaks harsh words, coming closer, her eyes threatening.

"Ler!" I call out, only slightly embarrassed that my voice squeaks when I do.

He turns and talks to the woman. She shakes her head, argues with him for a moment, and then leaves.

Maybe the question shouldn't be how much more I can endure, but rather how much longer I can stay alive. That's at least the fifth knife that someone's pulled on me since I got here.

I stop nibbling the food and move closer to Ler. He's happily engaged in conversation. Conversation is something I haven't had all day. I yearn for it, strangely. To say words, to hear my thoughts formed into speech, to see others understand those thoughts. Speech is the power to take another's mind down the same track as your own. Words change, just for a moment, what the person is thinking about; words put your thoughts into another's head. In graduate school, I may have not had much verbal communication, but I could always write and read.

Now, my brain is in a vacuum. The only person in this world who can understand the words I speak is avoiding me.

If only Lydia would talk to me. I would be nice, just to hear myself talk.

* * *

The next day proceeds as the day before. We wake up at the crack of dawn—once again I'm strangely refreshed and alert in the early morning—and we're off. We push the same rickety old carts.

Instead of going on the road away from the portal, this time we go on a trail that heads in a perpendicular direction, straight to the tall mountain peaks that tower over and surround the village. As we approach, a small pass between the towering rock faces comes into view.

Through the pass, a panorama of a huge valley opens in front of us. A valley. It's close, just a few miles away. Valleys have always been better sources of food than mountains. It doesn't make sense why the people stay up here if they live this close to a valley. Mountains aren't paradise. Dangerous drop-offs, wild animals, lots of winter snow.

These people are either stupid, or there is something dangerous down there.

Danger seems to be far from Ler's mind right now, though. He whistles as we walk along the mountain face for an hour. Just when I'm about to collapse from exhaustion, we stop in another flowered meadow. I sit down and sink my shovel into the ground. Nothing like another long day sitting in the hot sun and digging up unpalatable roots.

I'm more alone that I ever was in Pittsburgh, even after Tara dumped me.

I pull up a plant. This one has green flowers and a very strong scent. It is a strange anomaly, something that evolution should have eliminated a long time ago. Green flowers don't belong—they don't have the visual cues needed for making it to the next generation. Ironically, this flower is thriving, and I'm the one whose genes will be eliminated—a fat guy with eyes that everyone hates, and no hope for a future in a world I don't belong in.

This particular flower is doomed, too. Wrong place, wrong time. I snap the green off the plant and throw the root into the bag at my side. Maybe I can kill them all. Just another ten thousand to go. We'll see what evolution thinks of that.

Ler starts to sing. His voice is a strong bass, and it fills the air with sweet melody. For some reason, I smile. Ler can't be enjoying this either. I would never admit it to Lydia, but maybe if I could understand Ler, I might like him.

* * *

By the end of the day my head is pounding and my entire body aches.

What I need is to take some Tylenol and go to bed. Instead, I get to stay out with the village socialite, and tonight is a party. The music makes my head hurt, the headache pounding behind my ears with each strike of the drums.

I haven't seen Lydia all night. I can't even begin to guess where she might be. Maybe she's already been killed. This may be my last meal, and I'm in too much pain to enjoy it.

The evening slowly cools; the fire turns to embers. My head continues to throb as people retire for the night. I hear a baby crying. A woman is carrying the baby away from the party. Two other women accompany her. I sit up straight. One of them is Lydia.

Ler isn't paying attention to me. He raises a glass of wine and several others raise theirs as well. The dim light of the fire shows the large smiles on their flushed faces.

This is my chance. I have to talk to her.

I sneak away and follow the three women through the village until they reach a small house near the village center. They go in and moments later I see the dim light of a fire.

I'm going in to get Lydia. Crickets chirp, but otherwise the night is silent as I approach the door. I'm not sure how it will all work, but I need to talk to Lydia. We need to get out of here before we're both dead. Surely she understands that now.

The moon rises above an ominous peak to my right, casting long shadows all around me.

I take a deep breath and raise my hand to knock on the door. Hopefully she'll talk to me after what I said the other day. But, if she won't, I'll apologize. Surely, she misses speaking English. We need to be smart.

A large hand catches mine before it contacts the wood.

Ziru.

"Karu." His whisper is stern. I can't see his face.

Before I can say anything, he drags me off the porch and away from the house. I don't have a chance to fight him—not that it would do any good if I could. It was dark when I followed the women here. I'm positive if he takes me away that I will not find my way back.

Using what must be superhuman strength, Ziru drags me all the way back to the house I share with Ler, who stands waiting in the doorway. Ziru starts shouting before we get to the threshold of the house. Ler bows his head and nods as Ziru gives him a verbal lashing. It isn't Ler's fault, of course. I was the one who tried to run away.

Not that I want Ziru to start yelling at me.

Eventually, he stops his rant and leaves. Ler motions to the fuma skin, and reluctantly I get ready for bed. Maybe I can stay awake and sneak out again after Ler is asleep.

No hope of that. I'm asleep the second I'm wrapped in the skin.

* * *

I'm alert the moment the light streams through the window the next morning.

152

Something weird is going on with this fuma skin. I've never fallen asleep or woken up so fast in my life. But that's what's happening. Every day.

But something else isn't right.

Screams. People are screaming.

I roll out of the skin.

Ler, still as naked as I am, throws my clothes at me.

"Karu!" His voice is urgent. The screaming gets louder.

My fingers fumble as I put the unfamiliar tights and tunic on. We run out into the dim morning light moments later.

A crowd is gathered near our house. It isn't a quiet crowd. Shouts and screams fill the air as we run.

The people are gathered around the body of a woman—I recognize her as the woman who was with Lydia last night. Her body is mangled, naked, and covered in blood and bruises. She's dead.

I try to look away, but I can't—my eyes stay riveted to the body. Who could do such a thing? Ler runs over and falls next to it. The minute the people see Ler, they look at me. I stand awkwardly, gawking at the body, feeling the heat of their stares.

Arujan, the man with the wild eyes, steps out of the crowd. He shouts, pointing his finger at me and yelling. Others start to yell. Arujan's face turns bright red.

I'm frozen, my heart rate increasing like I just realized I have a paper due tomorrow. Sweat beads on my forehead. Should I call out for Ler?

Someone grabs my arm, and I jump. It's Lydia, suddenly at my side. Her hair is wild, and she looks as angry as the rest of the crowd.

"Karl," she says, in a whisper so intense I can hear it clearly over the raucous crowd. "What have you done?"

What have I done?

I don't have a chance to answer her. Ler leaps away from the corpse and sprints to us. He says something to Lydia, and she nods.

Then she screams. "Run!"

I don't need to be told twice. I run.

I'm not a sprinter or a distance runner. I hate running and I'm an overweight graduate student. But I have never run faster in my life. I hear people behind me, and I push myself as hard as I can. A few knives whistle past my head. Ler says something under his breath. He's right beside me.

This is it. This is the end of us. I'm frantic as I stumble over the rocks and tree stumps. Any minute hands are going to pull me down. I'm going to be slaughtered.

The mob is getting closer.

Ler's hand finds a place on my back and pushes me forward. With his hand there, each of my strides becomes longer than before, and each step is faster. I watch

153

as each foot contacts the ground only to lift off again. Ler is fast, and he knows these woods. We run away from the village, zigging and zagging through the forest.

Eventually we can't hear the crowd behind us. Ler stops and we duck into a thicket. I collapse onto the ground, pulling every oxygen molecule from the air in great bursts of breath. Ler sits beside me saying nothing.

I close my eyes, embarrassed by the tears that stream down my cheeks. I can't believe I'm alive. My body starts to shake with relief.

After a while, my breath returns to normal. The sun makes it over the peaks. Ler motions for me to get up and we start down a trail, walking this time.

We walk for hours, weaving through the trees. I have no idea where we are, but eventually we come out into the clearing. There is a small cave here, and a large, white animal rests inside it.

A fuma—the animal whose skin I sleep in every night.

Ler pulls a knife out of his tunic and throws it at the animal, striking it in the jugular vein. A second knife in the thigh takes it down. The smell of fresh blood fills the air.

Blood. That girl. The image of her mutilated body. I bend over and throw up.

When I look up from my vomit, there is a rustle from the bushes and Ziru and Lydia emerge. They have another man, a woman, and a baby with them.

Lydia glowers at me. Her eyes are puffy and her wild hair is sticking out in every direction.

"You've ruined everything."

"Excuse me?"

"You snuck away last night? Went wandering through the village?"

"I was coming to talk to you."

New tears splash onto her cheeks. "Did you see what he did to Cadah?"

I did, and I don't want to talk about it. We don't have time for drama. Lydia must agree with me now. We need to get out of here. We need to go home.

"We need to get moving if we're going to make it back to the portal before the sun goes down."

She doesn't hear me. "She was so nice to me," she mumbles.

"Lydia, we need to go home," I say again, louder this time. The panic from our first day here is back. I have to get through to this girl. She has to take me home! I don't need to understand the situation or how she feels. Not now. I need to get home. I want to eat a normal meal, to be with people I know and care about.

"Karl—we can't leave yet. Not now."

"Yes, we can. Right now." How could she want to stay here? "We are going to die! What has to happen before you're ready to acknowledge that we'll both die if we don't get out of here?"

She stares blankly in front of her.

154

I'm going to die because of this stupid girl. "How can you stay here one more minute? You're going to die, Lydia!"

She looks away again. She's good at that. This isn't fair. She has no right to gamble away my life.

"I need some space," she says in a voice so quiet I have to take a step closer to hear. She cowers, like she thinks I'm going to hit her. Ziru and Ler both stop what they're doing and look at me. I take a step back and put up my hands.

"You can't be serious."

"I'm sorry, Karl."

That's all she says, and she turns and limps into the cave. I stand helpless, frozen by the glares from Ler and Ziru.

Stupid girl.

I spin away from the cave and walk away from the idiots.

The easiest path goes straight down the mountain. My mind is so fuzzy with rage I can barely think. Lydia isn't going to take me home. The thought of tagging along on a journey to another remote village is ridiculous. This isn't right. People aren't allowed to hijack other lives like this. People can't just control where others go. It's not my fault I'm here, and I can't fix it.

I don't know how long it is before the mountain stops, though I'm a little calmer when I get there. A three-foot drop-off separates the mountains from the valley forest. The drop-off runs as far as I can see in both directions. I run my fingers along it, and it is rock, but it's as smooth as glass. The same trees and shrubs grow on each side of the divide. Did an earthquake cause this? How is the boundary so smooth?

How far does it go?

I walk along the edge. It continues as far as I can see, the forest undisturbed on either side.

I don't worry about my way back. They'll come for me soon enough.

A twig snaps behind me. They're already here. Couldn't they have given me at least a little more time? I keep walking. I hear another snap.

They can't take a hint, can they?

"Ler!" I yell. "Leave me alone. I don't want to talk."

Nothing.

I look behind me, and a large, white predator cat moves out from behind a tree. Ler is nowhere to be seen.

For the second time in this miserable day, I run for my life. This time, though, there isn't a steady hand to push me forward.

Are there any sticks around? A rock or something I could use to defend myself? I scan the ground around me. While I'm distracted, my boot hits a slick spot of moss and my leg goes out from under me. I fall, over the edge and off the mountain. My hands hit hard in a pool of water, and I yell as the rocks cut into them.

I use one of my injured hands to grab a small, sharp rock from the stream. It isn't much, but I'll use it and I'll fight. I roll my body over, scrambling to a sitting position as the cat leaps off the ledge, its claws out and mouth open.

Light flashes out of the corner of my eye. A knife. Several knives. The knives lodge in the cat's neck as it flies toward me. And then it hits me, knocking my body back into the stream. My head slams into a rock, my vision goes fuzzy, and then everything goes black.

27 Regret

Lydia

I lay still on the hard ground and stare into the darkness, but in my mind, I only see Cadah. Her mangled body. Why would Arujan kill her?

Not that she was perfect. But she was a human being. Someone who was nice to me. And Cadah was nice to Mara, even if it was against her will.

I hug my legs tight against my chest. The cold from the cave floor seeps through my clothes. I think of Cadah turning to take Mara back to the village. I think of her rolling her eyes behind Ore at the meeting. She was cute. She was my friend. She's gone.

The crunching of rocks underfoot lets me know that Ziru and Tran are coming to join me. Tran's perpetual smirk makes me sick. He seems to sense my distaste and stops at the entrance. Ziru walks slowly across the cavern and sits down next to me. Mara is also in the cave, but she's hiding in another room, invisible in the shadows with her baby.

"It's a day for weeping," Ziru says. "But we do not have long to mourn."

"She was really nice."

Ziru nods. "Her mother and I were long-time friends. Despite her youth, Cadah was a fine young woman. Much like her mother."

Where does he get his strength? Why isn't he breaking down? He comforts me, when I hardly knew Cadah. He puts a foot forward, but I want to disappear.

"She would have been your daughter in law," Tran's whiny voice echoes through the cave.

Ziru bows his head. "Yes. No one has lost more than my son today."

My heart aches for Ler. The man who saved Karl's life. The man who is out there following Karl as he wanders around the forest trying to cope with what just happened.

"How could Arujan convince people Karl did this?" I ask.

Ziru sighs. "The people expected this to happen the moment they first saw Karu." He sounds accusatory—like this is my fault.

157

Tran decides to join us, but at least he sits on the other side of Ziru. "For Arujan, your arrival was a disaster, fortuitous only because you brought the traitor with you. He's used the people's prejudice to create a rift against you. Seeing Karu sneak around at night was all Arujan needed to get rid of you." There is no mistaking who Tran blames for Cadah's death.

What do they think we should have done with Karl, if not bring him along?

"I should have never come."

"It's not your fault," Ziru puts his strong hand on my shoulder, but I shrug it off. It's my fault. All of this. Karl is probably right; we shouldn't go to Keeper. We need to go home before anything else happens.

"He just wanted to talk to me." The tears come again. "I've been avoiding him. I'm the only connection he has to his world, and I've been avoiding him."

"People who saw him sneaking around, weren't surprised to find someone dead in the morning," Tran says. "What an idiot. No one wanders around at night alone. It's too dangerous."

I don't say anything more. I knew how Karl would feel about me hiding from him, but I avoided him anyway. I planned to leave Watch and go to Keeper without ever telling him.

"What do you think Arujan will do next?" Tran asks Ziru.

"I don't care," Ziru says. "We will move forward. We cannot defeat Arujan, but Lydia will be able to soon. We are living in the days our predecessors dreamed of, the days of the Blue Princess."

I should tell him I need to go home, either now or after Keeper. But I can't bring myself to say it. They're counting on me. I either abandon them, or keep Karl trapped here against his will.

My hand reaches into my tunic, but it doesn't find a phone there. Ever since the accident, I've always had that phone to remember Mom, her voice, and the conversations we had. She has stayed with me, encouraging me and telling me what to do.

But the phone isn't here. I'm alone.

Tran and Ziru keep talking, but I tune them out and hug my knees tighter. I close my eyes and wonder where my phone is now. Is it sitting on the trail to Double Arch? Did someone find it and throw it away?

That night I called Mom, it was my fault that she died, too. When she took her eyes off the road to answer the phone, someone pulled up beside her. By the time she said "hello," she was being pushed into the guard rails and then off the bridge.

When the police found her, she was still clutching the phone, and I was sitting anxiously on the other side, hearing nothing but water lapping against the side of the river bank. She mumbled something about a man with blue eyes and a long, blond ponytail and then she was gone.

If only I hadn't called her. If only my seemingly urgent request could have waited until she got home. I don't even remember what it was. If only I hadn't called.

If only I had talked to Karl.

Ler runs into the cave, breathing hard.

Ziru and Tran jump to their feet. "Where is the traitor?"

Ler shakes his head, his hands on his knees as he catches his breath. "Leopard trap," he manages to say.

A pit forms in my stomach. "Karl's been eaten by a leopard?"

"No."

"Then where is he?"

"He was forced off the mountain," Ler says, still breathing hard. "And captured."

I push myself off the cold ground.

We have to fix this. Ler looks at me, but I don't see anything but pity in his expression. He isn't going to fix this; he expects me to do that. I'm supposed to fix everything.

Everything I touch dies, and yet I'm supposed to be the princess that fixes everything.

Ler clears his voice, but I don't wait to hear what he says. I run past him. Out of the cave. Down the mountain path. The men follow, but I don't wait for them.

I haven't run on my knee like this in months. It hurts with the downhill, but I ignore the pain and push myself harder. I step on a rock and my knee twists and buckles. My hands plunge into pine needles, which pierce my face and palms. I skid to a stop.

My knee hurts. A lot.

The men to catch up seconds later.

"Are you all right?" Ler asks.

I shake my head. I try to push myself up, but my knee can't hold any weight.

"It's not too much further." Ler picks me up and carries me like a little girl. My knee throbs. I've ruined the surgery and the months of recovery, and I'm a world away from a doctor.

And Karl is gone.

Ler carries me like an infant along a trail next to a ridge. But it isn't just any ridge. The entire mountain looks like it has been raised three feet, and the rock face is as smooth as glass.

"What is this place?" The shock of the scenery almost makes me forget about my knee.

"The border," Ziru says. "No one from the valley can cross it."

As Ler follows the trail, I watch Karl's footprints. The stride suddenly gets longer—he was running.

"The leopard saw Karu before he saw it."

"Why was there a leopard here?"

"Wynn uses leopard traps to get people off the mountains. Leopards prey on fuma, but the fuma are agile among the cliffs and generally avoid them. However, if a leopard can force them down the mountain, the fuma loses its ability to maneuver. Wynn uses leopards to force people off the mountain and into his hands. He has captured some people in this way over the years. No one has ever returned."

Ler stops at a small stream. A large leopard lies dead in the water just below the ridge. Blood seeps from knife wounds around its neck, dripping into the water and joining the current into the valley.

"When he saw the leopard, he started to run," Ler says. "I tried to catch up. I was just about to release a knife when Karu slipped and fell off the ridge. Five men took him away. There was nothing I could do."

"Knives don't pass through the border by themselves," Ziru says. He takes one of his own knives and throws it at the leopard. It stops in midair just above the ridge and falls to the dirt. "What you did was right."

"Is there any hope of us going to save him?" I'm cradled in Ler's arms, unable to walk, unable to be a princess.

Ziru shakes his head. "Child, we don't know if he's alive, or how many men are down there. We are safe up here, but not down there. The legends say that you will lead us off the mountain against Wynn. But you must be ready first. We need to go to Keeper."

"But maybe if we got more men?"

"After Arujan's speech this morning, do you think anyone from the village would put their lives at risk for Karu?"

I stare at the leopard, the image burning itself into my memory. First Cadah and now Karl. He's not going home.

I shift positions in Ler's arms and pain shoots up my leg. My knee hurts. A breeze rustles through the trees. It's quiet here, and it should be beautiful. But it's not. Not anymore. I look at the leopard one more time, and then I bury my face in Ler's chest.

* * *

Tran looks up from skinning the fuma when we get back to camp. He's butchering the animal for its meat and skin, which has taken him almost all day.

"What happened to Lydia?"

"She hurt her knee," Ler says.

"Can she walk?" Tran is upset. For once, I don't blame him.

Ler shakes his head.

"She can't even walk? How will we get to Keeper like this? What are they going to say when they see her?"

"I don't care," Ziru says. "We either go back and die fighting Arujan, or we go to Keeper."

Tran mumbles something I don't hear, but Ler ignores him and carries me into the cave.

"We'll have you women sleep in here." Ler puts me down gently across the cavern from Mara and Jarra. "We'll sleep outside. Arujan probably won't look for us, but we shouldn't be too certain."

He turns to go, but I don't let him leave. "Do you think I'm the blue princess?" I ask.

"Yes." He's so confident—even when everything he loves is falling apart around him. It doesn't make sense.

"Why can't I do anything the legends said I would do?"

Ler's response is unexpected. He laughs. "How did you get here?"

"Through the portal."

"Just as the legends say. We're going to Keeper and you'll learn the secrets of the mountain. You will defeat Wynn. You're the princess we have been waiting for."

I watch him walk away. I try to believe him.

At least he doesn't hate me. I saw lots of people who hate me today. Karl, the crowd, Arujan, Tran.

Me.

* * *

I don't sleep well, but finally the first morning light sneaks into the cave. My entire body aches, and I can't move my left leg at all.

I try to push myself up, but only end up crying out from the pain before I can stop myself. I bite my bottom lip, hoping I didn't wake the baby.

"Are you hurt, Lydia?" Mara's voice is barely audible. She crawls over to sit next to me. Jarra must still be asleep.

"Yeah. I hurt my knee yesterday when I ran down the mountain."

The pain subsides a little and I manage to push myself into a sitting position against the edge of the cave. Neither Mara nor I are ready for a 100-mile journey.

"You walked with a limp before."

"Yeah, I reinjured my knee running after Karl."

"How did it happen the first time?"

"It was during a game." Describing soccer to Mara doesn't seem worth the effort right now. "There was an accident."

I don't tell her it might have been on purpose.

"How did you survive with a hurt leg? I've never heard of a village leader who would support an injured woman."

"Things are different where I come from. No one is sent away just because of an injury. People treat life as a sacred thing."

"How strange," she mutters. "Society is the sacred thing in the valley. Is it true you're an Azurean?"

"I don't know. I'm not even sure what that is."

"Someone like Wynn."

As if that tells me anything. I thought Wynn was bad, too. We sit in silence for a moment.

"Mara, do you mind if I ask how you got here? The others said no one from the valley can get into the mountains."

"It's because of Jarra's father, Anu. I met him when I was small. We would meet and play in secret in the forest. When I was older, he moved off the mountains to be with me. He had to stay in hiding because he would have been killed otherwise."

"Why?"

"Valley people hate mountain people. At least Wynn does. When I was pregnant, they found Anu and killed him. I hoped they wouldn't harm the baby, but just days before Jarra was born, the man in magenta arrived in town.

"I tried to get away, but then I went into labor. As soon as Jarra was born, I heard a commotion at the front door. I was still in pain from the delivery, but I had to act, or I would lose Jarra. I grabbed him from the midwife's hands and ran. Without traveling papers, I couldn't go to anywhere else in the valley. My only hope was to hide in the forest."

"How do you know he came for the baby?"

"There was no other reason for him to be there. And he chased me. Since I know the forest so well, I thought I could find a place to hide. But the man in magenta was too quick for me."

"You'd just had a baby!" The look in Mara's eyes tells me her story is not exaggerated. I'm not sure who the man in magenta is, but he doesn't sound like someone I want to meet.

"I was close to the mountain border without anywhere else to go. That was when I remembered an old tale Anu found shortly before he was killed. It said that someone from outside the mountains could cross the barrier if they stood on someone from the mountains. If they were not forced, that is. We had planned to try it after the baby was born, back before Anu was killed.

"I ran the last few steps to the border and put Jarra on the ground. I stepped on his screaming little body, and the barrier to the mountain disappeared. I'd been at the border hundreds of times, and the barrier kept me out every time. That night, standing on Jarra, it let me and Jarra in, just as the tale from Anu said it might. The man in magenta was stuck outside. He yelled and slammed his ax on the invisible wall. I left him there and wandered to the village. That's where you found me."

162

And saved her life. Again.

"I wish I knew how to help you," Mara says quietly.

"You need to take care of yourself," I say. "But we can help each other. I'm not sure if the mountain is a safer place than the valley."

"I think it is," Mara says. "I've never seen people worked up about a beaten woman before. Did you see how many people gathered? And how they were all angry at Karu?"

"It wasn't Karu who did it."

"Well, in the valley it wouldn't matter who did it."

I shudder. "Is it true that Wynn has been alive for hundreds of years?"

Mara shrugs. "I think so."

"You've never seen him?"

"No. I've just seen the Man of Wynn, the one who wears magenta. He comes to our town to talk to the town authority, who is my father."

"What is a Man of Wynn?"

"The most powerful men in the world. Well, except for Wynn. My dad is powerful when the Man of Wynn is away, but he has to do things the man in magenta would like."

"What is the man in magenta's name?"

"We don't call the Men of Wynn by their names—only by their color."

"Oh."

"It's the only thing I've ever known," Mara says. "I didn't know that things could be different."

That is a pleasant thought—things being different. I think back to my last Thanksgiving with Mom. We stayed at home that year. Dessert was lemon meringue pie. Everything was perfect: the sweet aromas, Mom's laughter, the security of my home.

I hadn't known things could be different.

But they are. When I came through the portal, I felt like I belonged here. Do I still feel that way? Cadah is dead, and Mara's story doesn't give me a lot of hope for Karl.

Mara and I sit in silence, holding hands. Taking solace in each other's company. It's another few hours before the men wake up. Ler and Tran strap the new fuma skin to their shoulders and Ziru puts me on it. It makes a hammock, and I'm going to lie in it all the way to Keeper.

I feel every bump and twist as a stab of pain in my leg as the cave disappears. I grit my teeth and close my eyes. 100 miles to Keeper.

28 Recovery

Karl

I groan in pain as the cart hits yet another bump in the road. I've whacked my head so many times, and still each new bump manages to hurt. It won't be long before I sustain a brain injury and lose my ability to think.

Not that it matters. No one cares how well your brain works when you're dead. You spend an entire lifetime storing memories and facts and experiences inside that brain. Then, in a matter of seconds all of it is gone. You can't upload the memories to another system, you can't share them with anyone else. All that work. All that memory. Gone.

That is about to be me. Eaten by the strange bacteria who live in this strange place. My body will puff up as my cells are ingested, and then I'll be thin again. Skin and bones. And then, bones.

It's probably just as well. My brain hasn't gotten me anywhere. I thought I was going to become a famous scientist. I even had a paper with Tara that could have been good, if it hadn't all beeen a fraud. Instead, it led me here. Eight years of post-secondary education and I'm naked, nailed into a box inside a horse-drawn cart that's bumping down a road.

My body aches and I'm so hungry that I've stopped craving food. My lips are cracked and my mouth is dry. It's hot in the evenings, cool during the day, and I'm so delirious I don't know how many days I've been here.

The cart hits another rock, and my head bounces against the hard wood. Again.

Pain. More pain. It has to end soon. The human body can only take so much before it stops fighting.

It's strange, the little things that affect our lives. Evolution makes sense when you think of it as a whole. The strongest and smartest survive. The weak are preyed upon. But that big picture isn't important for the individuals.

An aleatory meeting with a soccer girl led me to a world with a recondite culture and language. Despite all my work, I left behind nothing but a sullied reputation due to another chance meeting—with a girl from England. Then I was chased by a snow leopard in the middle of the summer to be captured by a bunch of crazy men.

Random. Parsimony doesn't explain it. I didn't achieve scientific greatness. I didn't live up to Mom's expectations.

No, while life was pushing me around, I spent my life pushing people away. I hated Andrea for years. Did she betray me, or did I abandon her in her moment of need? What would have happened if I had run after her?

I didn't call Pearl back. Was she too pushy, or did I just keep her distant?

I even shoved Tara out of my life at the first chance.

Dad always told me that a life full of people is a life worth living.

Now, dying in a cart in the middle of nowhere, I decide he was right. More than anything, I want to let Pearl know where I am. I want to visit Dad and tell him I'm sorry.

I try to shift my body, but it doesn't move. It hasn't moved in days. My left leg is probably broken. I probably have a few cracked ribs.

My eyes close. I try to stop thinking. Death. Will it take away the pain?

The cart hits another rock and my head bounces up. Everything goes black.

* * *

I wake up with a stab of pain. My body is covered in sweat. The cart is stopped. I groan. Consciousness brings pain. I close my eyes and wish I was still unconscious.

People start banging on the box, which doesn't help me feel any better.

Light streams into the box, blinding me. In my mind, I hear a flight attendant announcing, "You have reached your final destination." Flying. I flew in an airplane. I soared high above oceans, traveled across continents. It was fun to fly. Lots of life was good.

The board cracks as they rip the box open.

Two men yank me out of the cart by my shoulders. I scream as my body straightens for the first time in days. Then men try to get me to stand, but I can't put any pressure on my legs and so they drag me across a bridge. Toward a castle.

I'm pretty sure my shoulder is dislocated.

A castle? I can barely get my eyes open.

I squint. It's a castle, like you might see in Europe. Behind it, I see mountains in the distance, barely visible against the horizon.

The men slow as they approach a large iron gate. Two short men step out and open the doors, bowing slightly as the men drag me past them. We go up a short staircase and into a large room with a high ceiling and open windows.

The men loosen their grip, and I drop onto the floor.

This is it. My last moment. I think of Mom, and tears trickle down my face. Will I be with her today?

I don't move. Every breath hurts, slow and raspy. It feels good to breathe, despite the pain. Living. It's a miracle to be alive. I take another breath.

Footsteps echo in the room. Approach. Stop. Silence.

Breathe in and out.

Yelling.

I force myself to look up, and the pain from the movement nearly makes me pass out. A man with long, greasy hair is standing next to me. He wears a long black robe with a black sash tied around the middle, which sways as he yells at a man across the room, also in a black robe with a yellow sash.

I've seen the man with the yellow sash before—he was the primary interrogator in the mountains after my capture.

The yells rebound around the room as another man enters. This man also wears black. He has an orange sash. He crosses the room, stops in front of the man with the black sash, and bows. His right knee touches the ground; his head touches his left knee.

The man in orange has glowing blue eyes. Is that how my eyes look in this strange place? I don't like it. I lower my head, overcome by pain.

Hands grip my shoulders and push me into a sitting position. I cry out, but the man in black speaks to me quietly, urgently, ignoring my cries. I stare back into his dark eyes. If only there was a way to turn off a few pain neurons.

The man shakes me, speaking rapidly. "I don't know what you're saying, you stupid idiot," I croak. "Let me lie back down or kill me quickly."

My words evoke a smile. I don't smile back.

The man in black lowers me gently to the floor. Maybe it's finally time. I close my eyes and picture Mom standing next to me. I wait. When I was 10, I caught the flu really bad, and Mom spent hours next to my bed talking to me and comforting me while I was sick. Mom is here. She will take care of me.

My heart beats faster, and I try to swallow my fear. Cold, clammy hands touch my forehead. I don't move. I won't fight death. There is no reason to struggle against the inevitable.

I don't move a muscle, waiting. Feeling as long as I can feel. Focusing on each breath. There is no sound around me. I breathe in, and out.

My leg doesn't hurt as much. Weird. No, my leg doesn't hurt at all. Maybe the broken bone finally severed the nerve. But no, I feel like I can move it. I do, and it doesn't hurt. My leg feels whole.

Impossible.

I keep my eyes closed and continue breathing. Pain starts to dissipate from the rest of my body. My head clears and my shoulder stops aching.

The man with the greasy hair sits next to me, his eyes closed as he sits like Siddhartha finding nirvana. The other two men watch, unmoving.

With each second that passes, I feel strangely stronger. Cuts mend, bruises fade, cracks in my lips seal. I sit up.

Who is this man? Did he give me some kind of drug? Am I hallucinating?

I must be despite the fact that my head seems clear. The man's long, glossy hair hangs over his face, hiding a small nose and dark eyes. If I didn't know better, I'd say his facial features look similar to Lydia's. I must be dreaming. I'm making this all up. Maybe this is what it feels like to be dead.

I take another deep breath, letting the air fill my lungs. Strong, healthy lungs. Wheezes gone.

What kind of illusion is this?

Black eyes suddenly meet mine. The man nods, his face expressionless. He touches his left breast with his right hand. "Wynn," he says.

"Karl," I say, repeating the gesture.

Wynn smiles and stands to speak to the other two men. They haven't moved for a long time. "Karu," he says to them, and they both bow their heads. Wynn starts to speak, his nasal voice loud again, the strange sounds echoing around the large room.

The walls of the room are made of the same stone as the cool floor. There are no decorations; the only light is provided by a few high windows, which are ten feet off the ground. The ceiling must be at least 25 or 30 feet tall. Wynn's voice fills all of it.

He goes to the man with the yellow sash, who has paled considerably. Wynn stops talking as he approaches, and the man with the yellow sash fills the void, speaking rapidly and waving his arms. Wynn reaches down and brushes the stones with his fingers before he gets to the man.

The man in yellow tries to back away, but he has nowhere to go except into the wall. Wynn reaches out his hand and merely touches him. But the touch is the touch of death. The man screams and drops to the floor. He writhes in pain, and he screams. It can't be more than a couple minutes, but it feels like forever. Finally, the room goes silent.

This must be a hallucination. I taste bile and my eyes swim. Is this man me, just meeting the finality of death? Am I outside my body, looking on?

Wynn unties the sash and pulls the robe from the corpse, leaving it naked in the corner of the room as he walks back to me. The man in orange stands next to me. The breeze blows his robes so they hit my naked body. I must still be alive if I can feel that. I take a step away and I can't feel the robes anymore. Wynn stops in front of me.

He speaks softly and the man in orange reaches out his hand and takes the robe from him, turning to me.

I would rather stand naked in front of these men, rolls of fat and all, than to wear that dead man's clothes, but I have no choice. The man in orange forces the robe over my shoulders. I shudder as it comes around me, barely fitting my overweight figure. The robe is moist from the dead man's sweat and smells like urine.

Wynn puts a thin hand on my shoulder and studies my expression. Then he takes the man in orange's arm and puts it around my shoulder.

"Buen," he says. He points at me, "Karu," and then at the other man, "Buen."

And with that, he walks out of the room.

I'm alive.

Moments ago, all my senses screamed, and I was on the brink of death. Now, I'm healed and whole. It's impossible, but it's what my brain says is true.

Buen says nothing as he leads me out of the great room into a dimly-lit stone corridor. Not that there is anything he could say that I would understand.

Buen has a scar on his clean-shaven face. He walks with a limp. I think he's older than me, but I don't think by much. His body is in much better shape than mine. Tanned skin, sculpted muscles. He could be on the front page of a magazine, except for the scar. Nothing Photoshop couldn't fix.

My stomach roars, and Buen smiles as the sound echoes down the hall. He says something I don't understand.

At the end of the corridor is another large room. This room is similarly tall and barren of decorations; it has a large table in the center of the room. Buen whistles, and a bald man comes out of a back room. This man has a prominent scar on his cheekbone and wears nothing but a blue wrap around his waist. Buen speaks to him and the man leaves.

Buen walks over to the table and sits down, motioning for me to follow suit.

Buen looks at me, and I avert my eyes. It's disconcerting, how his eyes glow. Can I trust him? I don't understand why I'm alive. I don't know why the other man died.

We sit in silence. Eventually five men enter the room. Each has an identical shorn head and blue waist wrap. They each carry one platter of food and set it on the table. They bow and retreat out of the room. Buen gives no indication that he even sees them enter the room.

This food smells good—not at all like the garbage they expected me to eat in the mountains. But Buen doesn't move, and so I don't either. Is this a test? Will I kill over dead if I eat this sweet-smelling poison?

Buen sits still until all the men in blue have left the room. Then he smiles and says something as he fills two glasses with reddish juice. He picks up one glass and motions for me to do the same. This is my new role: mimesis.

"Piunt Wynn," Buen says, bowing his face reverently toward the drink and the food.

I repeat the words, but he shakes his head. "Piunt Wynn," he says again.

It takes another five tries before he's satisfied with the awkward words that come out of my mouth.

We drink. The cool liquid fills my dry mouth. It's sweet, but also tart, unlike anything I've tasted before. I drink most of it, and then, after checking to make sure that Buen has already done so, dig into the food.

It's a feast. Roasted bird, prepared with unique, expensive-tasting spices. A variety of vegetables, and six different kinds of breads.

The meal highlights the pitiful existence of the mountain people. This world isn't a world with only bland food and hard labor. This world has luxury.

I'm full too quickly. Buen whistles and several men in blue wraps enter the room and clear the food away. We walk out of the room.

I'm clothed, fed, and not in pain. I feel good, though I still smell like urine from the robe. But I'm alive. And healthy. Years of scientific research hasn't prepared me for this moment. I can't explain what just happened to me. First the portal, and now this. There must be some kind of explanation, but I don't know what it is.

We leave the dining hall and the main castle tower. Our exit leads us onto an uncovered causeway where the sun beats down on us. The breeze cools the sweat on my skin in the places where the robe doesn't fit too tightly, which isn't very many places.

The walkway is made of stone with three-foot walls on each side. Over one wall is a twenty-foot drop down to a moat, which surrounds the castle.

An open garden is below us to my right. The garden is surrounded by three castle walls and three towers. Long stone paths lead through an assortment of plants, some of which I recognize from my recent meal. Most of them, however, are foreign to me. I don't see any plants from the mountains. People in the garden care for the plants, all of them with the same shaved head, scar, and blue wrap.

The tower we are leaving now is by far the largest. The others are smaller, but taller. It's a long walk between towers—this place is huge. A fortress out of the middle ages. Stone walls, open windows, servants, and gardens.

As we approach the second tower entrance, Buen points to the third tower and says, "Wynn." He makes a few hand gestures. I'm not to go anywhere near Wynn's tower.

That means that I'm probably going to be staying here. How long will I be here? Am I a prisoner?

I will have to learn the language. But it's up to me now. I have a fresh start, and I'm going to make the best of it.

We enter the second tower and Buen leads the way up a winding staircase. After four flights of stairs, we enter a long hallway lined with large wooden doors. Each door has writing etched into it.

At the end of the hallway, Buen points to the writing on the door. "K-a-r-u" he reads, pointing at four symbols that have been carefully carved into the door. Seriously? They already have my name etched into this door with such ornate workmanship?

Buen raps on the door. A girl answers and bows like Buen did to Wynn. Buen gestures for me to raise my hand. I mimic the motion, and the girl steps quietly to

169

the side and we walk into the room. She wears the same blue wrap the men servants wear, but she has hair—her black hair is long in a braid down her back—and she wears a loose-fitting tank top that covers her down to her midriff. She's small and slender, probably about 18. She doesn't meet my eyes as I enter the room.

Like everything else in the castle, this room is huge. A large bed stands in one corner, a shower and bath area on the opposite wall. A wardrobe is dwarfed against the far wall.

Buen speaks to the girl, motioning to me. Our eyes meet for a moment, and then her eyes return to the floor. When Buen stops talking, she bows and walks over to the wardrobe. It's full of black robes, identical to the ones Buen and I wear.

She takes one of the robes off its hanger and sets it gently on a chair next to the wardrobe before she returns to where I'm standing. Buen wanders to the window across the room. I move to follow him, but he shakes his head and I return to the center of the room.

The girl steps up to me and grabs my robe. I step back and put up my hands. "Hey!" I say. "What are you doing?"

The girl jumps and steps back, averting her eyes. She says something quietly, and Buen walks back over. He glares at me and motions towards the girl. It doesn't look like I have a choice here. Besides, I'm sick of this robe that smells of someone else's sweat and urine. This time I let the girl strip it off. She has to pull hard to get it away from my fat body. Talk about an awkward first meeting.

Naked now, the wind from the breeze through the room cools my skin. It should feel nice, but I'm too self-conscious to enjoy it. I stand in the middle of the room, unsure what to do as the girl puts the dirty robe away and retrieves the new robe she selected earlier. Even though I've been naked for the better part of the past week, I feel more self-conscious now.

When the girl turns around, she seems surprised to see me watching her. She motions to the bathing area of the room. I walk over, but I have no idea what to do. Everything is made of smooth stone, there is a hole in the wall and in the floor. I look back at the girl stupidly.

Her eyes go to the floor and she speaks quietly. Buen laughs and says something in return. She walks across the room and pulls a rope next to the hole in the wall. A stream of cool water comes out of the wall and hits my bare skin. I gasp as the water hits me, but it's refreshing.

The girl hands me something that turns out to be soap, and I bathe. Even though I'm bathing in the open in front of these two people, I almost enjoy it. It gives me a chance to marvel at the change in my body. It was so bruised and broken, but now my skin is new and soft. All traces of my suffering are gone.

When I finish, the girl hands me a towel and helps me put on the new black robe. This one is just as tight around my middle, but I'm glad to be clothed again.

Buen leaves his spot at the window and gives me a once-over. He nods his approval and then walks around the room, pointing at everything as if explaining what each thing is. There is something that could be a toilet, the large bed, the washing area, and some kind of adjacent room in a corner.

Done with the tour, Buen speaks to the girl, and she bows and retreats into an adjacent room. There isn't a door on it, and it isn't lighted. Then Buen leaves, and I'm alone.

Is he coming back? Is the girl still here, or does the that door lead out of the room? Is there something that I'm supposed to be doing?

I look out the window. It's about 80 feet down to the moat. The breeze rustles through the robe and cools my skin. That feels good.

I check out the adjacent room and find the girl sitting on a small mat. This isn't a room: it's more like a closet with nothing in it. She meets my eyes from the shadow of the room, and I blush and hurry away.

Since I have no idea what I'm supposed to be doing, I lie down on the bed and stare at the ceiling. Most of the castle walls and ceilings are bare stone, but I've noticed an etched pattern on at least one stone in every room I've entered. This room is no different. Above my bed is the same design, carved into one of the stones at the top of the wall. The etching isn't into the rock, however, which has been plated with copper. From here, I can make out the design enough to guess that it might be a man in a robe. His back is turned and fog surrounds him.

I don't study the design for more than a few minutes before my eyes get heavy.

Earlier today, I thought I would die. Now, I'm lying on a clean bed in a castle with clean clothes. I don't know what's going to happen next, or how long my life is going to be, but it's time for me to change. It's time for me to be better. It's time for me to think about others.

29 Redirection

Lydia

"Let's stop here," Ziru calls back. Tran and Ler find a large rock and place me on it. They put the hammock carrier I have grown to hate next to me. I give it a little shove, and it falls off the rock and into the dirt as the men leave.

"Thank you!" I call after them, straightening my sore body and trying to ignore the pain in my swollen leg. I hope I didn't offend them by pushing the carrier into the dirt. I'm grateful, though it has been a long five days, grinding my teeth in pain, mile after mile. The trail followed the border between the mountain and valley until this morning when it turned up a steep canyon. I'm hoping we'll find Keeper just up this trail.

Left alone in the quiet, I look around for Mara but don't see her. Scrub oak surrounds me. Now that we've turned up the canyon, it won't be far before the forest turns back into pine. Mountains tower in the distance. This canyon ascends a long way.

A breeze combs through my hair. I close my eyes and breathe in the fresh mountain air. I do love mountains. It's hard to remember that while swinging around in pain. It's just as beautiful here as it was at Mount Rainier.

I wish Brit was here. I hope she's doing okay now. I hope that the team ended up winning the PAC-12.

After a few minutes, the men return with some esculent plants. I take what is given me and gnaw on one of the roots.

"Are we getting close to Keeper?"

"Keeper is over this hill," Tran's voice is just as annoyed as always.

I'm surprised. We have an hour or so of daylight left, and if we are so close, why did we stop here? Surely the village has better food than this.

Tran laughs. "Our beet-red cripple thinks we stopped too soon."

I blush, but no one can tell since my fair skin has burned bright red in the thin mountain air. I can see it on my arms, and I can feel it on my face. Add my unruly hair to it, and I'm sure I'm quite the spectacle.

"Tran," Ziru says, and his voice is sharp. "We found the Blue Princess, and we have done our duty to bring her to Keeper. There are those here who will do the same, no matter what Arujan did when he was here."

"That's easy for you to say. You haven't carried her for the past five days. I don't think these people will believe this girl is the princess."

Tran can't be much older than me, and yet he calls me girl like I'm a three-year-old child. Yet, he carried me here, which makes me beholden to him. That makes me like him even less.

"Even if they're all on Arujan's side," Ler says, "their jail cells have to be warmer than sleeping out under the stars!" He laughs at his joke, although no one else joins in. Perhaps we are all are tired of shivering all night in the cold mountain air.

Tran glares at me when I toss the rest of the root into a bush.

I don't return his glare. His words echo my own thoughts. I look awful, and I have also wondered if anyone outside this small circle will accept me as a princess. Cadah told me all sorts of legends, but what happens when I don't live up to the hoopla? In this violent, desperate world, I feel like a fungible commodity, a hero ready to be swapped out for something more promising as soon as it presents itself.

We all jump at the sound of rustling in the trees.

"Ler! Is that you?" a high-pitched voice shrieks.

Ler stands just in time to embrace a young woman with long blonde hair. She laughs and holds him tightly. Although Ler doesn't show the same enthusiasm, he does hug her back.

"Hello Sharue," he says.

"I had no idea you were coming," she says, finally stepping back and pulling hair out of her face. She's an attractive woman, with features not too different from mine. The main difference is her straight, beautiful hair and her still-white skin. I stay still, hoping I will blend into the rock.

Ler doesn't respond, and Sharue's eyes dart around like a gnat, taking us all in.

Another girl comes down the path and stops at the edge of the clearing. She hides in the shadows, like Mara, wherever she is.

"We brought the Blue Princess with us."

Sharue's mouth falls open. "The Blue Princess! She shows up now? You can't possibly be serious." Her gnat-like eyes find me, and her face gets dark. "You think she's one of these two girls? The frizzled red-face cripple or the woman hiding in the bushes?"

How does she know I'm a cripple? I want to crawl under the rock I'm sitting on.

"She has the mark of the blue flower," Ziru says, standing up next to his son. His presence, though commanding, doesn't faze Sharue in the same way I've seen it faze so many others. She laughs and gives him a hug. The other girl stares at me. I shift uncomfortably on my rock and wish she would look somewhere else.

"What is the mark of the blue flower?"

If these people don't know about the mark of the blue flower, I have no reason to be here. Did Ziru make it all up?

"Show her the mark," Tran says impatiently.

I pull down my shirt hesitantly.

Sharue barely glances at me before laughing again. "Anyone can walk around with a strange mark. It seems like you've been deceived."

"She came through the portal; she has the mark. We have done as tradition demands and brought her here," Ziru says. His voice doesn't reveal any of the panic I'm feeling.

Sharue walks slowly to where I'm sitting, smiling in a way that makes me feel like I really am the little girl Tran thinks I am. "If she is a princess," she says in a voice one would use to talk to a young child, "then she must have blue blood."

I meet Sharue's cold eyes. "I have the mark, but I have red blood like everyone else."

"Then you admit to lying to these people?" Her expression is not friendly.

"I never lied to them," I say softly. "I came through the portal and they asked to see my mark."

Sharue takes my hand, her strong fingers closing tight around my wrist. She pulls a knife out of her pouch with her other hand. I try to move away, but I stop when my leg hurts.

"Then you won't mind showing me your red blood." She rests the blade across my palm.

"Dearest Ler," she says, her eyes locked into mine. "Don't your traditions tell you that the Blue Princess must have blue blood? It isn't a hard thing to check."

Ler doesn't stop her. I sit still, watching the dagger as it slices through the first layer of skin on my hand.

When my blood comes out red, will Sharue place the dagger in my heart? I've seen a lot of death these last few days—Cadah and Karl. This entire trip has been a disaster. Is this how it ends?

Sharue laughs again and puts more pressure on the blade. The next layer of skin splits and I cry out with the shock of the pain. Blood comes out of my hand. It seeps onto the knife blade and trickles down my palm.

At least I think it's blood. The liquid coming out of my hand is blue. A dark royal blue. The blood traces my palm and runs down my arm. Mara suddenly appears and pushes Sharue away from me. She wraps a white cloth around my hand. It's almost immediately dyed blue.

"You didn't have to cut her so deeply," Mara says softly, but she's ignored by everyone. I smile at her, but she doesn't smile back.

"Well Sharue," Ziru puts his arm around her shoulders. "That was the bluest blood I've ever seen."

My hand hurts.

"We'll take her to the chamber." Sharue's smirk is gone, and she's all business. "We can get you settled after that. You're planning to be here a while, right?"

I start at the idea of staying a few days before I realize I don't have to hurry back for Karl. Karl is dead. Probably. As anxious as I am to find out what is waiting for me in Keeper, I don't have any pressing reason to hurry. Aside from finding a doctor to save my leg so I can walk again.

Ler and Tran put me in the hammock carrier. I steady myself with my hand, which hurts, and try to balance my leg, which hurts. Every step of this journey leaves me more incapacitated.

After another long walk, the trail ends at the base of a steep cliff. Rugged rocks jut out of the ground and go up hundreds of feet, creating a solid wall of dark brown stone. Strong gusts of wind stir up piles of leaves next to the cliff, which fly around us.

Sharue pokes around in the piles of leaves until she uncovers a rock that protrudes about two feet from the ground.

"This is the portal." She motions for Ler and Tran, and they set me on the ground next to the rock.

I look around uncertainly. The men step back to stand next to Ziru. There aren't any trees for Mara here, and so she stands huddled next to the cliff, not quite blending in and clutching Jarra against her bosom.

I'm not the only one who wishes she were somewhere else.

Who am I fooling? I'm not a princess! I can't help these people. What I need is to go home and find a doctor. And a mental health professional to help me work through Karl and Cadah's deaths.

The hot sun beats down and makes me sweat, but the cool wind makes me shiver. I turn my attention away from my doubts to the small rock that is already collecting leaves again. It has a flat side, tilting away from the trail. A print of a hand is carved somehow into the middle of the rock.

A left hand. Maybe that is why Sharue cut my right hand.

I try to ignore the people watching me and run my fingers along the edges of the stone. I place my hand over the print. A flash of blue light bursts out of the rock, and I try to pull it back.

But I can no longer move my hand. Although nothing looks different, my hand is stuck, held on by some powerful force. The ground shifts. Then it dissolves. My legs drop beneath me, and in a matter of seconds I'm hanging by my arm, which is still

175

attached to the stone. And in that moment, my hand jerks free, and I drop into the hole.

I fall three feet before I hit a smooth surface and I slide on my backside down a long winding tunnel. Moments later, I come to a stop in a pile of dirt. I curl into a crumpled ball and moan. I hear rocks above me, and soon I can no longer see sunlight.

Eventually, my head clears enough for me to look around. I'm in a dim candle-lit chamber. It's shaped in a perfect circle, with a flat roof and a dirt floor. The walls and ceiling—made of smooth marble—reflect the light of five candles. The chamber is completely empty, with no hint of how there are burning candles down here at all.

There is no way I can get back up that slide—it looks like I'm stuck in here.

A small man appears out of nowhere on the far side of the room. He's short, bent over, and has bright white hair. He holds himself up with a cane, and in the dim light he looks transparent.

"Hello," he says in a soft voice that echoes around the chamber. "Is that you, Wynn?" He beckons to me, and when no other options present themselves, I crawl toward him.

"I cannot kill you here, Wynn, but I will not help you either."

"I'm not Wynn," I say.

"You are not Wynn," he repeats.

"No," I say. As I get closer the man looks more like a hologram, an illusion. I don't know how he can have any idea who I am.

The man frowns, his eyes looking at where my face would be if I were standing up. "You're here, which means something has gone wrong. Has Wynn killed Togan? Are you here to be trained?"

I'm not sure how to respond, and so I say nothing. The man nods after a moment. This man is a hologram, a memory. He can't see me, which is probably a good thing.

"This is only your first stop," he says, "on a journey of knowledge. Everything you need to know is in these mountains, protected by magic. Only a true descendant of Togan, like yourself, can access it."

My heart quickens at the mention of my descent, but I don't let my hopes get too high. After all, how could I be descended from Togan? Did he have a mistress in America like Kinni? That doesn't explain the blue light and my appearance in Seattle. Togan lived hundreds of years ago—he isn't the key to finding out who my parents are.

"Knowledge is hidden in chambers located in these mountains," the man continues, and I try to concentrate. "It's no easy journey to get to each of them. But once you do, you will know everything you need to know to take on Wynn."

I don't say anything. I don't want to take on Wynn right now. If I could walk again, I'd be happy.

The man nods. "Today, let me start by telling you a story." He motions for me to sit, but I stay lying in the dirt.

My name is Cylus. When I was young, this world was different than it is today, the day that I make this memory. There were many groups vying for power, and the whole world was in a constant state of turmoil. I lived in a town near these mountain borders. Our town was small, and so we avoided most of the conflict.

We lived an agrarian lifestyle and survived from day to day. My father never owned land, and so he worked as an agricultural hand for many of my growing years, until drought forced him to find new work. He began as a carrier, taking goods to nearby settlements to trade.

The new work allowed my father to provide for my mother and I better than he had before, but wealth did not translate to happiness. It was soon rumored that my father had a mistress in every city, and relations between my parents became tense. I dreaded the days my father was home, when the mother I loved would tremble and submit to beatings from my father.

When I turned 11, I was old enough to accompany my father. To a young boy, such as I was, the journeys were fantastic. Each new place we visited was so different than the small town I had known all my life. Many lands were frequented by war, but the people rebuilt their lives after each sweep of destruction.

My father felt no obligation to hide his adulterous behavior from me, though he often sent me on various delivery errands while he seduced women across the countryside. It was not a safe time for a young boy to be driving a cart alone, but my father didn't care.

One day, father sent me away on a particularly long errand. I had a cart full of goods, mostly vegetables, and I was to take them to a settlement about four miles away. It was already late in the afternoon, and so my father expected me to figure out shelter for the night and return the following day.

I had never been on the trail before, but it was supposed to be a direct route, and the pony was fresh. The trail came near these mountains, which were said to be completely uninhabited.

As I approached the midpoint of my journey, I was attacked by a leopard. The animal overturned my cart and killed my pony. In my attempt to defend my property, I was mortally wounded.

I watched the leopard eat my pony as I sat bleeding out the last moments of my life. I cried then, for the hard life I had lived and for the way I was going to die. I wondered if my mother would ever know what had happened to me.

In that moment of despair, a man emerged from the bushes and the leopard ran away. The man had graying hair and a kind look. He bent down and rubbed dirt between his hands.

"Stranger," he said, "what are you doing here?"

"I was to deliver this produce to the next village," I stammered.

The man did not hurry but walked slowly to me. His hands touched my shoulders, and the pain subsided. In a matter of moments, I was miraculously healed.

"You're not of age to be traveling this road alone," the man said.

"How did you heal me?"

The man's smile faded. "You must never tell anyone what you saw today, do you understand?"

"My produce is lost. What will I tell my father?"

"You will tell your father the truth about the leopard, but not about you."

"He will beat me," I said, "and I will die anyway for not fighting and dying along with the pony."

At my words the man looked concerned, and I knew he regretted his decision to save my life.

"Do you want to return to your father?"

I shook my head. "I have no choice. My family is poor, and I have no skills for an apprenticeship."

"You have a choice now," he said. "You must never tell anyone what happened here. I will free you from your father."

The man found and killed a rabbit. Again, he rubbed his hands in the dirt, and he made the rabbit's body look like my own, but mutilated, as it had been. He put the body near the cart, and gave me a name and supplies.

"You must go and avoid all contact with your father," the man said. "He will think you died here, and he will not bother you again. There are apprenticeships in the cities, even for young boys like you. Go, and never mention the hemazury you saw here today."

I had no choice but to do what the man asked. I traveled alone for days until I arrived in the cities. I found work with the man's friend, and I learned how to provide for myself.

The work was hard, but I was happy. I learned several trades, as I could never stick with any one thing too long, and the next several years passed quickly.

Cylus stops and laughs. "I'm getting carried away," he says. "You're in the middle of a war and have limited time for an old man's stories. You're here, which means that you have blue blood. It also means that something has happened to Togan. Perhaps he has been killed, and I have died. That means that many of the secrets about hemazury have been killed as well."

178

I shift in the dirt. I have no idea what the old man is talking about.

"I will help you with most of hemazury's secrets. There are three more of these caverns throughout the mountains. Do you know about the pine trees that stand in a perfect circle? They're up the trail in this canyon. That is where you will go next.

"But," he says, shaking his finger, "the secret that Wynn would do anything to know has died with Togan. I'm sorry, but I will not reveal that secret to you."

Okay. So there is some secret that he isn't going to tell me. Is there anything that he *is* going to tell me? He's told me that there is magic in this world, but that hardly seems helpful. How am I going to make it to these pine trees if I can't walk?

"Do you have any injuries?" Cylus asks. "I'm sure that you have something minor? I'll teach you some hemazury, but be wary and use it carefully at first."

Something minor? I'm sure I have some minor injury, but I can't find it with all the major injuries that I have.

"The dirt has power in it," he says. "Take a little of it, rub it between your hands, and feel it. You will need to concentrate, to feel the dirt, become the dirt, and then you will tell it what to do."

Feel the dirt?

Cylus disappears.

Feel the dirt. That's what he had to tell me.

There is no one else here, and there's no getting out. I might as well do what he said—it can't make things worse than they are.

In the story, the man healed a boy who was mortally wounded. That isn't me yet. Is there any way I could do something like that? My hands are covered in dirt. I rub my hands. The dirt gets into the cut from Sharue and smarts like crazy.

It feels like dirt. Nothing happens.

What does he mean, to feel the dirt? It doesn't make any sense.

I get a new handful of dirt. I rub my hands together, and again the dirt smarts around my cut.

I close my eyes and concentrate. Feel the dirt? What am I feeling?

There it is. It's slight, but when I think about the dirt, I feel like I did when I first entered this world. I focus on the feeling; I imagine what the dirt might feel like between my sweaty palms.

The feeling grows stronger, and the room around me fades until I'm no longer aware of it. All that exists is the dirt in my hands.

And I feel like I'm the dirt.

The dirt doesn't have many thoughts. I don't see light or hear, but I feel. I feel concerned. Something is wrong. My hand is cut.

And then I understand. I can see the broken arteries, the veins and detached cells. I can feel the blue scabs on the opening of my hand.

I want to fix it.

I focus on the wound, and the dirt helps me know what to do. I push the scab and feel it slowly detach from my skin. Blood seeps out of the newly-opened wound, but I don't feel worried about the new blood. Instead, the dirt guides me, and the skin regrows until the blood flow has stopped. I shift my focus, and I feel movement under my skin as veins and arteries reattach. I don't see the healing that is happening with my closed eyes, but somehow, I see everything. I understand what is happening. I feel my body changing with each new thought that I pursue.

Commanding the dirt to heal the wound takes all of my concentration. Minutes pass, although I don't know how many. When there is nothing more to do, I stop focusing on the dirt, and I regain consciousness of the room around me again. I'm still alone; the dim candles are still burning. I'm still sitting on the ground. But my hand is healed. The skin is smooth and new.

Cylus reappears.

"You can stay here for as long as you like," he says. "The exit will take you home when you're ready." The rock stump reappears next to me, the same hand print visible on its face. "I will see you in the grove of the pine tree circle."

He disappears again.

I sigh and stare at the rock. I'm hungry, and I do want to leave.

But, I also don't want to go back and face everyone again. Not crippled.

I wonder if I could fix my knee. If I can heal my knee, then perhaps things can start to work out. Maybe what Cylus said is real. Maybe my connection to this world is this hemazury stuff.

I get more dirt in my hands. I rub them together, and this time it doesn't smart because the cut is gone. I put my hands on my knee, and I feel concern and know things are wrong. I explore my knee, and I see that it's really torn up. I don't know what to do, though.

Frustrated, I touch my other knee. By exploring my good knee, I start to understand what is wrong with my hurt knee. I understand what needs to happen to fix it. It takes a lot of concentration, and I have to switch back and forth often, but I start to make changes, letting the feelings from the dirt guide me as much as my own thoughts.

This is crazy. This is real.

I'm a princess. I can help these people.

This is what I want to do. My whole life, all I've wanted is to play soccer, to live up to Mom's hopes for me. I've traveled the world with her to watch soccer games; I've spent my life on the field developing my skills. The soccer field has been my home, it's where I've belonged.

But, now, I feel a purpose and a desire that isn't soccer. I want to learn hemazury. That doesn't mean I love Mom any less. It doesn't mean I don't want to hold my phone in my pocket and remember her all the time.

No, I'm not leaving her. Everything she taught me about soccer will help me on this journey.

It's time for me to branch out on my own, to spread my wings away from the soccer field. I'm going to learn how to be this Blue Princess.

And I'm ready.

To be continued ...

Acknowledgements

Writing is an amazing journey that would be impossible without the influence of so many people over the course of generations. Although it's impossible to know when my journey started, I want to express gratitude for a few notable people along the way. My 3rd great-grandmother Mary Ann was known for her love of reading; her son, my 2nd great-grandfather Edmund, was taught to love books very early in his life, and that love was passed down for generations. On the other side of my family, my great-grandfather James moved his family next to the university so my grandfather could get a college education. After that, all of my mom's family went to college. I love these great ancestors, and I'm grateful for their sacrifices that made it possible so I could grow up in a home where education and reading were placed front and center.

When I decided to write a novel, my dear wife thought I was crazy (and she was right). Still, she was supportive anyway, even through countless terrible drafts and long brainstorming rants. She has been my sharpest critic, and my greatest accomplishment has been writing something she wants to read. I'm also appreciative of my children's enthusiasm. The time they spend writing and telling their own stories keeps me going on mine.

And then there are all the other people who have encouraged, edited, and helped along the way. Though there are too many to name everyone who has helped, I want to thank my superstar beta readers and the amazing editing team at CookieLynn Publishing Services. Additionally, many twists, turns, and inspiration for this story came from the classes and great people at the Storymakers Writer's Conference.

Finally, thank you for reading! It's amazing to me that you would be willing to read my work. Thank you! Thank you!

About the Author

I grew up reading all the time. Yeah, I'm the guy my 5th grade teacher nicknamed "Mr. Read-a-thon." Now that I'm a father to six energetic children, I do a lot of reading out loud to my kids, while the others, who are supposed to be in bed, sneak into the hallway to listen. I love reading, and I love writing.

When I'm not buried in a book, you will find me with my family, either hiking in the mountains, working in the garden, or destroying the kitchen doing a crazy science experiment.

Don't forget to visit my website, https://rgenecurtis.com. Thanks for reading!

Made in the USA
Monee, IL
23 June 2021

72087544R00111